MY
PERFECT
HUSBAND

BOOKS BY GEORGINA CROSS

GEORGINA CROSS

MY
PERFECT
HUSBAND

bookouture

Published by Bookouture in 2024

An imprint of Storyfire Ltd.
Carmelite House
50 Victoria Embankment
London EC4Y 0DZ

www.bookouture.com

ISBN: 978-1-80019-901-9
eBook ISBN: 978-1-80019-900-2

To my friends in New Orleans and our old stomping grounds.

PROLOGUE

You don't think that I see you, but I do. I watch you standing up there, a cool breeze rustling through your hair, the night falling around you like a shroud, your eyes lifted to the heavens as you stand on that balcony. You're happiest against the night sky. You've climbed to the top of those rickety steps before, and I should know as I followed you that time too.

But you're not alone. You've asked someone to join you, and the two of you gaze out at the view, the moonlight resting upon your shoulders, a glint of it highlighting your cheek as you lean against the railing, his elbow touching yours. He's too close.

The words that rise in my throat... *Come down.*

The words that I should have said instead: *Watch out.*

Because the wood is old, and the balcony creaks, and the first of those rotten boards groans and cracks and splits, and you reach out your hands as if you're looking to hold onto something, wanting to hold onto anything, the swaying and buckling of the railing causing you to pitch sideways, then down.

And this man beside you, the person you've asked to be with you tonight... Your eyes widen because you've realized he won't be enough. He won't be able to steady you. He can't get you to solid ground.

And I leap forward. I jump from my hiding place, my arms outstretched, thinking that maybe I can catch you. I can save you. I can run across that grass and reach you in time. Prevent you from smashing into that hard, unforgiving earth, from that sharp crack against your skull. I can help. But will I be fast enough?

ONE

"I brought you coffee," Alex says, and he places the ceramic mug on the bedside table.

It's my favorite mug, the one with the large red heart and thick white handle, the mug my husband reserves just for me.

I scoot over and make space for him on the bed, and he sits, the mattress sinking slightly beneath his weight. I prop another pillow behind my head, and Alex smiles. My husband is often gentle with me in the mornings.

He's dressed, his hair wet from the shower, the crisp green notes of his Irish Spring soap clinging to his skin. He's one of those cheerful, painfully exuberant, *seize the day* kind of people who wakes up at 5 a.m. with absolutely no need for an alarm clock. While the neighborhood is quiet, a dark gray hush blanketing our streets, Alex will relish the early hours of dawn, having already sipped his coffee before stepping into his running shoes and looping through the neighborhood for a jog.

But I have to be dragged out of bed, my hand reaching for the snooze button more times than is necessary as I squeeze my eyes shut against the harsh morning light, my groans of protest against the start of another work week, a Groundhog Day of sorts with projects and endless group chats. My latest design project is due this afternoon.

But this morning is worse somehow. I feel... different.

I'm staring at the ceiling—still under the covers, yes—with an unease that stirred me long before my husband appeared in the doorway, a prickle that ran up and down my arms long before my alarm clock went off.

At first, I thought it might have been the clang of my husband's spoon against his cereal bowl. Or the click and shut of the door when he returned home. The neighbor's car revving to life below our bedroom window. The normal, routine sounds that might have woken me but could have been easily disregarded as I rolled to one side and curled into a ball, a soft puff of air releasing from my mouth, that hazy, dreamlike state where my worries lie temporarily suspended. I normally cling to those extra few moments of sleep.

But the nudge against my ribs is still there. A hollow thumping that grows louder.

It's a foreboding—it has to be. It's the only explanation, the knot in my throat tightening. A sixth sense of what is to come, I just don't know what it is yet. My life changing forever, and again.

I reach for the coffee, but my hands are unsteady, and I wrap them tighter around the mug. Bringing it to my lips, I wait for the warmth of the dark roast with its splash of milk and dash of sugar to cross my tongue like a balm. But the blood in my hands runs ice-cold.

Alex sits patiently. He waits for me to say something, anything. Details about a bad dream or a crick in my neck, for my thoughts to slowly take shape, for the words to tumble from my lips.

But how do I explain what is happening? That I might... what? Be experiencing a premonition, a gut feeling? An anomaly that has never happened to me before? Certainly not when it should have happened all those years ago, when we first learned that Ellie was missing and time was of the essence.

Where had the warnings, the unsettled notions, the gut feelings been back then?

The silence stretches between us. A car door slams outside.

"Did you sleep okay?" he asks.

"It was okay," I murmur.

"Any dreams?"

I lift my eyes to his—his gray, soulful eyes that are unlike mine, which have become a dim, muted green over time. Sadness has had that effect on me.

"Strange dreams," I tell him. "But they're always strange. Like yours."

Alex knows all about my sister, and I know what worries my husband at night too.

He smooths the hair from my forehead, the strands still damp from sleep, my body becoming its own hot water bottle while I snooze, something he'll often tease me about but he doesn't complain when he can curl up beside me during the many freezing nights in Evanston.

We live in a suburb north of Chicago, the wind often whipping off the shores of Lake Michigan and blasting down our tree-lined streets, the neighbors' kids running past our house with their bright, splotchy cheeks. One day we hope to have our own children.

Winter has mostly come and gone in Illinois and it's nearing the end of April, but there will have been frost on the ground this morning and Alex will have worn a beanie over his head while he jogged.

I don't run. I refuse to run. To me, life is already hard enough as it is. My sister never got the chance.

· · ·

Ellie, my younger sister, with her long, red hair like mine. A small, silver hoop that she kept pierced through the top part of her ear. As children, we would argue sometimes.

Ellie was twenty years old when she was last seen, on an independent streak that had her living hundreds of miles away in New Orleans to study music. She covered bands at night and wrote reviews for a local magazine by day. She was gaining a real following.

One night, Ellie stepped outside a music hall to share a smoke. Her co-worker went back inside, but Ellie never did.

I wish my sister would just come home. I wish we knew what happened to her. But there is nothing, no word, no sign, only radio silence, and the not knowing is often the cruelest of all.

Alex coughs lightly, and I cradle the coffee in my lap, not knowing how I would cope, how I would manage, if I had never met my husband.

"I love you, you know," I tell him.

"I love you too."

I nod. I should check in with him too. "How was your run? Did it go okay?"

He flexes his shoulders at this. "I made it to Lighthouse Beach and back. Seven miles total, if you can believe it."

"That's great." And that *is* great. It's quite the run, and I marvel at how Alex can do it, all that expended energy while I remain trapped beneath the covers refusing to move, refusing to start my day. Running has become my husband's therapy.

"I made it around Northwestern's campus and a bunch of students were already out there," he says. "I don't remember getting up that early when we were their age."

"Probably because we were too hungover." I smirk.

He smirks too, but soon his mouth tugs down. "Such bitter-sweet times for us, you know?"

And my heart tightens. Bittersweet then, and certainly bittersweet for us now.

Alex and I met our senior year in college after my life had already turned upside down. My sister was missing, and I didn't know what to do, how to help my parents, how to move on. A group of friends encouraged me to attend a Grief Share program that wasn't far from campus. And with name badges on our shirts, a table with paper cups filled with lukewarm coffee, I learned that Alex was missing a sibling also, a younger brother, and I couldn't quite believe it.

Here was someone my age, walking and breathing and living through the exact same nightmare as me. Here was someone who could understand what I was going through. At that moment, Alex felt like a godsend.

My sister went missing while she was at college in New Orleans while his younger brother, Clive, stopped checking in while hitchhiking in Texas. Clive was backpacking, heading to Houston to look for work.

I have yet to meet Alex's brother, and Alex has yet to meet my sister. But one day, I hope. One day.

Alex touches my knee. "Are you sure you're all right? Do you need anything?"

I gesture to the coffee, to the morning routine we've kept after so many years together, and say, "I'll be okay. Just a few more minutes and I'll be downstairs."

Our home office, a sitting room at the front of the house with a large bay window that overlooks the garden, offers us the ability to work from home while we complete our graphic design projects. It's funny that Alex and I both chose to follow the same career path.

My husband looks at me. He hesitates before standing, as if he's not quite sure he believes me, that maybe he shouldn't go down and fire up his laptop but sit with me a little while longer instead.

And a thought occurs—is Alex having his own gut feelings too? His own premonition?

I swallow. I should try not to read too much into things.

"I'll be fine," I tell him. "Honest."

It's another moment before he leaves, the padding of his wool socks against the floor, the creak of the stairs as he makes his way down to the kitchen, and I steady myself. *Not every day has to be a crisis, Lauren. It's going to be okay.*

But there was that feeling, wasn't there? I should know things are about to change.

My phone rings, and it's not the house phone—unlike so many people we know, we still keep a landline, a cordless in our kitchen and in our bedroom, in case it's Ellie who needs me or it's information about Clive. It's my cell phone that rings, lighting up on the bedside table, the ringer kept on high so I don't miss a thing.

I stare at the screen: an undeniable New Orleans area code in the phone number. The Caller ID reads New Orleans Police, and my chest tightens, ice pricks beneath my skin.

I'm pretty sure I've stopped breathing. I don't want to hear what the police have to say.

Ellie's missing person's case went cold years ago, and the detective who originally worked with us has long since retired. We haven't had much of an update since.

Unless...

I look to the top of the stairs but my husband hasn't returned. If he heard the loud ringtone, he must think it's someone from work, or it's my dad calling from his room at the senior living center.

I want to shout for Alex to come back, for him to sit with me, to help me. But if this call is about Ellie, and I'm almost positive it is, I need to hear what they have to say first.

I set aside my coffee, but the bottom of the mug hits the

edge of the bedside table, hard, and the hot liquid spills out the top. At the next buzz and ring, I swallow.

This is it. They found my sister.

She's alive.

She's dead.

Maybe someone saw her wandering along the side of the road, and they've rushed her to a hospital. They will tell me she's going to be okay. We can come see her.

Or it's what we've been dreading the most, and a fishing boat dragged the remains of her body into a net. Or she washed up along the mouth of the Mississippi River. A dog pawed at a field and unearthed her bones.

I've imagined this call so many times, but now that it's here, now that they're calling, I'm not ready. My vision goes black. I'm faint.

The phone is on its fifth or sixth ring before I finally have the courage to answer.

"This is Lauren Capshaw," I say, and I'm surprised I am able to utter this much.

"Mrs. Capshaw. This is Detective Frank Rayburn with New Orleans P.D."

I press my hand to my stomach. I swear the room tilts.

"Can we speak for a few minutes?"

"Yes," I tell him, but my voice is hoarse; it comes out a whisper.

"Mrs. Capshaw," he says. "I'm so sorry to tell you this, but we've found your sister."

TWO

My body runs cold, a wave of panic cresting inside my lungs.

"Mrs. Capshaw, we found Ellie's remains."

My chest hollows out, the blood rushing to my ears.

"A construction crew uncovered her body. They were working on a run-down home that's been neglected for years. They came upon your sister."

A run-down home that's been neglected, and I shake my head. None of this makes sense.

My body shakes, and I can't stop, the tears spilling from my eyes.

"Mrs. Capshaw, can you hear me? Your sister... Ellie Duncan."

And I draw my knees beneath my chin. I double over and sob. My sister is dead. She's gone. Ellie is never coming back.

I stare at the door, waiting for Alex to materialize, willing for him to run into this room. He'll tell me that this is another bad dream. He'll stand beside our bed with my cup of coffee the way he always does, wiping the tears from my eyes as he assures me that none of this is happening, that I'm imagining things. The detective's words will disappear into the ether, sweet relief filling my lungs. It will be a normal Monday morning.

Yes, it's been twelve very long years—we still don't know what happened to my sister, which will always be frightening, but Ellie will remain safe, her status unknown—but at least I can still cling to the string of hope that binds me to her.

But not this. Never this.

I sob into the phone.

Ellie...

My younger sister with her eyes the color of jade. The dark flash in them when she's angry, the bright shimmer in her gaze when she laughs. The way she likes to tuck her hand beneath her chin when she's listening to someone. The indie rock music she loves to blast in the car.

As kids, I would call her Ellie Bellie.

She begged Dad to build a treehouse for us in the backyard, and at night we would climb to the top as she told us ghost stories. I was always frightened of the stories, but Ellie never was.

I press my hand against my chest and cry. I cry until my throat hurts, my face hurts, my heart splitting in two.

"You've got it all wrong," I tell the detective. "It's not Ellie—it can't be. You've made a mistake."

He pauses. "Mrs. Capshaw, I'm afraid we matched her dental records."

Her dental records, and now I know I will be sick. A retching sound escapes from my mouth.

"She was wearing the same jean jacket her roommate described seeing her in when she left the apartment. The jacket was on her body."

I shudder—*her body*. I'm not sure if this pain will ever stop.

"We also found a couple of photos inside the jacket pocket. I need you to take a look at them."

I sit straight up. "What photos?"

"I'll text them to you. She's sitting at a table with two men. Maybe you will recognize one of them."

Another desperate glance at the door, and I nearly scream. Alex must have heard me crying by now.

A sound from below, and it's my husband. He's talking. He must be in the office on a work call.

"Mrs. Capshaw?" the detective says.

And I ask, "What happened to my sister?"

"We'll know more soon, but we believe she died the same night she went missing. Where she was found, the property was abandoned. It's not far from the music hall where she was last seen."

Something changes in the detective's voice, as if he's sucked air between his teeth, an inhale of sorts, and I realize that he's trying to be patient, he wants to be sympathetic, but he's also eager. A body has been discovered, and he has a lead. With the photos, he's ready to track down this lead.

"I understand this is difficult," he says, "but can you look at them, at the images? I'll send them to you right now."

"Yes, send them."

The first image arrives with a ping, and then another. I place the detective on speaker to look at my screen, then enlarge the first photo, my heartbeat a sledgehammer against my neck.

The photo is crumpled and faded on one side—evidence of the humidity and conditions where Ellie was kept hidden, the vicious Louisiana heat along with several cold winters—and the image is hazy, the quality poor. I remind myself it's a photo that's been taken of another photo.

It's not lost on me that this is something that was found on my sister's body.

In the photograph, Ellie sits between two men, and seeing her face, her smile, her bright green eyes, her lips pressed together with a red glossy tint, most likely from that cherry lip balm she loved so much... it almost takes my breath away.

She looks happy, but the flush in her cheeks could also be from the half-empty Bloody Mary glass sitting before her, the celery stalk and skewer of olives tipped at an angle. I didn't think she liked Bloody Marys. On the table is a small clutch of flowers. Pink camellias.

Those flowers... and the unease is here. It trickles across my skin, a sickness that flourishes inside my belly. There is some kind of meaning right there.

I touch the screen and trace the curves of my sister's face. She wears a thin gold chain around her neck, and despite the faded photograph, I would recognize that necklace anywhere, the letter E that rests at the center, a gift from our parents when she came home a month earlier for her birthday, a month before she disappeared.

One of the men has his head turned, his hand lifted as if he wasn't quite ready for the camera. Plates of food are set before them, what looks like eggs Benedict and slices of toast. They're enjoying brunch.

The other man leans closer to my sister. He's around Ellie's age and keeps his head tipped toward her, his arm wrapped around the back of her chair in a way that could either be seen as endearing or slightly possessive, depending on how you want to look at it. His mouth turns up in a confident grin, as if to say he's claiming her, as if to say, *This gorgeous girl is mine.*

I study his hair, his eyes, and there is a twinge of something, a recognition perhaps in the slope of his nose, his dark eyelashes, the delicate rise of his cheekbones. My sister keeps her head tilted toward him too. She liked this man.

They're sitting outside at a restaurant, the recognizable wrought-iron railing of a New Orleans balcony behind them, the sky overcast in a flat sheet of gray. All three of them are wearing long sleeves, which makes me think the photo was taken in November, when the weather was finally beginning to cool in Louisiana. Ellie was last seen the week before Thanksgiving.

I look again at the flowers, at the bouquet.

Enlarging the next image, I halt... This can't be right.

I'm choking, panicking, my gaze zooming in and out. There is no way this can possibly make sense.

Because the other man faces the camera now, his long and somewhat shaggy hair swept across his brow, whereas in the first image his long strands hid much of his profile. He has the same thick lashes, the same high cheekbones as the man who sits closest to Ellie. They could be brothers.

And I'm trembling because I know those eyes... those gray, soulful eyes that have peered into mine.

I know that look.

It's just that he's grown older, and so have I.

Over the years, I've become accustomed to his shorter hair, the cropped haircut and clean-shaven face that he says he prefers these days over the scruff of a younger twenty-some-thing-year-old.

In those photos, sitting next to my sister is my husband, Alex.

THREE

"Mrs. Capshaw?" the detective says.

I've stopped breathing, I'm close to hyperventilating now, and I clasp a hand over my face to try to muffle the sound.

"Are you looking at the images?" he asks. "Did they come through okay?"

"Yes, I see them."

"Do you recognize either of the men?"

My mouth parts, the bewilderment springing to my eyes.

"Mrs. Capshaw?" he repeats.

And I startle. "I need to call you back. I need a moment."

"I understand. But please let me know—"

But I've hung up. I don't want to hear any more.

I rise from the bed, my knees trembling, to check the hallway beyond our room. I can still hear Alex downstairs, his morning routine, his day moving forward just like any other. He has no clue.

Alex was there, but he shouldn't have been.

This is impossible. I don't know what this means.

I take a few steps, but I'm cautious, stealthy, my blood running hot then cold.

Am I frightened of my own husband? Do I have reason to be?

Footsteps below, and it's Alex. He moves toward the kitchen; he's no longer speaking on the phone.

The staircase and its polished steps, the single flight toward the bottom, and it feels like an eternity before I can reach the floor. I bite down to keep the dizziness at bay, fighting to banish my sometimes paralyzing fear of heights.

This is one flight of stairs, and it's supposed to be nothing. It's something I should be able to work through and get over. That's what Alex told me at least.

I find my husband at the kitchen counter, the white, subway-tiled backsplash behind him, the tile we installed ourselves last spring. It took weeks, much longer than we'd expected since we didn't often take on DIY projects, but I'd thought it would be a good way to save money. Something we could handle, a fun activity for us to do together after work.

It had been my idea to select the white tile, a kitchen makeover I'd seen in a magazine, and I'd shown the pages to Alex. He'd simply agreed; the sharp, clean brightness would work well with the rising morning light. With him standing there, the brilliance of the white is now a stark contrast to my husband in his dark sweatshirt.

Alex, his back turned to me, rinses out the French press at the sink, dusts a scattering of coffee grounds into the basin. Rubbing his hands together, he wipes the remaining residue from his fingers.

But I stay where I am, my feet frozen, my ribcage hollowed out until I fear it's empty. I'm outside my body, detached, my world flipped inside out as I tell myself this isn't happening to me. It's happening to someone else.

I have become someone else.

And so has my husband.

.   .   .

I don't know what to say, what to launch at Alex and question him about first, but I need to see him. I need to see his face, for my eyes to land on his so I can fully register what is happening, to comprehend the seismic shift that has occurred: the difference between our lives from a few minutes ago and now. The truth and betrayal that are being forced out.

Maybe there's a good explanation, I beg. *Alex, please tell me you have a reasonable explanation.*

But my husband didn't know Ellie, always said that he wished he'd had the chance. Over and again, through the years, that's what he told me.

Somewhere in the home office, a phone buzzes—it's Alex's. He must have left it behind when he finished his work call, and it strikes me that he doesn't keep his ringer on high, not the way I do, my phone on constant alert to find out if there is any information about Ellie. Is he less eager to find information about his missing brother than I am about my sister?

Alex's cell buzzes repeatedly, and it might be the detective calling him. He might have questions for him too. But I need to talk to my husband first. I need to ask him about meeting Ellie, thinking that I can warn him, let him brace himself for the news before it comes at him from out of nowhere, just as it did me.

Alex rinses out his coffee mug; he's taking his time, swishing the soapy sponge around while he periodically looks out the window to the cold Illinois sky. A lone tree in the backyard rustles, its gray branches knocking together in the breeze. But in here, I am stuck in space and time.

He doesn't seem to register my presence, and if he's aware of his phone buzzing, he doesn't move to answer it. The water going down the drain might be overriding any other sounds.

"Alex?" I call, but my voice breaks. I try again. "Alex...?"

He lifts his shoulders—he's heard me—and he turns off the tap. "Hmm?" he says softly and turns around.

But I shudder. I can't do this. Once I cross this threshold

and confront him, our marriage will never be the same. Our *lives* will never be the same.

My vision tilts sideways, and my steps wobble. I hunch over and sob.

Alex is in front of me in seconds, his arms wrapped around me tight as he cradles my head in the palms of his hands. He pulls me against his chest, and his touch is protective and loving. He is so strong and warm. Alex has always been my rock, and over the years, I have tried my best to be his. I've tried to help him find his brother too.

"Lauren, what is it? Was it a bad dream? You could have told me—"

"No. It's not a bad dream."

"What's happened?"

I sob. "It's Ellie."

And it hurts to say these words out loud, the second half of my sentence that, tragically, will not end with my sister being found safe and sound.

I crumple against his chest, and it's becoming difficult to breathe, my mouth and nose pressed against the thick cotton of his sweatshirt, my words coming out muffled, more desperate. I try to say, *Let me go.*

But Alex clutches me harder, with a grip that is so tight, and I panic. I'm locked in, unable to break free, and a white-hot fear flashes through my insides: Alex isn't comforting me but smothering me.

"Lauren," Alex says. "Is your sister okay? Do they know what happened?" He sounds moments away from crying himself.

Is he crying for me or for Ellie?

I break loose and pull back, finally able to gulp in a mouthful of air. Alarmed, he looks at me and he's shocked, apologetic—he didn't mean to squeeze me so hard. Perhaps I imagined it.

He cups my face and lifts my chin to his, and I gaze into those eyes that I adore, at the man I've depended on during so many nights when I've anguished over Ellie. Alex's face is pale, his gaze huge and round.

What are you hiding? I want to scream. *What do you know?* The accusations are here, the pressure undeniably building inside me, ready to burst.

Alex searches my face, and with the warmth of his hands against my cheeks, my neck, I find myself caving. I want to melt against him. I want him to comfort me, the way he's always done. I need my husband.

The look he gives me is so intense, it's filled with so much concern, that I sob all over again. I see my husband, don't I? The man I love is right here in front of me. It's that steadfast look that I thought I could always depend on and trust. I know him—right?

Alex repeats, "She's okay, isn't she?" And his voice shakes. "Tell me that she's okay."

"She's not," I tell him. "Ellie is dead."

Alex leads me to the kitchen table and helps me onto a chair, and I'm thankful that he's gotten me off my feet as I don't trust myself not to collapse to the ground.

Was it just my imagination or did my husband's knees buckle when I told him? Was there a falter in his spine when I said that Ellie was gone?

Alex sits at the table also. His face has gone white as a sheet.

I shove my hand against my mouth, my knuckles pressing against my teeth. *How do we move forward from here? What am I about to learn about my husband?*

"Was that the police who called?" he asks.

I nod, recounting to him parts of what the detective said: the run-down house and the construction crew, the location that's not far from the music hall. But I stop short of telling him about her dental records, about her jean jacket.

And I don't breathe a word about the photographs. *Why don't I?*

Because I'm buying time—that's what this is. I know this instinctually. I don't want to go to this uncharted territory just yet.

I should say something, and my mouth drops open to tell him, preparing to fire off my list of questions after which I will show him my phone and those dreaded images. I'll watch as he stares, as he explains what we're looking at, that maybe, just maybe, everything can be all right again.

But I don't say much more, and my husband squeezes my hand. He asks me questions instead: What else do I know? Are there any other details about the house and where it's located? Do they know what happened? But I don't know much else—I hung up on the detective.

"I'm so sorry," Alex says. "Lauren, I am so, so sorry." His genuine concern overwhelms me.

Down the hall, the buzz of his phone picks up again, and this time, he hears it too.

"I'm not answering that," he says, dismissing it as if it could be another work call, a pointless interruption that would be considered abhorrent and rude if he were to leave me at this moment and answer his phone.

The buzzing stops, and my cell phone lights up next, my ringer on high, always on high, and the pair of us jolt, the shrill tone rising in the air between us.

The Caller ID reads New Orleans Police.

"You should answer that," he says.

But I shake my head. *No, Alex, I really don't think you want me to.*

"Lauren? Your phone?" And Alex must misunderstand my look, my hesitation, because he says, "I'll take it. I'll talk to the police. I can do this for you and get the rest of the details."

He is so chivalrous to me.

But I'm unable to speak, and the call rings out.

Alex's eyes widen. "You should talk to them, Lauren. Your sister..."

Down the hall, his phone starts up again—a whiplash of our heads as we register each sound—and Alex is ready to stand, ready to spring from his chair to fetch his phone. "They're trying to reach you through me. I'll answer."

"No," I tell him. "Wait."

I shake as I rise to my feet. I finally know what I must do, and I cross the kitchen. Alex follows me. He practically hovers by my side as if ready to catch me if I fall. He's afraid to let me out of his sight.

"I have to show you something," I say.

In our home office, his workstation sits across from mine, the morning light shining through the bay window and across our matching pine desks with our double monitors. It's quiet outside with the neighbors' children having already gone to school.

"What's going on?" Alex asks. His voice hitches, his concern shaping into something else.

I unlock my phone and email the images to myself, careful to lean away from him and keep the screen tilted. But it's pointless, ridiculous even, since he's about to see the photographs for himself. I will print these images on large sheets of glossy paper. We will stare at them, the photos haunting us for the rest of our lives.

I slide the mouse along the foam pad and wake up my laptop; Alex bought the mouse pads for us, picked out the matching, ergonomic design months ago. *They should let us rest our wrists better*, he said. *You work so hard.* Alex has always been considerate like that.

On my desk I keep a framed photo of us from our wedding

day, and I have to turn my head. I can't look. It was one of the happiest days of my life, when my mom was still with us, and my dad was trying his best to be happy. But there was a hole in our lives, a missing piece of our family: Ellie.

I sob again as I think about my dad. I will see him later today. I will have to tell him this horrible news, that Ellie isn't coming back alive, and it could destroy him. Letting Dad know could kill him, this lie that surrounds Alex also, and my father is already not doing so well. What if he responds like Mom did and dies of a broken heart too?

My heart hurts. My head hurts. Never in my life have I wanted so much for my husband to hold me and reassure me. But that may no longer be an option.

I log into my email and open the attachments, the files springing to life across my screen. Steeling my nerves, I bite down to keep going.

The thud of my heart is so loud I imagine that Alex can hear it, that the whole neighborhood can hear it, that everyone will know what is happening, that our world is about to suddenly, and irreversibly, come crashing down.

I send the images to our office printer with a hard click.

Alex watches quietly, and within seconds, the printer lights up, the first image rolling out onto the tray. The second image slides out next.

I lift the printouts and stare at each one. I'm seconds away from screaming, from wailing to see these photographs enlarged, as if they could have ceased to exist, the images erasing in the last few minutes, the detective made a mistake, but it's real.

The photos are real, the tangible paper hot in my hands as they shake. My sister's radiant face smiles up at me.

And there it is again—the turn of my husband's head. That man who sits with them.

The proof is right here.

FOUR

I present the images to Alex, and he frowns. He doesn't quite understand, not yet, his eyebrows stitched together. But his eyes skate back and forth, a blanched look spreading to his temples, a tremble setting in his jaw.

Alex's hands shake too. He flips to the next copy, the one where he faces the camera head-on.

"What... what is this?" He struggles to swallow, and I see where the Adam's apple catches and is stuck.

"Where did these come from?" A line of sweat stretches across his brow.

"You tell me."

Alex doesn't meet my eyes but flips again and again through the printouts, despite the fact there are only two images, a freneticism quickly taking over in his movements. It's as if he thinks that the more he checks, the more he flips, the greater the chance the images could change, that they could morph into something else with the next rotation. This isn't what this seems. It's a trick of the eye, and I'm playing a cruel joke on him.

This would be the cruelest joke of all, dear husband.

Alex's hands are trembling so much that I'm afraid he's seconds away from dropping the pages to the floor.

He staggers while I watch. I wait for Alex to explain, for him to tell me something that could stick. Or he'll say something outrageous like, *The photos have been altered, Lauren.* We're both graphic designers and we know how easily this could be done in Photoshop. He'll claim, *I know this sounds crazy, but that's not me. It's got to be a doppelganger.* He'll grasp at straws.

But I know the truth: that man is not a look-alike, and these images have not been altered. That is, in fact, my husband with my sister.

Alex was in New Orleans, and the police have pictures of him *with Ellie.* They found those pictures *on her body.* They will question him, and I will be damned if I don't ask him the same questions too.

Alex backs away... one step, two... and I have no idea where he's going, what he thinks he's doing. He wouldn't just leave, would he? He wouldn't just bolt without offering me some sort of rationalization.

Alex, explain yourself! I want to scream.

I snatch the printouts from his hands as if I'm afraid he could destroy them, that he could be seconds away from hiding them, which is ridiculous. The police have the originals, and the images are saved on my phone; they're forever backed-up to the cloud. I could print a thousand more of these if I wanted to.

The thought of the photographs blanketing the walls of my home makes me sick. I want to hurl something at my husband. I want to throw something large and heavy at his head. Hurt him.

I love this man.

I don't know this man.

From this point on, he is a stranger.

I shake the pages at him. "Tell me everything."

He jumps. He cowers. He lifts his hands in his defense. "I know how this looks..."

And with those words, I do everything I can not to scream at him. "You knew Ellie. You met her. You *lied*. The cops found these photos in her pocket. They found her body, and these were *with her*."

Alex looks like he's going to be sick next, and the circumstances must start clicking inside his brain, the implications slowly dawning on him.

"When did you meet my sister?" I ask. "How well did you know her?" I stare at the man who smiles at the camera. "And this other person? What does he know?"

Alex's eyes turn red. "I should have told you. I'm so sorry. From the very beginning, I should have said."

Yes, Alex, you really should have.

"You know how long I've been looking for my sister. How many years we've waited for answers, and *you knew her*." I can't stop; I'm speaking through tears. "All this time, you knew something huge about meeting her, and you didn't tell us. You could have told the police. It could have led to—"

"But I didn't hurt her!" he cries. "I wanted Ellie to be found safe and alive too."

And that's the confirmation I was looking for. His words rip a hole right through me. This is real—it's horrifyingly real—and I cradle my head with my hands. Of course it's real.

Alex pulled off one of the most ultimate betrayals to me and my family. He almost got away with it completely.

Because Alex said he only knew my sister by what I've described, the photographs I keep framed in the house, my favorite one I display above the fireplace, the one that is less than six feet away from us in the office next to a piece of pottery that Ellie and I picked out on a girls' trip to Mexico.

Alex has seen her missing person's flyer, for God's sake; a stack of them rests inches away from me on my desk, the next batch ready to be mailed out. I keep a Facebook page about her in case anyone wants to send us a message, a tip, or a confession.

On the anniversary of her disappearance, I monitor the well wishes that pour in with notes from friends and former class-mates, messages about missing and loving her, strangers telling us they hope we find her too. Alex periodically helps me to check the messages. Her former roommate, Carmen, helps out too.

A year after Ellie went missing, I met Alex at Northwestern University; he'd transferred from a small school in Florida. We fell in love. Months later, he traveled with my family to New Orleans to help us retrace Ellie's steps.

Alex has gone through family photo albums saying how much we look alike, with the same red hair and freckles, the same narrow chin. He's told me more than once how much he wishes he could meet her.

He talked to me about Clive too, how for years he's been worried sick about his whereabouts, what could have happened to him, if he's alive and well, his desperate search for his younger brother. He misses him...

And a sharp kick hits my gut. I stare once again at the photographs.

The familiarity that is so obvious between the two men. The pieces of that day that are clashing and colliding together inside my head.

It's him. Of course it's him. I know who this other man is.

And the pain strikes me, one hit after another. As I realize this other harsh truth about that day, another piece of my world shatters forever.

FIVE

It's Clive—the other man in the photograph. That's who sits closer to my sister, the one with his arm wrapped around the back of her chair, his dark hair and the slope of his nose that are so similar to his older brother.

The last time we talked, Alex said, *he was heading west. Clive was always traveling and looking for work.*

Clive stopped in New Orleans first. Alex must have gone there to meet him.

They met with my sister.

I didn't recognize him at first because in these photographs, Clive's hair is shorter and so different from what Alex has shown me in the past, photos from their last family get-together, a beach trip where they'd crowded around a table at a seafood restaurant, a bucket of beer placed between them. The brothers posed for the camera with matching sunburned noses.

I point at the printouts. "That's Clive," I splutter to Alex.

"I can explain," he says, and he steps forward.

God help me, I flinch and draw back. "You were all together. *The three of you.*" I cry so hard that I can barely see my husband through my tears, but his eyes pinch, I know that much, his eyebrows drawn upward. It's dawning on him that the ruse is up, that I'm afraid of him. I don't believe a word that's coming out of his mouth. He will have to tell me and the police everything now.

"Lauren, please."

I don't know where to look. I can't bear to see his face.

"What... is... going on?" My voice is a croak.

"My brother, Clive. He met Ellie while he was out watching some band. He was traveling through New Orleans, and they hung out a couple of times."

"And you?"

"He called and asked me to come down. He wanted to see me before he took off again, so I went. I thought it would be fun."

I speak through gritted teeth. "You *sat* with her at a restaurant, Alex. My sister had pictures of you on her *when she died.* How do you explain that?"

"I don't know."

"This whole time—"

"I didn't know she was your sister when I met you."

"Bullshit."

"I promise you, I swear."

"When were these photographs taken?"

"November." He looks to the ceiling, thinking. "Sometime in November."

"So it was right before she died?"

"It was the same day." He makes a face, then clarifies, "It was earlier that day."

"You saw my sister *the same day?*"

"It wasn't like that. My brother said he'd invited a friend last minute, and Ellie showed up. We ate, and that was it. She took off. She said she had to go to work. I left town the following morning, and Clive left soon after that. Neither of us went to the concert that night. We didn't meet up with her again, I swear. I don't know anything."

"Then why did she have pictures of you?"

Once again, his eyes dart around the room. "I don't know."

"Who took them?"

"One of the waiters. Ellie had this camera with her. She said she always had a camera for work."

And that part is true: my sister carried a Nikon around with her for photo shoots and interviews with bands, evening events at clubs. But taking photos during the day and at brunch with two men she barely knew? I don't think so.

I think about the way Clive sat close to my sister, that self-assured grin of his, his arm draped around her chair.

"They liked each other," I tell him. "You saw how close they sat. How can you be so sure your brother doesn't know anything, that he didn't go out with her again?" And I halt. My breath catches. "Oh my God, is that why Clive took off? Is that why he disappeared? He knows what happened to my sister, and he ran away? He's been hiding all this time?"

Alex's cheeks flame red. "No, that's not it. Believe me, that is *not* it. He left for a job in Houston, something his friend set up for him, and it was months later. We stopped hearing from him months later. Please, Lauren, don't think like this. My brother has nothing to do with Ellie. He disappeared long after she did. It's not connected."

My mouth drops open. *Believe him? How can I ever believe him again?*

The timeline is stringing together; realizations about that weekend are coming together, hard and fast.

Ellie went missing and it was a year later when Alex said he moved to Chicago. He was taking a graphic design class at Northwestern and he saw a bulletin board in the hallway with a flyer describing the Grief Share program.

He told me it was serendipitous there was a meeting that same afternoon, that he would go, that we would meet...

He found me.

The fear is irrational, it's ludicrous, but the thought is there, pinging hot and sharp in my brain. Alex knew who I was, and exactly where I'd be.

I've never been to a meeting like this, he said. *I'm so glad I came.*

Alex knew my sister. Did he come looking for me next?

"After we met, you told me about Ellie," he says. "But I didn't realize it was the same girl, not then, not at that time. I didn't realize she was who we'd had brunch with in New Orleans. I'd moved to Northwestern and an entire year had passed by then. I was so worried about Clive—we didn't know what had happened to him. You still couldn't find your sister. It seemed crazy—it *is* crazy. It's a total coincidence that we met."

"And in Evanston?" My breath is ragged. "At Northwestern, of all the colleges in the world?"

"I know," he says. "What are the chances?"

The chances are slim—he has to know that. The sheer improbability of it, the massive fluke that would bring him into my life.

"I should have told you," he says, "but I was afraid of how you would react. We were dating, and I'd already fallen for you, I'd fallen for you so hard. And then I saw a picture of Ellie, and I didn't want you to think... If I told you that I knew her, that we'd met, and so many months had passed by, I was scared of how you would react... how it would seem..."

"That it would what, seem suspicious?"

His eyes bulge. "*No.*"

I glare at his stupidity, his complicity. "Alex, we could have told the police. It would have been another clue, something she did that day, and we could have retraced her steps better. Every piece of information is crucial—you knew that and you still kept it from me, from my parents, *from the police*," I sob. I want to rip the hair from my head. "What else do you know? What else have you lied to me about?"

"We—Clive and I—we don't know anything. We didn't do anything."

"But why not tell me? Why not speak up? This..." And the doubt swirls thick and rancid between us in the air. "It's like you're hiding something. You're covering up for something." I jab my finger in his direction. "You're covering up for him. You know what he did to my sister."

"No, please don't say that."

I step away, and the room is tilting again.

Alex meeting me, making me fall in love with him, then marrying me, while his younger brother hides somewhere covering his tracks, is the evilest thing. A vicious act for how sordid these brothers could be.

I stare at him, at this stranger, and I realize the shift that has occurred, the gaping hole that has breached between us, the destruction he has caused that might never be repaired, the deception that might never be forgiven. This monumental omission that my husband has made for years.

I woke up this morning with that strange feeling... and it's coming true. The strange notion that something wasn't quite right as I lay in my bed and stared at the ceiling.

Alex was with Clive... and the two of them spent time with my sister.

My phone rings again, and the sound cuts between us. I hold my breath.

Alex lets out a long sigh. "What will you tell the police?" His face crumples, and it's as if he's resigning himself to his fate, that I will spill everything. "It's okay," he says. "I understand what you need to do, if you tell them."

I meet Alex's gaze. "The police probably want information from you. Confirmation about the photos, that it's you and your brother. I bet the detective already knows this, and he's matched it to Clive's missing person's file."

Alex scrubs his face with his hands. "I'll talk to him," he says, and he reaches for my phone.

But I draw back. No way am I handing my phone over to him. Alex can use his own.

I'm positive my husband is being considered a person of interest, along with his brother. There could be possible obstruction of justice charges too, withholding information.

The search for Alex's younger brother is about to take on a whole new meaning.

My phone stops and the room falls silent. The detective is giving up for now. Maybe he's thinking about placing a different call—

My dad.

I have to go to him. I can't be here anymore. I need to talk to him before he learns about Ellie from someone else.

I rush to the staircase. I will change my clothes. I will find my car keys and drive to the senior care center. I will sit with my father, and together we will cry.

But I wobble at the first step—that damn unsteadiness of mine coming back. This fear of heights. Because if I'm not careful, if I let my mind spin, things can go topsy-turvy, especially when I think back to my childhood, to some of my most unsettling memories, and the screams will seep into my brain. *Lauren!* my sister will shout, my mother's cries following afterwards.

I take a deep breath.

It's only two floors, Alex told me when we first viewed the house. *You can do this, I know you can. It's mind over matter. I'll help you.*

It's only two floors, I repeat to myself now, and I grip my hand around the railing. I was never afraid of heights as a kid, was never worried about a single flight of stairs back then... but that all changed. It changed on that hot summer's day. We were only kids.

Ellie...

It's her voice coming back, and I remember all over again what has happened, that my sister is dead, that this is the biggest crisis of all. Ellie isn't coming home. She will never crank up the dial and blast loud music in the car. She will never laugh or beg me to step out of my comfort zone.

I tried stepping out of my comfort zone once and look at how that turned out.

I lower my head. I'm not sure if I can get through this, if I have enough strength to survive this. This is far too much for me to handle, too much is happening at once, the multiple crises stacked on top of each other. I could break. My sister's death is already devastating enough.

Alex stands behind me. He lingers before placing his hand on my shoulder. And this time, I don't pull back. My body is numb.

I want so much to slip between the cracks of these stairs and leave this place. I will go somewhere far away and disappear, pretend that none of this is happening.

"I'm sorry," Alex repeats again and again. "I am so sorry." He leans in and his breath is warm and close on my back.

"She's gone, Alex," I say softly. "My sister..."

Alex tries to hold me. He moves to wrap his arms around me, but once again, the pressure is too much, his presence is too much, and I break loose to get away. I reach the next step. "I have to see my dad."

"I'll go with you," he says.

"No."

I need to get away from this person. I need to be with my father. I close my eyes.

Mind over matter, I repeat to myself. *You've climbed these stairs so many times before. You just came down to find your husband.*

But everything was in slow motion then. I'd left the bedroom and stumble-walked down the steps as if someone else was in charge of my body, the detective's words, my disbelief in what was happening with a mad propulsion to find my husband and face him, to have him answer me.

Alex doesn't reach for me again. He stands, motionless, as I take the next step, dropping the printouts to the floor, the pages fluttering beyond my feet. My husband can have them for all I care. He can stare at the images. He can agonize over how much our lives are about to change.

When I reach the last step, the top of the landing, my breath heaves in and out. I can do this. I will keep moving.

In the bedroom, I fling clothes from the hamper, tossing aside a hanger, a balled-up set of pajamas, before rummaging through a shelf and finding a pair of jeans. I tug a sweatshirt over my head.

I'm in the bathroom next, knocking over bottles of lotion and lipsticks, Alex's shaving cream, the items scattering across the counter with several of them dropping to the floor. I ignore what spills, not knowing what I'm doing, what I need in this instant, but I will finish getting dressed. I will leave this house.

I find an elastic hairband and pull my hair back, my arms hollow, my elbows knocking together as if everything about me has become unsteady. I have become unmoored. I'm not here, but hovering on the other side of this mirror watching this happen to someone else, another Lauren. A stronger Lauren. But my reflection stares back. It's only me in the glass.

And what I see is shocking: my eyes are swollen and red, my cheeks streaked with tears. I think about my sister's green eyes, the energetic light that once shone within them, and how her eyes will never shine again. Her eyes are closed forever, and I hunch over, realizing they've been closed for a very long time.

I brace myself against the sink, and Alex steps into the bathroom. But I can't bear to be near him, the scent of his laundered sweatshirt and the clean, fresh soap, and I push past him to the bedroom.

"Lauren," he says. "We should talk."

I ignore him, searching the floor for my shoes, kicking at a pile of clothes before I finally spot my shoelaces among the mess and pull my shoes on.

I struggle my way down the stairs, my hand sliding against the polished wood of the railing as the dizziness rushes at me with full force. I worry that I will trip over my own feet and tumble over, that Alex will have to scoop me up from the floor. He will have to come to my rescue. Not anymore.

A framed photo from our wedding day hangs on the wall, and I avert my eyes. I lower myself to the last step and see my husband's running shoes that have been kicked to the corner. An end table is by the front door, a beautiful dark cherry wood with a hand-blown vase displayed on top. The vase, a gift from Alex last year for my birthday.

It holds the latest bouquet—camellias that Alex brought home yesterday, like he often does—the colorful blooms that came wrapped inside delicate paper. My husband, always the romantic.

There were pink camellias set in front of my sister on that table, flowers that were given to her. Another coincidence? There have been too many of them.

I shove aside a stack of mail on the end table and find my car keys. My jacket I grab from the hook. I shut the door with a heavy thud, not turning back to see if Alex is following me, not caring if I've left him on the landing to stare.

On the porch, the cool air that reaches my cheeks is a shock, and I hurry down the path. Halfway toward my car, I nearly stop, realizing how alone I am, how terribly alone I am without Alex, his absence punching right through me.

But I can't stop. I can't go back inside, not to him. It's just that I always thought if this day were to come, if that dreaded phone call were to arrive, my husband would be by my side. Alex would be the one to help me get through this. He would help me as we comforted my dad.

Not anymore.

SIX

Sitting in the parking lot, I try to gather my nerves before entering the senior living center. Cutting the engine, I drop the keys to my lap and look down, tracing the letters of my sister's name along my skin.

It's a tattoo I had inked on my left index finger shortly after the one-year anniversary of my sister's disappearance, a reminder to never forget, to never give up hope that we would one day find her. The cursive letters forming her name—the elegant script of the *E* and the two looping *l*s—run along the patch of skin. The needle had pressed against bone.

The tattoo is blue, Ellie's favorite color. And seeing her name, running my fingers along it, always makes me feel connected to her. Despite everything, and especially over the years, I still feel responsible for her.

Give me strength, Ellie. Please give me strength.

I find Dad in his room, in a wheelchair facing a small desk, the furniture that comes standard in pretty much every accommodation at the Oak Manor Senior Center. The sun lifts higher in the sky now, a mid-morning light that streams through the window and shines upon my dad's face, his thinning gray hair.

Whoever was the last nurse to check on him didn't position him toward the window, and I wonder why since he likes to watch the birds flutter and peck in the bird feeders. It's one of his most favorite things.

We moved my dad here five years ago after my mom died and we realized he needed more care. He stayed with us for a few months, but it soon became apparent that we couldn't watch over him as often as we should, not with us both working full time.

His doctor suggested an assisted living center, where nurses could help with his mobility. They could provide plenty of activities to keep him busy, keep his mind engaged, and Dad agreed, although the decision for me was an agonizing one.

Dad simply patted my hand and said he could meet new people this way. He could show them pictures of Ellie and ask if anyone had information, if anyone had seen her.

But Ellie went missing in New Orleans, remember? No one here knows a thing. It broke my heart to see Dad stare at me and blink.

I no longer ask him if he remembers specifics about that week, or anything about those months that followed. His memories now fluctuate, the details swirling inside the frustrating, muddled fog of his brain. But every once in a while, he will remember something. He will bring up a random memory or he'll make a comment, as if someone has stirred it up for him again, as if someone might have whispered in his ear and brought up the past.

A stroke has made things more difficult recently too, and it's upsetting to see my dad this way, especially when he was always the strongest person in our family. He led the charge after Ellie went missing, handling most of the media interviews and ordering hundreds of extra missing person's posters. As the years passed and there was still no word, Dad took care of Mom until she grew quieter and withdrew into herself. Eventually, her sadness ultimately overwhelmed her and she was gone.

Now, I hover in the doorway and watch my dad. He is so peaceful right now, and I don't want to disturb him.

On the desk is a picture of my sister, and I realize that's what he is looking at; he must have asked the nurse to turn him in this direction so he could gaze upon his youngest daughter.

My hand lifts to my chest. Does he already know? Did Dad wake up with some sort of harrowing gut feeling too?

"Hi, Dad," I say, and slowly enter the room. But he doesn't turn his head.

I kneel in front of his wheelchair, hoping this will get his attention, but it takes a few more seconds before his eyes register, and he looks at me, his face slowly crinkling with a smile.

"Lauren! Good morning."

He's so cheerful, and that, combined with the relief he still recognizes me—that part of him, thankfully, remains intact—makes me swallow hard to keep myself from sobbing. Within seconds, I will tell him the unbearable. I will be tearing this man's world apart.

A weight tugs at the corner of Dad's mouth and his smile disappears. "Lauren, what is it?"

I tell myself I don't have to say anything, not yet at least. I can save him from this grief a little while longer. Better yet, I don't have to tell him at all. I can protect him in this way, a kindness that only I can offer. I can shield him for just a few more hours, and wouldn't that be understandable, the right thing to do?

But it's a delay tactic, I know it is. Dad needs to hear this from me, no one else. I need to tell him what's happened to Ellie.

A woman appears in the doorway—it's Sheryl, the head nurse, with her astonishing head of blond curls and a penchant for wearing brightly colored scrubs. She is kind and dotes especially on my dad. Sheryl has worked here for years.

She nods a sad smile in my direction before she shuts the door, giving us privacy.

Earlier, when I entered the lobby, I was such a mess, my shoulders shook as soon as I saw Sheryl. She reached for me, and I collapsed against her, telling her about my sister, about my need to travel to New Orleans. She wrapped me in a hug, and the fact I let Sheryl hold me instead of my husband hit me square in the chest. It should have been him right here, right now. It was always supposed to have been him.

In the lobby, Sheryl rocked and soothed me, the way I wish my mother could have done for me too. I cried for every person in my family who was missing.

With the door shut, it's now just me and my dad, and the hallway noises disappear as Sheryl's footsteps retreat. The only sounds are the heater clicking on in the corner and Dad's quiet breathing. It's warm in here, and I tug at my sweatshirt.

I take Dad's hand into mine; his fingers are thick and knobby, the blue veins pressed against his skin. "Dad, it's Ellie..."

And he stares at me for the longest time. He doesn't blink. But then a light shuts off somewhere inside him, and I know he sees it—Dad feels it—the god-awful truth that is written across my face.

He whimpers, and it's such a low, anguished sound, so heartbreakingly guttural and deep, it threatens to destroy me too.

It's the sound of a father who has lost his child, the pure shock and agony of it.

For the rest of my days, it will be the most tormented sound I've ever heard.

.   .   .

I sit with Dad for a long time afterwards, the two of us holding hands, the heater clicking off, then on again.

I don't share the details about the state of Ellie's remains, the specifics about her bones. He protected me before, and now it's my turn to do the same. The photos with Alex I obviously skip over too. My dad will understand this even less than me, and I still don't have enough information to drop this bombshell on him yet.

There is a knock at the door, and it's Sheryl returning to check on us. She says the doctor is on her way, and it will soon be time for Dad's medications. A grief counselor will also meet with him and they will give him special care the next few days and weeks.

"We will watch over him," Sheryl assures me.

I don't think I can leave my dad just yet. I'm not sure if it's the right thing to do, and I hesitate, but the nurse rests her hand on my shoulder while she motions for two other staff members to enter the room. "We've got this, Lauren. Go do what you need to do."

Dad peers up at me from his wheelchair. "Find out what happened," he says, crying softly. "Bring our Ellie girl back home."

And I hug him. I kiss the paper-thin skin at his temple while picking up the scent of his morning coffee, the leftover hint from his shaving cream.

"I'll bring her home," I promise him. "I will bring Ellie back to you."

Sheryl keeps her arm wrapped around my shoulders as she helps me down the hall. "We'll check on him nonstop," she says.

My grief threatens to knock me to the ground, and I stumble. With every step, I'm moving away from my father, and it's excruciating. I'm leaving him behind.

"It's going to be okay," Sheryl repeats. "We're here for him. We're here for you too. Call us anytime and we'll give you updates."

My teeth rattle. I am very, very cold.

"Oh, sweet girl," she says. "I'm so sorry this is happening to you." She tucks my head against her shoulder, and it's a welcomed, loving touch.

I don't want to leave Sheryl's side. I don't want to leave this nursing care staff who has become an important part of our family. I don't want to exit those sliding doors either and go back into that world, to that parking lot and the dark, dangerous cities and towns where vicious things can happen—where vicious things have already happened. Where people can go missing. Sisters too.

Sheryl asks, "When do you leave?"

I pause. "I haven't looked at flights yet, but probably this afternoon."

"Alex is going with you, right?"

I hope she doesn't notice my hesitation. "I think so, yes."

"This is such a huge loss." She swallows. Sheryl has tears in her eyes.

Her expression is so loving, so caring, that it touches me to see her grieving for us like this. Sheryl really is kind, the way she watches over the residents as if they're a part of her family too, an extension of great-aunts and grandparents that she helps comfort each day.

Sheryl has greeted me during so many of our visits. She's listened to Dad talk about Ellie. She's held out so much hope for us.

My girl has a fighting spirit, Dad always tells her. *Wherever she is, she'll fight her way through it, I know she will.*

The nurse looks at me. "When you get back, please don't think you're alone, okay? You've got us too. We're here to help, and we will definitely help with your dad. You have Alex also.

And tell Alex he can come find me too, the next time he stops by."

An anxious flutter presses against my ribs. "Alex comes here without me?"

"Yes, about once or twice a week." She sounds slightly surprised. "I thought you knew."

"No..." I say slowly. "I didn't."

"It's really sweet of him," she says, and offers me a smile. "So many of our residents don't have a lot of visitors, and then there's Alex spending so much time with his father-in-law."

It *is* kind. It's exceptionally generous of Alex to show my dad this extra support, and my heart swells for my husband. I think of the times when he told me he was going to the gym, and his trips to the grocery store that took longer than usual—he must have been checking on my dad.

But why didn't he say anything? Why not let me know that he was stopping by? It would have been nice to have updates, to have an extra peace of mind that Dad wasn't spending too much time alone, especially when I couldn't always get away from work. I've always led more projects than Alex. I would have loved to have known this about him.

I look at Sheryl, my unease stirring soft and slow. "When Alex is here, do you know what they talk about?"

"They stay in your dad's room, mostly. Alex isn't usually here for very long." She pats my arm. "There's no need to look startled, Lauren. It's touching. Truly. You're so lucky to have your husband. Not a lot of people care the way he does."

I swallow the tears. *But he didn't care enough to tell me the truth.*

I don't go home straightaway—I can't. I change lanes without looking, brake hard at red lights without noticing how close someone might be behind me. I'm driving on autopilot, recalling every turn, speeding up at every intersection before slowing down again.

Alex is kind. Alex is wonderful. *You're so lucky. Truly.* And yet, something doesn't sit right with this latest information either.

What a difference a day can make, how inside out my thoughts have become about my husband. If I hadn't learned about my sister, if I hadn't seen those photos of Alex and Clive, the brother he insists is still missing, I would have loved Alex even more for his visits. I would have been filled with pride that he would care for my father this way.

I'm positive I would have gone home and hugged him, wrapped my arms around his neck and repeated the same sentiments: *I am so lucky. Thank you.*

And Alex might have brushed it off. He might have said, *It's no big deal. It's the right thing to do. I care about your dad, Lauren. We're a team, remember?*

How many times has Alex said that we're a team?

I punch the gas, a tremble running through my neck. My husband and these details he's been diligently keeping from me.

I'm on Chicago Avenue and crossing Clark when I see the tennis courts up ahead, the grand stone façade of the Technological Institute of Northwestern University. Without realizing it, I've returned to my old stomping grounds, my college of four years and Alex's senior year, the community center that is just around the corner, with the Grief Share program where we met.

The sports field with its wide pitch of grass comes into view, followed by a block of residential halls, including the one where I used to live. Alex would meet me right there on that sidewalk as we walked to class.

I turn north, away from campus, and head for the lighthouse, the beige, sandy beach to my right with the steel-gray waters of Lake Michigan in the distance.

A steady wind whips across the lake with rows of white

caps surfacing, the darkness of the water ebbing and flowing beneath the rippling waves. An elderly couple walks arm in arm along the shore, their hair blown back, their heads pressed forward, the pair of them stepping into the wind. The sky and its great expanse of blue soars behind them.

It's quiet. The parking lot, for now, is mostly empty, but the beach will fill up later with students bicycling over from class and parents bringing their little ones from preschool. The weather should be nicer by then, the sun beaming down with its rays of warmth, springtime valiantly trying to venture into this hemisphere. Families will lay out blankets and snacks, coolers and thermoses of water, their dogs kept on a leash. Students will study in groups or run around throwing a Frisbee to let off steam. They will laugh with one another. Life will move on, but it will move on for everyone else. Not me.

My eyes circle back to the parking lot. This is where Alex said he ran this morning. He jogged through this area before he returned home while I stayed beneath the covers.

I trusted everything about my husband then. I find myself still wanting to trust him.

Lowering my head to the steering wheel, I cry. I miss my sister so much. This shouldn't have been what happened. This shouldn't have been her story.

Ellie should have been able to build a career. She should have been happy, had the chance to fall in love. Maybe even have a family.

My phone rings, and my first instinct is to ignore it, the way I've ignored all the other calls and messages. But I check it and see my screen is lit up with a string of missed calls, Alex's name showing up, as well as that dreaded phone number with the New Orleans area code.

I shouldn't put the detective off any longer, I know I shouldn't. I should answer him. He will think I have something to hide too, and my stomach twists because maybe I do.

SEVEN

"Mrs. Capshaw," Detective Rayburn says. "I've been trying to reach you."

"I had to see my dad. I had to tell him."

He hesitates. "Of course, I understand. I realize he hasn't been doing very well."

"No, he hasn't." And the tears fill my eyes. "Telling him about Ellie... it was horrible. It's not what we ever wanted."

"Mrs. Capshaw," the detective says, and the urgency returns. "Did you recognize either of the men in those photographs?"

"Yes," I say. My eyes squeeze shut. "It's Alex. My husband."

He doesn't sound surprised, and of course, he already knew. "We matched Alex's image to information about your family. It's been a few years since those pictures were taken, but that's definitely Alex Capshaw."

"It's also his brother," I confirm.

No surprise from the detective there either. "I understand that your husband kept this from you? That you didn't realize they had met your sister?"

"That's right." I look up. "Have you spoken to Alex? What did he say?"

"He finally answered his phone." The detective does little to hide his frustration. "I spoke to him a few minutes ago. As you can understand, I needed to hear his side of things."

His side of things.

"And?"

"Mrs. Capshaw, why do you think your husband kept this from you?"

My cheeks flare hot with a sudden need to defend him, for a desire to explain my husband. "Alex said they only met the one time. They barely knew each other. He didn't realize she was my sister until we'd already been dating a while. He didn't want to upset me..."

"Do you know why your sister would have those photos on her?"

I pull at a loose piece of string on my sweatshirt. "I don't know. She might have liked Clive. She might have printed them for work. Maybe she wanted to keep them to remember him by if he was leaving town soon, I'm not sure."

I search the beach, my eyes skimming across the sand. The elderly couple has moved on, and the beach is empty again.

"I understand how this must look, Detective," I tell him, "what you must think. But maybe there's a chance this is nothing. That it's all nothing. *Right?*"

"Your husband has agreed to travel to New Orleans and talk to us," the detective says. "We need to know a few more things. How soon did Alex Capshaw see her before she disappeared? What about his brother? Have either of them concealed anything else? We're checking on their alibis."

And that's good. That's very good, and my heart settles a notch. Maybe they will discover that Alex is telling the truth, that he wasn't at the music hall. He was nowhere near Ellie. They will find proof, someone who used to work at the hotel or a credit card charge from when he and Clive went to dinner. There could be something from twelve years ago that will corroborate his story. I shiver at the word *story*.

It won't explain or forgive why Alex kept knowing Ellie from me, but we'll learn that he's not the one who hurt my sister, that Clive had nothing to do with her death either.

"We need to know what your husband was up to while he was in town," the detective says. "His brother's movements also. But getting in touch with Clive Capshaw is proving to be difficult."

"Because he's missing."

"Yes..." And the detective pauses. "But that's what I'm trying to understand. Your husband said he's been missing for years, but no missing person's report has ever been filed. There is nothing official about Clive Capshaw in the system."

"But the last detective..." I say.

"Henley."

"Yes, Detective Henley. He knew about Clive. He knew we were looking for him."

"But he was mostly focused on your sister's case. He wouldn't have had a reason to look into Clive. He probably didn't think it was possible for these cases to be connected since he had no way of knowing that Clive was in New Orleans at the time of your sister's disappearance. As you are well aware, that information was kept from him. Alex said the last time he heard from his brother, he was somewhere in Texas."

My head aches, a throb settling somewhere behind my eyes.

"Clive Capshaw has gone off the grid since then," the detective says. "No social media, no credit cards. It's like he's on the run. Either that or something happened to him."

My thoughts spin and spin into a dark, spiraling hole.

"You know about the efforts that were used to retrace your sister's steps," the detective reminds me. "Everything the police did in their initial search, how Ellie left her apartment that morning and went to work. But no one knew she'd stopped somewhere first. There was nothing in her calendar about meeting someone for lunch. No one came forward about seeing her at the restaurant either. New Orleans is a busy place, and she would have seemed like any of the thousands of tourists who visit the city, especially in the French Quarter. We didn't have a lot of CCTV cameras back then. And without your husband coming forward, without him saying anything about that day, we didn't know where else to check. Who else to ask. We didn't know about this incident."

This incident, and I tighten my hands.

"But it was only brunch," I say. "Ellie went missing, but it was later that night. She came home after work. She went out again to the concert."

"Alex and his brother could have met up with her. Maybe they saw her."

"But everyone was interviewed. We would know if they were at the show."

"They could have met up with her. Maybe they followed her down the street."

An image of them following her to a run-down house in an abandoned lot sends shivers right to my core.

"Mrs. Capshaw, does the description of the house where Ellie was found mean anything to you?" he asks, as though reading my mind.

"No," I answer. I stare again at the beach, my hands trembling in my lap.

In the days and months after my sister went missing, we searched everywhere, or at least, I thought we did. From the concert hall near River Road where she was last seen, through the grid-like pattern of neighborhoods and businesses that stretch across East Carrollton, and past Loyola toward Ellie's apartment. We posted Ellie's missing person's flyers on light poles and stop signs, in any shop window where it was allowed, including several locations where we didn't ask permission.

We went north to the neighborhoods of Jefferson and Metairie too, our posters tucked beneath our arms, walking the streets in the heat, crossing parking lots with rain slinging sideways. And always there, always present, a mere four blocks from the music hall, swirled the ominous, brown waters of the Mississippi River. So many secrets churning within those murky depths, so many unknowns.

Could she have slipped and fallen? we wondered. After leaving the concert, did someone hurt Ellie and dump her body into the water? Did Ellie float out to the Gulf of Mexico and then...

I never liked to think about what happened next.

But my sister didn't make it that far; that's not what I've learned at all. She was dumped at a dilapidated house in some neighborhood—a neighborhood I swear we searched. She was abandoned and left alone.

Did she say anything to you? I remember Alex asking. It had been more than a year since Ellie had gone missing and he was with us during a follow-up trip to New Orleans. At night, he helped my family pore over case files as we kept hoping, kept praying, that someone would come forward, that someone would remember a new detail. We would never stop trying, my dad would always remind us. It was a hope we held onto.

Ellie's co-worker, Rachel, repeated the same details that she had described to the police.

We smoked a cigarette outside. I thought she was coming back in for the rest of the concert, but she didn't. She didn't tell me she was going somewhere else either.

We visited Ellie's roommate too.

Carmen had moved out of the apartment by then, saying it was too painful with memories of Ellie, the dinners they'd cooked together, the chicken they'd tried not to burn. The afternoons they'd spent on the sofa studying.

Carmen said she was too frightened to stay in the same place, as if the apartment itself had been cursed, like it was bruised and haunted and ruined after what had happened, never mind that Ellie had last been seen across town and nowhere near their place.

The apartment they shared is located close to St. Charles Avenue, which also makes it close to homes and businesses, but Carmen said she no longer felt safe walking home at night. She was terrified that someone could be watching her, waiting for her, ready to pounce in the dark. They would snatch her the same way they'd snatched Ellie.

We need you to be safe, Mom would tell my sister. *Walk in pairs. Be vigilant, look around you.*

And Ellie would roll her eyes. *We're not kids anymore. We know how to take care of ourselves.*

And sitting with Carmen that day, Alex asked, *Did Ellie say anything to you? Did she tell you about someone she'd met?*

He was so gentle, so kind, and I remember being grateful that he was by our side, that we had someone with fresh eyes to help us lead the way for a change. Dad was so sleep-deprived by then and worn thin, Mom too. We needed someone new to help guide us through the investigation.

Mom was on anxiety meds by then and drinking a lot also, and she slept very little, consumed by not knowing what had happened to her youngest daughter. She spoke hardly at all, keeping to herself and waiting for the bottom of her world to drop out again and again, for the police to say that Ellie's body had been found, that she would never be able to hold her daughter in her arms.

I wasn't coping so well either, and having Alex's support became a much-needed and tremendous relief. I kept hoping that Alex would hear something we hadn't picked up on before, that he would point out something we hadn't noticed. After all, he was asking the same questions regarding his brother's missing case. His search for Clive was running parallel to ours. At least, that's what I thought back then.

Sitting across from Carmen, we listened as she blamed herself.

I should have gone with her, she cried. *I shouldn't have let her go by herself.*

I held Carmen's hand. It hurt to hear her torment herself all over again, and I reminded her that it wasn't her fault. But Carmen was devastated, and she remains devastated, ever since that morning when she came home from her boyfriend's place and realized Ellie wasn't there. She hadn't slept in her bed. There was no note, no text message, and Carmen made that first worried phone call to me. A phone call that would change our lives forever.

In the months and years after my sister went missing, Carmen routinely checked on us, and each time we were in New Orleans, she helped us with the search.

I should have gone with her, Carmen sobbed and repeated.

But she went out all the time for work, I reminded her. *You couldn't have known.*

But she asked me to go. And I told her no. What kind of a friend does that?

Mom hugged her while Alex listened. And then Alex leaned in close. He practically perched himself on the edge of his seat and said, *Don't blame yourself, Carmen. We're so glad you're safe. If you'd been there too, who knows what could have happened? We wouldn't want you hurt too.*

I look up flights on my phone, but it's difficult to view the details on my screen. I'd much rather be home, sitting in front of my large monitor.

But I can't return to the house just yet. I need to sit in my car and settle my nerves first.

Detective Rayburn asked that I send my flight details as soon as I'm booked. As for Alex, I have no idea when he plans on leaving.

"He's being cooperative," the detective said, as if that could make any difference to me. "Anything he tells us will help."

I find a flight leaving Chicago at one o'clock this afternoon and landing in New Orleans three hours later. I can meet with the detective this evening and learn what else he's discovered.

What else will the police learn by then about Alex and his brother?

I can't stop my fear and anxiety surfacing about taking this flight, and my finger hovers over the screen. Can I do this? Can I really get on the plane and return to that city? Because on top of everything else, my fear of flying—and worse, my fear of flying alone—could shatter what's left of me.

We usually drive south to New Orleans so I can avoid boarding a flight, but the journey is long. And with time being of the essence and the detective asking me to be in New Orleans as soon as possible, I have no choice. I must do this. I must book this ticket.

Whenever I had to fly, Alex was the one to sit beside me. He would hold my hand and tell me that everything was going to be okay. He would say, *I'm here with you. Nothing is going to happen. People fly every day.*

But another voice loops in my head, and it's Ellie. We're kids once again, and she's telling me not to be afraid. She's telling me not to look down.

But I look anyway, and someone screams. My world goes dizzy, and Mom runs from the house, her face twisted in horror. She hollers our names. *What did you do? Girls, what did you do?*

I shake the memory away.

Clicking the screen, I purchase the ticket before I can

change my mind, then send a message to my team at work asking if someone can finish the project that's due by the end of today. After what's happened, there is no way I will be able to focus, to make the necessary changes.

I assure them only a few tweaks remain, that most of the project is ready to go, and I receive a response within seconds that it will be taken care of. My simple, vague explanation of needing to take leave for personal reasons does the trick, and no one pries. No one asks for an explanation. My colleagues understand that everyone has their days, their need for taking breaks, for having mental health days. My co-workers know full well about my search for my sister.

I start the engine and tell myself to go home. I will pack. I will make this dreaded trip to New Orleans, even as my hands tighten on the wheel.

But what if Alex wants to talk? What if he's still at the house?

I no longer know the man who will greet me on the other side of that door.

EIGHT

"Mom, Dad, this is Alex, the guy I've been telling you about."
Leading my new boyfriend by the hand, we step into my
parents' house. The heat is on, and it's warm.

It's been a hellish time for my parents, and Mom and Dad
have barely had the capacity for visitors, or for much of
anything else except looking for my sister, but I want them to
meet. It's important that they meet. Alex means that much
to me.

I've already explained to them about the Grief Share
program where Alex and I met, the program we continue to
attend, the sessions I wish my parents would try out also, my
mom especially, but they refuse. Dad thinks that every second
he spends sharing his emotions with other people is less time he
can spend looking for his daughter. And as for Mom, she
acknowledges my requests by anxiously dismissing me with her
hands.

Mom can't bear to take on another person's hurt, is what she
tells me. She doesn't want to hear about other people who have
lost loved ones. She can barely cope with her own loss.

She stands beside my dad wearing a blouse that hangs loose on her frame. Her hair is limp and dull, whereas only last year she would have had red highlights added from her monthly appointments at the salon. She would have asked the hairdresser to match her color to the auburn shine of my sister's, as Ellie's hair has always been brighter than ours. But those efforts have stopped. A lot about my mom has stopped.

Dad has lost weight too, and his belt is cinched tight at his waist. With his reading glasses pushed on top of his head, I assume he was staring, shoulders hunched, at his laptop even after we pulled up. I bet he's spent the entire day sitting at the dining room table, searching and clicking for anything related to my sister.

In my parents' kitchen, we work together quietly, throwing together a simple meal of pasta with sliced tomatoes and hunks of mozzarella, a side salad too, and some baked bread. We sit down to eat and I can't help feeling nervous. I'm a senior in college and somehow I'm still anxious about bringing home a new boyfriend. But I know there's another layer to all of this.

Because in my newfound happiness, in this mere sliver of hope, I find myself riddled with guilt. How can I have a partner, how can I possibly begin to fall in love, to share my life with someone, when we still haven't found my sister? How can I move forward when Ellie's life is standing still?

We're meant to be, Alex says to me sometimes. *We were meant to find each other*.

On the way to my parents' house, we stopped and picked up a couple of bottles of wine, plus a small pot of geraniums for my mom, something to cheer her up. It was Alex's idea to buy the flowers, and she accepted them with a timid smile, her hands wrapped around the gift.

At dinner, she doesn't say much, just picks at her food, topping off her wine glass more than anything else, and I worry about how the alcohol will mix with her sleeping pills later, if she should be drinking so much in the first place. I slide the wine closer to my end of the table.

Dad picks at his pasta. He sips at his water. It's not long before he asks Alex about his brother, Clive. "I'm very sorry to hear about what's happened."

"Thank you, Mr. Duncan. I really appreciate that."

"Have you heard anything?" Dad asks. "Any updates?"

He shakes his head. "Nothing. My brother said he was planning on crashing on a friend's couch when he got to Houston, but we don't know if that ever happened. I haven't been able to locate this friend either. Clive was always on the go, checking out new places; he's a free spirit in that way. But there have been no phone calls, no emails, and it's not like him. He wouldn't go this long without talking to me. He wouldn't leave me stranded like this."

Alex quiets, and the tremble in his voice is something I've heard from him before—it's agonizingly familiar. Because when Alex talks about his brother, he sounds a lot like me, like my parents, distraught and frightened. We're at a constant loss with what is unknown.

Because no matter how many times you repeat your story, it hurts like hell with every detail. Nothing can soften the blow, no matter how much time has passed, whether it's been months or years. Sharing with someone else doesn't lessen the pain.

I place my hand on top of Alex's, wanting him to know we understand, that he is among understanding company—my God, is he with understanding company. We feel every ounce of his pain.

"I thought that maybe he might have left Texas and wandered down to Mexico," Alex says, giving a tight laugh. "That's what I keep telling myself, that maybe he's a beach bum and living his best life somewhere. He has no phone, no internet, and he's loving every minute of it. But the moment I see him—I admit, the moment we find him—I will wrangle his little neck. I'll be so angry, but then I won't be able to stop hugging him."

Dad nods, and I do too. If Ellie has done the same, if she's taken off to backpack around Europe, if she's trekking through Nepal or the Outback in Australia, and she hasn't bothered to call, we will be furious. We will yell at her and question her lack of consideration. But then we will be overcome with such relief. We will finally know that she is okay, and we will forgive her. Our lives will go back to normal. That is what we want more than anything else, for Ellie to be safe, for everything to be normal.

"And the police?" Dad says. "They haven't been able to tell you anything?"

"Nothing." Alex shakes his head again. "And it's frustrating because I don't feel like they're looking for him very hard either. They don't seem to care. Since there's no evidence of foul play and he's an adult, they said that maybe he doesn't want to be found. That maybe he packed up his one duffel bag and left, headed for the road, and will contact me in a few months' time. But I can't just sit around and wait, you know? I can't relax because I know my brother wouldn't do this—he wouldn't *not* call me. Something is wrong, I know it is, and I have to keep looking. I have to keep searching. All these chat groups and hospital visits... I keep asking around. I try to go back to the Houston area whenever I can."

Dad says, "You're going through so much."

"And your parents," Mom says, and I startle at hearing her voice. "They must be so terrified." She has tears in her eyes.

I glance worriedly at Alex as this is something I haven't told my parents yet.

"My dad has been out of the picture since we were kids," he says. "And my mom died a couple of years ago."

"I'm so sorry," Dad breathes. "You're doing this all on your own?"

Alex smiles. "But I'm not alone, right? We have each other, don't we?" He looks to me, to my mom also. "We're in this together."

* * *

Alex's car remains parked out front, and I hesitate before unbuckling my seatbelt and stepping onto the street. A tricycle from one of the neighbors' kids is abandoned on the sidewalk.

We fell in love with the neighborhood the first time we saw it, the houses that were built in the 1920s with their painted front porches and low fences separating each backyard. Sidewalks lead to the playgrounds and nearby schools, and not far is the quaint main street with its coffee shop and delicatessen. A row of picture-window boutiques that sell stationery and women's clothing, plenty of silk scarves.

It's a short walk to our favorite café, the one Alex and I love to visit on Sunday mornings, where we can sit in the small courtyard and share breakfast if the weather is warm enough. We were at the café just last weekend, but with a chill in the air, we grabbed a table inside.

The neighborhood hosts block parties during the spring and summer months, with families handing out sidewalk chalk and cupcakes for the kids. We shared a cooler of beer with other couples on our street, and we kept glancing at each other, contented smiles that this is where we want to raise our children one day.

Traces of yellow chalk remain on the sidewalk, and I step over the streaks that are left behind, the arch of a giant rainbow with a pot of gold on one end, remnants from the last block party that haven't washed away.

On our front porch is a wooden bench that Alex built

several years ago. He carved our initials in the corner. Beside it is a small table I picked up at a thrift store and painted turquoise.

We've spent so many nights sitting on that porch, talking about our lives, about my sister and Clive. At some point, we inevitably fall silent, our minds drifting to *what if?* Where are they, and what are they doing now?

One time we laughed and cried while coming up with alternate universes where we could imagine our siblings. Fantasies that were far better than the awful worst-case scenarios that often slip into our minds.

Ellie is a hippie traveling through Spain, I said. *Or she joined the Peace Corps and is somewhere remote.*

Clive grew out his hair and surfs all day. Alex laughed. *Either that or he's working for the CIA. Or he's a performer in the circus.*

We laughed, and my husband held my hand as we sat, the cool night air surrounding us, the chirping of crickets lifting from the grass. I wasn't alone then. I was able to love and comfort my husband too.

I open the front door and listen for Alex, wondering which room he's in, what he's up to. The staircase is empty, and the printouts are missing. He must have picked them up and has been studying them. He's wondering how he can fix this mess.

In the kitchen, I find him pacing with the phone pressed against his ear. "Yes, that will work." His head lifts, and he registers my presence, adding quickly, "Thank you so much," and hangs up.

I stare at him, and he stares at me. Alex is wary, nervous. Jumpy.

"Who was that?" I ask.

"A hotel in New Orleans. I booked us a place."

I fold my arms. I won't be able to stay there, not with him. I'll have to find somewhere else.

"I talked to the detective," he says.

"I know."

"I'm helping with the investigation."

"You're helping them now, is that it?"

He flinches. "Yes, Lauren, I'm helping with everything."

I turn away, not wanting to hear any more. "I need to go to the airport," I tell him, and backtrack for the stairs.

"Wait, hold up. We need to talk."

I can't bear to listen to him. I can't bear to hear him come up with the next story, another excuse, a far-fetched scenario—I'll know it, and he'll know it—and it will hurt too much to hear him fumble with his words, his attempts at filling in the gaps, far, far too late.

I'm at the bottom of the stairs, once again wrapping my hand around the railing. My gaze wavers, the warped visions returning, and I curse at myself again.

The flight of stairs gives way to my parents' backyard, a flat piece of grass, and I'm crying.

Ellie, I say and stare at the ground, *what happened?*

It's not my fault, Lauren. You know it's not my fault.

Blood seeps from the boy's arm, and it's bent at an angle. Our mother's shouts reaching my ears when she bursts from the house.

I grip the banister harder. Alex is right behind me.

"I thought we could take the same flight to New Orleans," he says. "We can go together."

I don't respond.

"Please—"

"I already booked my ticket."

"When do you leave?"

"Soon."

"Stop." And there is a rush of air at my back. Alex is reaching out to grab me, to stop me, but he drops his hand. "We can do this. We can work through this. We're in this together."

And I halt. "Are we, Alex? Are we really in this together?"

He doesn't answer, and I don't wait another second before I pound up the steps, my knees no longer shaking, my mind willing me to go on.

I head for the closet and pull out my suitcase, tossing in my clothes, an extra pair of jeans, a few sweatshirts, some underwear. I have no clue what the weather will be like in New Orleans, so I add a couple of short sleeves too. Some of the clothes I fold while others I heap into a pile. There is no suitable wardrobe, no understanding of what is appropriate when traveling somewhere to bring back your sister's body.

"I'm coming with you," he says.

"No."

"Tell me your flight time and I'll book the same one."

In the bathroom, I grab my toiletries, my hairdryer, a full-sized bottle of ibuprofen; I chuck them in, then zip up the suitcase.

"I'll book my own flight," he says. "I'll join you tonight."

He tries to take the suitcase from me, and I balk. But it's not to stop me; it's so he can carry it. He wants to help. He would carry it out to my car if I asked him. My husband, the gentleman.

I grit my teeth. *But it's an act. Our entire marriage has been an act.*

I lug the suitcase down the stairs, fighting my way through the dizziness.

"Let me drive you," he says. "Let me take you to the airport at least."

"No. I will get there on my own."

I roll my suitcase to the office, then rummage through the desk drawers until I find what I'm looking for: my blue binder, Ellie's binder, where I keep newspaper clippings about her case, photos, and notes that I've copied from Detective Henley.

Updates that have become fewer and farther between over the years.

Later today, I will go back through this information. I will add the latest notes from the new detective.

I slide my laptop and the binder into my backpack and fling the straps over my shoulders. Glancing around the room, I search for anything else I might need, something I'm missing, something I want—and, yes, I'm missing something huge: I am missing my husband by my side. I'm missing my sister.

My lungs ache; tears sting my eyes.

Alex is behind me. He says, "I should go with you. You know I should."

I feel for my car keys that are in my pocket. My purse I grab from the floor.

"Let me sit next to you and help. You know how you are about flying."

"I will manage on my own."

"Hear me out—"

"Please don't," I snap.

"We'll find out who did this. We'll find out who hurt Ellie."

And my hand freezes on the door handle. My heart breaks, my hand trembling. "I loved you," I tell him. "I loved you the moment we met. I thought you could help me, that I could help you too, that we could depend on each other. We could help each other get through everything. But it's all been lies, Alex. Our entire marriage has been nothing but lies, and I don't know what to think about us anymore."

"You don't mean that, Lauren. I know you don't. I never wanted to—"

"For this to come out?" I shoot him a look. "Well, it has. And now I have to leave, do you understand that? I have to go get *my sister*. I have to bring her body back home. Do you know how much this is killing me, what's happened? *She's dead*. Ellie is dead, and I should be focusing on her, on plans for her funeral, not this."

He cries, "You shouldn't have to do any of it alone." His voice is wet and throaty.

"I *am* alone," I tell him, and fling open the door. "You've made plenty sure of that."

NINE

The flight is on time, and I'm seated, doing my best to regulate my breath. My hands I keep wrapped around my armrests.

I purposely didn't select a window seat—I never, ever select a window seat—preferring the aisle, where I can keep my eyes bolted to the table that is stowed away in front of me, my gaze remaining glued to the clasp that locks in place. If I maintain a focal point, if I do what all the books and meditation apps tell me, I should be okay.

The plane shifts, and it must be the stacks of luggage loading into the hold from the conveyor belt. My heart jolts. We have yet to lift off the ground.

Other passengers shuffle down the aisle, and a bag or an elbow will occasionally knock into my chair, my shoulder. I shrink my body, keeping my legs tucked, attempting to make myself small, wanting to occupy as little room as possible on this plane. Because in this small space, I can convince myself I have the tiniest semblance of control; I can tell myself I'm going to be all right.

There is nothing I can do about the pilots—they have been trained properly and they will do their professional best. I have no control over the weather either, although I did overhear a flight attendant saying it will be a smooth flight to New Orleans with no turbulence, and the exhale from my lungs was long and steady.

The other passengers and what they're up to, their conversations, their books, and their laptops, their rustling and tearing open of snacks, these people are separate from me. We don't need to interact. We will sit together in this tiny metal can, and I will ignore them. I will tune them out, and they will ignore me also. I will let myself trust what is happening and try to let go.

And one thing is for certain: I will absolutely not look out that window.

The woman beside me pays me little attention. If she notices my focused breathing, how balled up I am in my seat, she doesn't glance my way.

She digs through her handbag instead, applying hand lotion, then swiping lip balm before she unwraps a piece of gum and pops it into her mouth, the spearmint lifting into the air for a brief second before the scent disappears with the quick blast of air conditioning from above. She pulls out her phone and scrolls, and I'm convinced this will keep her occupied until take-off.

I keep my phone shoved inside my purse. Alex hasn't called, but I wonder if he's followed me, if he jumped into his car and headed for the airport to chase me down.

At security, I kept looking around, my nerves skyrocketing, half-expecting to see Alex standing in line, his own ticket purchased, his face searching mine for forgiveness. He'd finally tell me about Clive.

But at security, there was no sign of him, and at the gate, I held my breath at every person who approached, their carry-on bags clicking and rolling in tow, thinking Alex would show up and grab the seat beside me. But my husband was nowhere to be found.

Alex said he would fly to New Orleans. He told the detective that he will help with the investigation. That he'll do what he can...

Alex wouldn't be a no-show, would he? He wouldn't skip out to find his brother now that their secret is out? How guilty would that make them look then?

I keep my eyes glued to the tray table. I fight to keep my breathing under control.

Most of the passengers have boarded by now, and the jostling down the center aisle has slowed. No one has tapped me on the arm, and Alex hasn't walked past and quietly said my name.

But he could be here, couldn't he? He could be on this flight, and I somehow missed him. He might not be meeting up with his brother after all since he wants to keep his eyes on me. He wants to discover what else I'll learn. It's what he's done for years, isn't it? Staying close. Staying close to the investigation. My family.

The plane rattles, a sharp shudder that seems to be closer to the cockpit, and the main cabin door is closing. We will be leaving the gate soon.

It hits me again that Alex isn't here. He won't be here to sit with me and tell me the flight will be over before we know it, that I don't need to worry about all that sky, all that distance, all those clouds and wind and vast nothingness below as we sit, like sitting ducks, trapped in our seats. He isn't here to hold my hand.

I try not to think about him. About all of it.

Because Alex knows the real root of my fear—my fear of heights—and the reason why I'm afraid. He understands why I'm slow to get out of bed in the mornings too, why he has to reassure me when some days are painfully worse than others.

It all happened so long ago. But the screams are still there, and they haven't gone away. My sister's screams, the boy's screams too. They're still seared into my memory. That hard, hard earth, and the body that lay twisted below. Our mother's look of horror. The huge sky above, and nothing to spill from our mouths but more lies.

* * *

"Come on, Lauren," Ellie shrieks. "Dad finished the treehouse."

We're in overalls and T-shirts, our hair pulled into ponytails and wrapped with elastic hairbands. *You're almost like Irish twins*, Mom always tells us. *Doing everything together*.

We were born eighteen months apart, which is close, but just enough of an age gap for me to use to remind Ellie that I'm her big sister, that I should be the one leading the way for most everything. But she is defiant. Ellie is loud and assertive. And with her being so adventurous and bold, spontaneous and daring, that means my sister is more popular too. She jumps straight in, no questions asked, and usually, friends will follow.

Months ago, Ellie convinced our dad to build a treehouse, and with those bright green eyes of hers, the energy and excitement she brought to the planning, the pleading and whining, she managed to get Dad to agree.

Ellie came up with part of the design too: a platform she insisted needed to be very high as the perfect lookout. She wanted to be able to see everything. The treehouse would require a ladder, and she wanted a roof—a proper clubhouse.

Dad looked up plans while Mom stayed silent, her mouth twisting in a way that said she knew something bad was coming. She didn't think it was a good idea, something so high. Someone could fall.

When Dad asked what I thought, I wondered why we couldn't convert the old shed at the end of the garden into a clubhouse instead. The shed existed, and it wasn't being used except for some pots and planters. Most importantly, it was safely on the ground.

But Ellie, at age nine, thought that a treehouse—*In an actual tree*, she said, giving me a stern side eye—would be far more thrilling and, therefore, more coveted by the neighborhood kids. She insisted they would come running from up and down and around the block, telling everyone it was the coolest treehouse they'd ever seen. They would beg to climb up there. They would talk about it at school, lavishing us with attention. And I admitted, that sounded pretty good.

We'll be able to look out over everyone's rooftops, Ellie said. *We'll get to determine who gets to climb up or not, who's invited. We get to make the rules.*

I agreed, and from that night on, Dad hammering in the mornings, then taking breaks for work, we would lie in our beds and dream.

It can be our rocket ship, Ellie said. *Or we're on the International Space Station. We can be Blue Angel pilots commanding the skies just like Amelia Earhart.* She'd only just learned about Amelia Earhart at school.

Now, with Dad's hammering and sawing finally at an end, and with the treehouse completed, Ellie runs ahead, sprinting the length of the backyard as I follow, my excitement catching up to join hers.

Ellie reaches the ladder. "This is so awesome," she squeals. "Don't you think so, Lauren? Isn't it the best? It's just like we pictured it."

It's just how *she* pictured it—not me, at that great height, and not the way our mom wanted it either, but Ellie got her way. Dad gave in.

We hug our father and thank him. He kisses the tops of our heads, our long skinny arms wrapped around his waist, as Mom watches us. She doesn't step forward from the back deck.

Dad has told her numerous times that it's safe, that the design is foolproof. He added multiple support beams to allow the bulk of the weight to rest on the thickest and sturdiest branches.

But Mom doesn't move. She stands warily, her arms folded.

Ellie grabs the ladder to climb.

"Be careful, girls," Mom calls out. "One at a time. Don't rush."

It's not as if Ellie is giving me a chance to cut in front of her. She scrambles to the top, her white tennis shoes digging into the wooden rungs that Dad nailed to the tree bark, and I watch her go, our dad too, our hands covering our eyes to shield our gaze from the sun. Up she goes, higher and higher.

"Come on, Lauren!" she shouts. "Come check it out with me."

She's on the platform next before she ducks inside the clubhouse. "This is so amazing," she shouts, racing from one side to the next, her face peering out from one of the windows to beam down at us. "There's a table and a bench and everything."

Ellie closes a set of window shutters with a hard click. She swings them open again. "Lauren, you have to see this!"

It's my turn to climb, and with the excitement, my nervousness, her insistent calls for me to join, bubbles pop inside my stomach. Within seconds, I'm scrambling to the top and reaching the platform to look across the yard.

I smile at Dad. I wave at Mom too. And on the other side of the fence, I spot the red patio furniture that belongs to the Henry family.

Someone passes behind one of the living room curtains. Is that Mrs. Henry? Will she bring her son outside and let him go round and round on his tricycle?

The movement in the living room stops, a muffled noise from somewhere in the house. Is that Mrs. Henry arguing with her husband again?

The Henrys' backyard remains empty, and whatever little

Cameron is doing, if he's coloring or playing, his toys spread out before him, it will only be a matter of time before his parents stop arguing, before he sees us at the top of the treehouse and realizes it is ready. He will beg to come over.

But he's too little, his mom has repeated. *Cameron needs to wait until he's bigger—*

And from behind me, an abrupt push.

My body flies forward, an unexpected jerk. A cold fear pierces my lungs, a thousand needles cutting into my skin.

I'm falling forward—this is it. I'll plummet to the bottom with nothing to stop me. Nothing but that hard, hard ground. That cold, dense earth.

But two hands are suddenly around my shoulders, and they pull me back, my scream cut off and swallowed at the back of my throat.

I rock on my heels, deliriously happy to be on solid footing again, my shoes digging into the plywood as I try to regain my balance. My mouth is still open, I'm trying to breathe—to scream—but there is no shriek, no sound, only my heartbeat exploding like a burst dam. I'm dizzy.

"Gotcha!" Ellie giggles, and she jumps back.

I look at her, my arms shaking, as she giggles again.

That was too close, way too close. I could have gone over. What was she thinking?

"Ellie!" Dad hollers at her from below. "What is the matter with you? Don't you ever do that again."

Ellie tries to laugh, to lighten what happened. "It was just a joke," she says. "Just a joke."

"Never, ever again!" yells Dad. "I want your word. Now."

Ellie's lips tremble, and she looks at me, her eyes widening. "I'm so sorry, Lauren."

I can't speak.

"I was just having a little fun," she whispers.

Dad hollers, "Ellie, I swear I will tear this whole thing down if I have to worry about you doing something like that."

"I won't," Ellie pleads. "I promise."

Mom shouts from the back deck, "Come down *right now*."

And I do what I'm told, I always do, and drop my legs to the ladder to scurry down. I wonder if Ellie will listen, if she will comply.

She is still begging for my forgiveness. "Lauren, wait... I'm sorry." She climbs down after me. "I won't do that. I promise you I won't," she says.

TEN

The humidity hits my face as I step through the sliding glass doors and exit the airport. I can't get out of that concrete block fast enough, needing to put as much distance between myself and that plane as possible. I remember the blessed relief as we touched down, the surface of the earth once again solid beneath us.

I lost sight of the woman sitting beside me as soon as we exited the jetway, my feet carrying me into the terminal as I didn't look back.

But then I spotted her near the baggage claim and our eyes connected for a brief second. She gave me a sympathetic smile, and I timidly smiled in return.

On the flight, she handed me a packet of tissues—I hadn't realized I was crying, my fingers lifting to my face and finding the tears dripping to my neck, an ache that threatened to explode inside me from the sobs I was fighting to hold in. I wasn't strong enough.

My sister... and her body... what remains of it. Ellie waits for me at the end of this journey.

The woman leaned over and said, "Whatever you're going

through, whatever's happened, I'm so sorry." And she lowered the window shade, thinking that perhaps the glare from the clouds and the white-hot sky was hurting my eyes, that maybe I'd want to sit and cry, mourn and grieve, in this little patch of dimness. She couldn't have been more right.

She had no way of knowing what was happening—maybe a breakup, a lost job, a family member in crisis—but she sat with me in silence, a companionship that said she needed nothing in return. She didn't want an acknowledgement. And I don't know if she understood how much this gesture meant, the reminder that there is still a lot of kindness in this world. There are still good people. There is still humanity left out there, we just have to look.

The plane lowered as we approached our destination, and with the window shade down, I was able to avoid the slow descent, the ground that rose toward us, the trees and buildings that would have warped and wobbled in my vision, my breath shortening into tight, panicked gasps.

I wrapped my hands around the armrests as we touched down, my gaze staring straight ahead, my spine straight. I wanted off that plane. I needed to get out of there and move and be free again.

I roll my carry-on quickly now and walk to the center concourse, where I will wait for my Uber. There is no wind, no breeze, but the steady, ever-present Louisiana heat circling my head, along with puffs of exhaust fumes from the cars passing by. A driver honks loudly as someone else whistles for a cab, the blast echoing against the concrete pillars. A bus hisses as it pulls out in front of another.

The air is warmer and stickier here than it is in Chicago, and it never ceases to amaze me—every time we've returned to New Orleans, we've been surprised by the heat at our necks, the humidity causing us to push up our sleeves. My thoughts drift to the reasons why Ellie would move here in the first place.

There's a sense of celebration to this place, she would always say. *Can't you hear it? There is music everywhere.*

And there *is* music. It streams from car stereos and overhead speakers playing festive jazz to welcome the tourists. And in the distance, past the interstate, past the Superdome, and far beyond the busier streets, tucked within the narrow grid of the French Quarter, the music drifts throughout those spaces too.

From within those bars and private lounges in the Garden District, the terraces that overlook the off-beaten path of the Marigny neighborhood, come the haunting notes of the blues, the smooth, low tones of someone's breath sighing into a saxophone. The beat of a drum the next street over can quickly speed up your pulse, your blood pumping.

Ellie came to New Orleans with such high hopes, so many dreams. I know now that she never left.

I lean against a concrete pillar, my head throbbing, as I wait for the latest dose of ibuprofen to kick in. My eyes ache, the sky beyond the arrivals area a sharp, bleached white from the clouds mixed with smog. I throw on my sunglasses to block the glare.

I check my phone. The Uber driver is less than two minutes away, and I step closer to the edge of the curb.

Soon, I'll be heading downtown to meet with the detective. I'll learn more about what happened to my sister, the run-down house where she was abandoned, the progress the police may have been able to make since this morning.

And will he know... Will Detective Rayburn have gotten any closer to understanding my husband's movements that night? Will he have learned anything about his younger brother and what they were up to?

Most of all, do I want to know any of that information myself?

. . .

Detective Rayburn stands from his desk to greet me. His work area is tidy compared to the chaos that surrounds him, his colleagues and their clutter and stacks of folders with pages spilling out, their fast-food wrappers and coffee mugs that have not yet been rinsed and put away.

Steel desks are pushed together in haphazard pods, and police officers roll back from their chairs to grab printouts from the copier. Several talk loudly into their phones. Others finger-peck at their keyboards, their heads lowered to enter their reports.

Detective Rayburn lifts a notebook from his desk. He keeps a single-file organizer with the information carefully tagged, a row of brightly colored sticky notes lining the edge. A framed photo rests beside his computer, and I assume it's of his family, his wife and two small children, the boys wearing matching red shirts, their hair combed to one side. They're miniature versions of the detective. Detective Rayburn catches me looking and suggests we grab a room down the hall.

"It will be quieter there," he says.

The detective is tall and slender but with a width to his shoulders that makes me think he was once a swimmer, or he could still be a swimmer now. His long-sleeved, button-down shirt is beige in color and tucked into a pair of brown slacks. He keeps his badge clipped at his waist.

His eyes are kind but intent, a light brown, perhaps hazel in the fluorescent lights. But there is a steely grit to his gaze too, a hard edge that makes me think he's seen a lot in his career, some good, some bad, some of it downright atrocious, and he may only be in his forties. Flecks of gray have not yet reached his hairline.

He closes the door behind us, and we sit across from each other at a table. He opens his notebook, flattening the pages with great care, with such purpose, that I'm reminded again of his determination to solve my sister's case as soon as possible.

"Your husband is arriving separately, I assume?"

"Yes. Maybe tonight." My voice catches. "Honestly, I have no idea. He should get in touch with you."

"We'll make sure that he does," he says.

I tighten my hands.

"We're trying to determine why your sister was at the house in the first place. We've learned a few things about the home and its condition since the property was in dispute for many years after the owner passed away. He left it to his children, and they couldn't quite agree on what to do with it. One brother wanted to tear it down and rebuild, hoping for a quick sale, and the other is perhaps the more sentimental one and wanted to renovate it, move in with his own family. The house sat empty and tied up in legal battles for quite some time. With each passing year, it deteriorated until the brothers finally reached an agreement. That happened a few months ago."

My mouth runs dry, my breath uneven. He's describing the background details, the setting, but in my mind, he also paints a bleak picture. This was Ellie's unknown resting place for years. It's where she was kept hidden as we walked block after block calling her name.

Where did we go wrong? How did my family not check this neighborhood well enough? We missed it, all of us. We failed her.

This is a big city, the first detective told us. *There are a lot of square miles to cover. Everyone is doing their best.* But we let her down.

"The property was in bad shape," Detective Rayburn continues. "With a cease and desist order in place, no one could enter the premises either. We've had a lot of storm damage over the years, hurricanes and tropical storms, and part of the house collapsed. The floor above the garage had a kind of raised area." He glances at his notes. "I've seen pictures of it, the original house. There was a section that rose up from the roof, kind of like a lookout point, like a..."

"Like a cupola?" I ask.

He nods. "Yes, a cupola. It was large with its own wrap-around balcony. The brothers said that's where they would spy on people when they were kids. They could almost see the river from there."

A lookout spot with an interesting view. My sister would have loved it. She would have insisted on seeing it despite the cease order. Any restrictions to keep back would have made her want to see it more.

Come on, Lauren, she would often plead with me. *Climb up here. You're missing out.*

But I would beg instead, *Come down, Ellie. You're going to hurt yourself.*

"The neighbors filed complaints," the detective says. "The house was an eyesore and dangerous for anyone who might wander in. Understandably, they didn't want their children to go near. As soon as the brothers reached an agreement, the case was settled, and a construction crew started clearing the debris last week. They pulled back Sheetrock and wooden beams. That's when they found your sister."

I close my eyes, trying not to picture it—not wanting to picture it. But it's there, the image now burned horrifically within my imagination.

Ellie with her long red hair like mine, but brighter. Her body forgotten within that derelict house, one of her hands possibly sticking out from beneath a cracked beam.

The perspiration lines my lip, and I must pale, my eyes squeezed together, because the detective says, "Are you all right, Mrs. Capshaw? Can I get you some water?"

I can barely get out the words. "Yes, please."

He returns moments later with a plastic cup, and I drink from it greedily, clutching the plastic and relieved to have something to hold, grateful that I can squeeze in the sides as I listen to the rest of the details. My tattoo with Ellie's name presses against the cup.

The detective says, "Are you sure you're okay to continue?"

I nod. I don't have a choice. I must do this for my dad, for Ellie.

It's up to me now, I remember sadly.

"Construction on the house is now halted. The area is marked off as we search for anything else: DNA from your sister's clothing, something that was left behind in the debris. Loose fibers, that sort of thing. We collected her driver's license and a debit card from her jacket pocket. A gold necklace—"

"I want that back," I say quickly, needing every treasured item that belonged to my sister.

"Of course. We'll make sure that everything is returned to you. As you know, we also found those photos."

I stiffen.

"Mrs. Capshaw... I need to speak with you about the condition of your sister's body. She had multiple broken bones with large breaks to her arms, her legs, and back. They're consistent with someone falling from a height. We believe the injuries occurred before the house collapsed, which means the breaks weren't from debris falling on her or from that part of the house caving in, but from a fall to her head, to the back of her skull. That's what killed her."

A crack to the skull.

My sister fell to her death.

It's been twelve years, and the police finally know what happened to my sister. Ellie lay there, shattered and broken, her body a mangled mess on the ground.

I pull the tissues from my purse and press them against my mouth. Finding Ellie will never be closure, no matter what anyone says, no matter the results of the final investigation. Finding Ellie's remains, retrieving her body, is just another complicated layer to our anguish, another heartbreaking step in our journey to bring Ellie home.

No, the closure, I tell myself, the reckoning, is what is soon to come, when we find out who did this, and we punish this person. When we find justice for my sister.

I cry, not caring that the detective is waiting for me, not caring that I'm shuddering in front of him, my face a blotched mess. The detective can wait for as long as this takes, and I imagine he has sat with other families and endured this same excruciating torment before.

I sob harder. Ellie fell to her death, and no one would have believed it. My sister with her love of heights, with her curiosity that led her up and away, with her constant excitement for what was ahead, and she plummeted to the ground instead. She fell to the earth. My sister, a shooting star, going out in an instant.

I crush the plastic cup in my hands.

A fall is what took her life. Not a horrific gunshot wound or a stabbing, or years of neglect from some demented kidnapper—my mind often slipped to those dangerous places—but a fatal crack to her skull. A topple from some great height was my sister's tragic ending.

Did Ellie see the ground as it rushed toward her? Did her world go blank the moment she landed? Was she in pain?

I hope she wasn't, and I pray that she had no idea what was to become of her, the years of darkness that would surround her body as she lay in wait. The ghost of her voice crying out to us from beneath that rubble. *Please find me, Lauren... please...*

"The cupola..." I say to the detective, and I splutter to get my voice under control. "That's where she fell?"

"We believe it was from that balcony. We've considered the possibility she could have been hurt somewhere else and then taken there to hide. But her breaks, her injuries, they're consistent with that height. It's also similar to another tragedy that occurred at the house."

"What other tragedy?"

"Someone fell from the balcony decades earlier. A family member of theirs, a great-uncle. He took his own life and jumped. There was no foul play," he adds. "But it was upsetting to a lot of people. Several of the neighbors didn't want to see the cupola anymore. They wanted it torn down to get rid of the bad memories."

Two deaths at the same house, and I shiver.

Did my sister know about this? Had she heard the stories? Had it become another haunted ghost tale within a city that is already so full of them? Ellie would have had a strong desire to check it out for herself. She always loved a good ghost story.

My sister, Ellie, the more curious one, the more adventurous one. Far more reckless than me.

Ellie would have gone up there on a dare, I'm sure of it. But then again, she wouldn't have needed much convincing. She would have wanted nothing more than to see that view. The promise of it, the allure, and she would have climbed those steps with such titillating excitement. The tragic history of someone jumping from the balcony years earlier would have only piqued her curiosity more.

"Ellie could have slipped and fallen," the detective says, and he meets my eyes. "Or"—he pauses, delicately—"she could have jumped."

I straighten in my chair. *He's not implying what I think he is, is he?* The suggestion about my sister lingers in the air.

"Or," the detective adds, "there's a chance someone pushed her. Someone went up there and killed her." He regards me carefully. "We just need to know what really happened. We need to know the truth."

Detective Rayburn's phone lights up, and he apologizes for having to take the call. He leaves the room and I don't move. I stare at the cinder-block wall that's painted an ugly, drab gray.

Ellie would *not* have jumped. I know she wouldn't. I can't imagine her slipping and falling either.

And in that quiet space, in that barren room without a single window, the air stifling and still around me, my thoughts fire off one by one.

Ellie climbed to that balcony on her own—no one forced her. Padlocked doors and *No Trespassing* signs be damned, Ellie crept across that property, believing she was stealthy, a tickle of excitement in her throat, the slight fizz of danger pumping through her blood and goading her on.

She found a way to get in, and that was the easy part. She discovered a broken window: teenagers busting in months before or someone looking for shelter, ignoring the cordoned-off areas just like my sister would. They smashed through the glass and tumbled in, finding rooms to explore, a place to sleep or take cover.

And that night, as the temperatures finally began to cool in Louisiana, when no one was around and the teens and drifters had apparently moved on, the house creaking and sagging in its various dark corners, my sister ventured inside. She wandered around and found the stairs. She climbed to the top, to that lookout point and balcony where she could stand beneath the night sky, a house where she shouldn't have trespassed, but she went anyway. Ellie climbed up and up, like a moth to a flame. She wouldn't have been able to resist.

Who stood among the shadows and watched? Who crept up behind her and pushed?

Besides Alex and Clive's whereabouts that night, should the police be considering anyone else?

Sitting and thinking, I crush the cup until it's in a little ball. For every second that I am in this room, I resent the detective for implying that my sister might have jumped. How could he think that? How could he speak those words?

I suppose it's because he has to. He has to look at every possibility, including the fact that someone took their own life from that exact spot years earlier. It's his job to consider every situation, the difference between suicide and an accident. Murder.

But the Ellie I knew as a child, my carefree, twenty-year-old sister who moved away to live in New Orleans, had so much going for her, so much potential. I can't imagine her taking her own life. I can't imagine her feeling such wretched desperation, such isolation and bleakness, that she didn't think there was a chance for things to get better, for anyone to help. That there could be no end to the fog and sadness that pressed in around her, the pitch-blackness suffocating her everywhere she looked.

She would have talked to me, right? I really hope she would have. I would like to think she would have told me if she was in trouble.

She might have come home and seen our parents, too. She might have said something to her roommate.

Did Carmen notice a change in her behavior, perhaps? Something that Ellie might have shared with her, a dark shadow that could have fallen over my sister in those last few months, a sadness she was struggling to break through.

She asked me to go to the show, Carmen said. *And I told her no.*

But Ellie also told Carmen she was excited about the band write-up that she would be turning in the next day. Her co-workers confirmed Ellie had already started the draft and saved it to their server. My sister wouldn't attend the concert and prepare a write-up if she was planning on ending her life, would she? She had plans—she'd made plans with us for Christmas. She promised she would come home for Christmas.

None of this sounds right, and none of it sounds like Ellie.

But, then again, how much do I really know about my sister? How certain can I be about every single thought she had from twelve years ago?

We were no longer living in the same house, but lived hundreds of miles apart. We didn't speak to each other on the phone as much as we wanted. She was busy with her life, and so was I. That's as simple as it was.

A month before Ellie went missing, she came home for her birthday weekend. Mom stood in the kitchen finishing her cake; Dad was busy wrapping her present, a jewelry box with a necklace that was tucked inside, a gold letter *E* at the center of the chain.

Ellie and I went out later for drinks with friends, and she got quiet at one point. She told me a strange story but then blew it off, saying it was no big deal, that she was overreacting again.

Living in New Orleans, Ellie said, *it's weird, but my imagination can go wild sometimes.*

The music was thumping, and I had to lean close, had to raise my voice. *What do you mean?*

She looked embarrassed. *I don't know. You know what? Forget about it. I bet I'm imagining things.*

What things?

It's okay, she said.

No, Ellie. What is it?

She stared into her glass, and her shoulders were tenser than before. *It's stupid, but I'll be walking home, and sometimes it feels like someone is right behind me, like they're practically on my back. But when I turn around, there's no one there. It's like they vanished. An apparition.*

I nudged her with a wary smile. *A ghost? Is that what you're saying? You're not trying to freak me out again, are you?*

She laughed. *No, this is different. It's something else. Like someone is watching me, maybe watching me from a window.*

My throat tightened. I no longer found this playful.

She shrugged half-heartedly. *It's nothing. Let's dance. It's my birthday after all.*

Had someone been following my sister? Or was it just Ellie's imagination? Had she heard sounds—maybe a neighbor clicking their front door shut, the hum of a streetlight, a stray cat darting between the bushes—and spooked herself walking home?

Someone could have pushed her, the detective said. *Someone might have killed her.*

Did Ellie—always wanting to be so trusting, always wanting to have fun—invite Clive out with her that night? Did she take him on a stroll through the neighborhood and then they climbed to that balcony? Did she lead him by the hand to show him the view, not knowing he might have seen her climb those steps before?

Clive said he wasn't staying in town for much longer, and she thought it would be a nice send-off, a late-night walk offering him a one-of-a-kind view of the Mississippi River. An experience that he could only get in the Crescent City, and she thought she was being kind.

Clive didn't tell his older brother about his plans, and Alex fell asleep like he said he had. Clive snuck out of the hotel. The gorgeous girl he'd met, someone he'd introduced to Alex hours earlier, and he wanted to see her again. Like a moth to a flame, Clive couldn't resist either.

Clive, and the way he sat beside my sister with that look in his eyes, his arm slung around her chair. A steady crush.

And up there, against that night sky, did something happen between them on that balcony? Did Clive come on too strong, and Ellie stepped away? Things got heated, and they argued. She told him no, and he was angry. He didn't like being told no. He pushed—

By now, the tissues in my hands are shredded into pieces in my lap, a mess of soggy white confetti that falls to my jeans.

A noise on the other side of the door, and it's the detective returning. He will have more questions. The door handle lowers, and I brace myself for what comes next.

What do I tell him? Do I say that Clive might be the one? Do I imply that this man—this brother-in-law of mine—is the one who could have hurt my sister?

ELEVEN

The detective clicks the door shut. "They're still running tests. There's a lot of debris and damage, a lot to sift through, but we should know more soon. In the meantime..." He sets a couple of printouts on the table, placing them side by side in front of me.

It's the same images, and it's torturous: their three faces staring up at me again. My sister's smile. The turn of my husband's head. Clive's grin.

Alex staring right at the camera.

The detective watches as I study them, and I'm still in shock. The photos are of an event that took place long ago, a gathering that I wasn't a part of, that I hadn't been aware of, that I wasn't *supposed* to be aware of, and the secret remained buried—just like my sister—for such a long time. The truth is coming out now.

Seeing these images for a second time doesn't help either. It's also more destabilizing in front of the detective, more surreal, the possible legal consequences extending far beyond the implosion of my marriage.

Sitting here, and being in this room with my sister's face, my future husband's... It's like falling through a fun house, everything tipped upside down. This mere blip in time when the three of them sat together, this sliver of history, and it's the exact same day my sister went missing, *hours* possibly before she died, not long before I would meet the man who would one day become my husband.

I grimace, the uncertainty growing like a vine and threatening to choke me.

Like I did this morning, I reach for the photographs and trace my sister's face. She was so beautiful, so happy, with no idea what was to become of her. Did she think of that day? Did she mention me? Is that how Alex knew that I existed?

"The original photos are being tested," the detective explains. "They're fragile, as you can understand, the edges faded, the paper crumbling in places. There was a lot of damage…"

And he stops. I'm grateful that he doesn't finish his sentence because with my sister's decomposing body, the weather, and the heat impacting them over time, the jean jacket material thinning and shredding against her, I'm shocked the photos haven't disintegrated completely. I'm surprised there is anything left, that a stained, white blotch didn't spread across the surface and cover their faces, the photos shriveling into a tight, soggy ball.

Instead, the photos lay protected inside her pocket, beneath the toppled roof and all that Sheetrock, those crumbled tiles. Ellie kept a clue for us all these years. She has a message.

And it's hard not to think about, but if the images had been destroyed, would that have been any better? I wonder. If they'd fallen apart into unrecognizable pieces, their images lost to time and all that changing weather, would my situation be any less horrendous?

My sister's body would still have been found, and that would have been devastating, but there wouldn't be this extra gash to my heart, this double-edged sword that implicates my husband and his brother.

I want nothing more than to turn back the clock. Make these images disappear. Keep my sister alive. Because without the photos, I could still be in love with Alex. I could still have my husband. I wouldn't have to know about the secrets he's kept from me. I wouldn't be going down this path alone, fearing I could lose everything.

I whimper as I already don't have much family left.

But then again, Alex would have kept on lying. He would have kept me in the dark for as long as possible, for the rest of our marriage, I'm certain. Whatever it took to protect him and his brother, and conceal what happened that night.

I scoop the pieces of shredded tissue together in my hands and crumple them into a ball. It's another moment before I look at the detective.

"Your husband remembered the hotel where they stayed," he says. "It's on Canal Street on the edge of the Quarter. We confirmed it. We also confirmed that he left the next day, just like he said he did. But his brother? He didn't take a flight, and there's no record of him buying a bus ticket. Your husband thinks he might have caught a ride, that he hitchhiked, and this is something he would apparently often do. It would have been cheaper that way. If he did, we would want to track that person down, of course. Confirm the date, confirm the driver."

"So, Clive was definitely in Houston?" I ask. "You know this for a fact?"

"We're still trying to determine that, if he arrived at all. But, Mrs. Capshaw, what we're most interested in is what happened the night your sister went missing, where Clive was, what he was doing during that time. What both of them were doing."

I nod, the sickness spreading with their absolute duplicity.

"We checked with the magazine where your sister worked, and she made a print request for that same afternoon," the detective says. "She put a rush order on these photos, which is interesting. Did one of the brothers go to the concert that night so they could meet up, so she could give them the pictures? Did one of them climb up to that balcony and push her?"

"Or maybe it was something else entirely," I say, surprised, once again, by my need to defend my husband, my inclination to pivot back and forth with my emotions, especially who I'm siding with in front of the detective.

After all, I've been married to Alex for eight years. I should defend him, particularly in front of the police. Didn't we make our wedding vows and promise for better or for worse, until death do us part?

My loyalty, whatever remains of it, still lingers inside of me somewhere, in the recesses of my mind, the corners of my heart, like a muscle reflex. My misguided loyalty still beats for my husband. But the connection, the existence of it, hangs by a thread. One more revelation, and I'm not sure how I will respond next.

"Alex and Clive stayed at the hotel," I tell him. "They didn't go out that night. Ellie went to the concert, and for whatever reason, she left early. She shared a smoke with her co-worker and took off. She'd already seen the band before, and she wanted to go home. She was tired. She owed her boss a write-up in the morning. She walked..."

My voice trembles, a faceless perpetrator looming in my mind.

"Ellie made it a few blocks, and someone watched her go to that house," I continue. "They followed her to the balcony. Maybe they'd seen her at the concert, and they lied to investigators about what time they'd left, where they'd gone afterwards. They followed her."

"We're tracking down everyone who attended the show," he says. "We're re-questioning them."

"Good."

"We're locating everyone who was seen in and around the concert that night too," he adds. "Anyone near the property.

Everyone will be questioned. But here's the thing: what happened to your sister could be a completely random act or it could be someone she knew. Someone she trusted to walk with into that abandoned house in the dark and go up to the balcony. Sadly, as you may know, crimes are often perpetrated by someone the victim is acquainted with. They can be lured more easily that way."

He taps his finger on the table. "Therefore, we cannot discount Ellie's connection to either of the Capshaw brothers. Your husband not disclosing this information to you at the time or after all these years is something that cannot be ignored."

My body tightens, and I look down, pulling the photocopies closer, their edges lining up with the end of the table. They looked so young back then, so carefree.

A pitcher of water is set in front of their breakfast and what's left of eggs Benedict and slices of toast. The flowers rest in front of my sister too, the small clutch of blooms tied together with a piece of twine.

Flowers, pink camellias.

A gift for Ellie.

The memory returns to my mind, several memories in fact. Those flowers, and the gesture that could be hidden within them, the potential symbolism.

Alex would have given me the same flowers. And he has. He has multiple times.

I told him that I loved him, and he told me the same. I believed him.

* * *

Light shines through the vase. It's gorgeous, and Alex places it on the end table near the front door.

He's returned from another trip to the grocery store, and I turn down the music.

Holding the latest bouquet of flowers, Alex smiles. It's another delicate arrangement that is wrapped in paper, and I grin at his sweet, romantic gesture.

My husband will often walk up and down the aisles of the grocery store, several loaves of bread in his cart, a selection of carrots and celery for a stew to perhaps simmer later, a bottle of wine, and he'll approach the flower section to take a look. He will take his time selecting another bouquet for me.

No reason, he says. "Thinking of you flowers" is what he calls them.

My friends tell me that it's sweet, but also sickening and obnoxious, nauseating even, they tease, while also admitting they wish their partners would do the same for them. Spontaneous gifts, something as simple as flowers. *Just thinking of you*, their partners could tell them.

My mom would smile when Alex brought the bouquets home, especially if there was a bouquet for her too. *You don't have to*, she would say, but then she would beam at me next. I think she was relieved that I'd found someone who was kind and thoughtful, someone who would always be there for me and help me to get through.

The flowers started on our first date and continued after that, Alex bringing me arrangements of carnations and daisies first, then orchids and tulips with their bright orange and yellow blooms. After we were married, he would bring home larger bouquets and place them on the kitchen counter, or he would surprise me with a gorgeous display in the living room. The glass vase is where he keeps the flowers now. *So you can see them when you come home*, he tells me.

The types of bouquets have meanings too, Alex informed me. For camellias, white is for someone you like or admire. Red is for a significant other. And pink represents a longing for someone, someone you miss.

On the anniversary of Ellie's disappearance each year, Alex

presents me with a bouquet of pink camellias. He never, ever forgets.

You miss your sister, he says. *I miss my brother too.*

Poppies are another flower that symbolize remembrance, and in some cultures, marigolds represent grief and mourning, ways to remember and honor someone. But Alex specifically brings me camellias, pink in color, and I have always cherished that he remembers Ellie with me, that he recognizes how much I want to see my sister again.

Alex's kindness—his consideration for what I've gone through, what I'm continuing to go through, despite his own worries about his brother—has always touched me. But now I'm learning there was a secret within those gifts too.

The pink camellias that were given to my sister. The ones placed in front of her.

Did Ellie's face light up when she saw them? Or was she shy at first, maybe even taken aback since it was supposed to be a casual brunch with men she'd just met?

Would she tell Carmen about the flowers when she got home later? Would she place them on the kitchen counter and mention that she might see them again?

But Carmen never mentioned a bouquet, and the bouquet wasn't listed by the police either, not during the initial search of the magazine office or the sweep through Ellie's apartment. She didn't tell her roommate about someone giving her a gift.

After the restaurant, where did she take the flowers? Or did Ellie leave them behind, forgetting them, or simply not wanting them? Alex saw her reaction, and Clive did too.

Pink camellias for my sister.

Pink camellias for me also.

But who gave them to her—my husband or his brother?

TWELVE

After leaving the police station, I find a small hotel in the Garden District off St. Charles Avenue. I'll be able to access the streetcar from here, which will take me closer to Loyola, Ellie's university, in the Uptown neighborhood where she used to live.

The streetcar will also run me to East Carrollton, where I can walk the additional blocks until I reach the music hall. It's where I can find that house.

But do I really want to see it? Do I want to see where my sister was left behind and forgotten?

I imagine the property that is roped off with yellow crime scene tape, the crumbled Sheetrock and bulldozers that are now halted in place, the workers gone and replaced with police officers and a forensic team, the news crews parked out front. The reporters will have their cameras and gear set up, looking for neighbors and police officers to answer their questions.

Have the reporters learned the latest from Detective Rayburn? Are they aware the coroner has identified the body? I hope not as the detective only contacted me this morning; he only just informed our family. But the media is swift, reporters can be relentless, and they will soon track someone down to talk. After all, the house has been marked with crime scene tape since last week. They've already reported that a body has been found, and the reporters will be counting down the seconds until they learn more details.

Has the press already tracked down the homeowners for a response? I imagine a joint statement from the two brothers, their solemn expressions about how stunned and horrified they are to know that something like this has been discovered inside their father's home, a home where they grew up. *We had no idea*, they might say. *Our thoughts are with the family.*

Will they ignore questions about how their great-uncle ended his life? This house being the location of two tragedies?

If only the brothers had stopped arguing, if only they'd stopped fighting for one second and agreed to work on the house sooner, and we would have known about Ellie sooner too. We could have found her.

And would that have been any better? Trading years of hope that she was alive and safe somewhere and dashing them with the knowledge that she is dead, that she has been dead all this time?

We could have already had a funeral and buried her. Mom would have known what had happened to Ellie before she passed away herself.

We would have known about the photos sooner too, and I clench my hands.

I assume the police will release a formal statement in the next day or so, most likely from Detective Rayburn when he announces that, yes, the body that was found has been identified as a young college student who went missing twelve years ago. The dilapidated property is where they believe her death occurred. If anyone knows anything, if they know anything at all, they should come forward. Every piece of information needs to be shared with the police.

How long before the reporters track me down next? My

phone is set on silent now. No more loud ringtone since my sister isn't coming home alive. No more need to rush to my phone at the first ring.

The reporters will be able to find my details easily as I've done plenty of interviews in the past. Ellie's Facebook page is open to the public and the media can send me a message. My design work is listed online.

How long before they learn about the questions surrounding my husband and Clive too, when the reporters discover the truth? And I feel faint, pressing my hand to my forehead.

Alex Capshaw knew the college student before he met her older sister a year later. Is this a coincidence? Or did he seek her out in order to discover what she knew about her sister's disappearance? He wanted to know everything about the case. The reporters will have all kinds of questions for the police, for me. The very same questions I'm asking myself.

The public will have a field day about this too, anyone with an opinion, with time to stand around and gossip, the perfect watercooler subject at work. They'll come up with their own theories about what happened, who did it, who's responsible. This case will be too intriguing, too scandalous and shocking of a story to pass up. Within days, Alex and Clive's guilt will be determined in the punishing court of public opinion.

And what will they say about me?

How could she not have known this about her husband?

The reporters could be standing outside the property this very instant. They might be interviewing the police for updated comments as they prepare to go live for the ten o'clock news. The neighbors could be out on the street also, their arms folded as they shake their heads, telling everyone and anyone who will listen, *We asked them to tear down this place sooner. We worried that something bad would happen.*

Something bad did happen.

I won't go anywhere near that house tonight, I tell myself. I'm not ready to lay eyes upon the collapsed property just yet. The hours I spent earlier with Detective Rayburn were more than enough, the walls of that meeting room closing in on me, closing in around my family, with every minute that ticked by.

What I want to do instead is lie down in this hotel room in the dark. I will lie in the quiet stillness and hide myself away for a few hours.

I requested a room on the first floor—finding one is no small feat in a city that is filled with high-rise hotels and lobby areas lined with banquet halls. The larger hotels are closer to the French Quarter and along Canal Street.

But this smaller bed-and-breakfast is tucked away in the Garden District, a home that was built in the 1880s and has since been converted into suites. With its black, wrought-iron fence out front, painted white columns, and a wraparound porch that leads to a courtyard behind the building, the home is the epitome of a Queen Anne-style mansion. The quarters where enslaved people lived have been torn down, thankfully, and so has the once-attached carriage house. The new owners introduced a large fountain and an extended garden in their place.

Outside my window, wide-leafed ferns press against the glass with rows of jasmine and azaleas filling the flower beds. Ivy twists up the brick walls and wraps around the gas lantern posts, the lanterns flickering their yellow-white beams upon the path.

A decorative crane made of solid cast iron stands regally in the center of the fountain, with one foot lifted and two spotlights shining up at it through the water. The courtyard is beautiful and serene, and the steady gurgle of bubbles would have typically been a soothing sound for me, but not tonight.

I pull the curtains together and step back from the window.

Years ago, we stayed at a small bed-and-breakfast similar to this one, but when I looked the place up, I discovered it had been turned into offices, which was disappointing. The hotel had been a haven for us during our many sleepless nights after Ellie first went missing, those nights stretching into weeks, then months.

When the reality hit that Ellie wasn't coming home right away, and that our stay would be extended, we moved into a semi-furnished apartment.

The rental property served our purposes with its small kitchenette, where we could sit down and make meals, even though we weren't eating much back then—we were too sick with worry. The sitting area became a mini headquarters of sorts, where Mom and Dad, mostly Dad, commanded the space and followed up with the police. We had stacks of missing person's posters piled everywhere. Packages left by local churches with containers of unopened food.

When Dad wasn't out searching, he was sitting beside Mom, their hands clasped together, the whites of their knuckles showing, as if Dad already knew he needed to hold Mom together. They invited reporters over for interviews, the police stopping by with their updates too. But those updates became less frequent as the weeks passed, and I could see it in their faces, their lack of eye contact with my father, with each of us, that their hopes of finding Ellie alive and well were becoming less likely with the minutes that were passing.

It was awful to see the diminishing hope.

We forged on, regardless, organizing more street teams and posting Ellie's missing person's posters everywhere we could. Carmen came over every day to help, recruiting volunteers and classmates from school. She helped answer the phones.

I was missing so many classes by then that I withdrew from Northwestern for the rest of the semester. Carmen took a break from her studies also, neither of us able to cope or concentrate, not with our exams coming up, not with everything that was happening.

The hotel room is dark, and the soft hum of the air conditioner hushes my mind with its steady white noise. I'm too exhausted to change out of my clothes, too overwhelmed to do anything else but lie on the bed and close my eyes. I don't bother to pull back the covers, wanting nothing more than to block out everything, for everything to disappear so I can go back to the beginning. So I can rewind the clock to when Ellie was still alive and she was still with us, Mom too.

In here, doors don't slam. Phones aren't ringing, and there is no detective staring me down, asking me questions. Tourists aren't stumbling and laughing down the hall either—not yet at least. It's nearing midnight, which is still early in New Orleans, even on a Monday.

The rooms on either side of me are quiet too, and so is the one above. They're either vacant or whoever is staying is already in for the night. The guests are courteous not to move around or talk too loudly. The house is old, and the rooms won't be as soundproof as the heavy, thick spaces of a larger hotel.

I wonder, briefly, where Alex is staying. I decide that I don't want to know.

Pressing my head against the pillow, I realize that I should have called my dad by now. I should have checked on him. But it's late, and the Oak Manor staff won't like it if I call at this hour unless there is an absolute emergency or we're in crisis—but then again, our family's been in crisis for a very long time.

This will have to wait, I know. These latest details are something I will have to tell my dad about in the morning. Because for now, he needs his sleep; he needs to recover after the shock of today, and so do I. I close my eyes and pray that no bad dreams will occupy my mind.

My eyes shoot open, and it's a strange, panicked feeling, those initial few seconds of consciousness when I'm not sure where I am, how I got here, what is going on.

I keep my body still, my arms and shoulders tense, as I lie in this space, in this pause, the darkness surrounding me.

This is definitely not my bed, and against that window, those are definitely not my curtains. The air here is different too, thick and humid and lying across me like a damp wash-cloth. The trickle of the fountain outside continues to fall with its soft, gentle bubbles.

It all comes back—a tidal wave crushing me—that I'm in a hotel in the Garden District. My sister is gone. My husband is no longer with me.

I turn my head. The glow from the alarm clock reads 3 a.m., and of course it is: the so-called witching hour.

The witches will come and get you, Ellie used to tease when we had friends for a sleepover. I hated when she said things like that, especially when I was more spooked than everyone else.

It will feel like someone is right behind me, like they're prac-tically on my back, Ellie said. *But there's no one there. It's like they vanished. An apparition.*

I'm wired now, jolted awake to be in this unfamiliar room, the knowledge that somewhere across the streets and city blocks, somewhere in this city, are the remains of my sister's body. She is alone too. Unlike me in this nice, comfortable space, she lies in a cold and sterile morgue, and that breaks my heart.

I can't get to her. I can't comfort her. I can't tell her that we will soon be bringing her home.

And somewhere close, near the riverbank and not far from

the swirling, brown, ominous waters of the Mississippi, is also the place where my sister's body was kept hidden for years. All that splintered wood.

The detective's voice whips around my head. *We cannot discount Ellie's connection to the Capshaw brothers. Your husband not telling you cannot be ignored.*

Alex, what have you done? What have you done to my family?

A sound from above, the distinct creak of a floorboard, and I rise to my elbows. The room above me isn't vacant after all.

Another creak, and I sit straight up—a frightening thought hits me at once. *Has Alex taken that room?*

He's above me. He's found me. He's found me again.

Alex has woken in the middle of the night, same as me. He's wondering if I'm awake too. He wants to talk, to see me.

For as long as we've known each other, we've been restless sleepers, our haunting dreams and endless worrying about our missing siblings.

I reach over and switch on the lamp, one side of the room illuminated with shadows cast over the other walls. My shirt is stiff against my neck, my jeans tight against the back of my waist. I will drag myself into the shower at some point and change into fresh clothes. I will figure out what to do next, go through my blue binder with Ellie's notes.

I rub my hand across the tattoo of my sister's name, but it no longer brings me as much comfort.

Another creak, and I look up again. The sound is followed by footsteps, a steady tread across the room as this person walks slowly.

Does Alex know where I'm staying? Did he guess?

He knows that I will have asked for a first-floor vacancy, and there aren't too many of those unless you venture toward the city limits and find a motel. Alex might have looked up the same place from before, all those times we traveled with my parents, when we visited Carmen and retraced my sister's steps.

Did Alex discover the hotel is no longer open, so he searched for something comparable, a location that is close enough to Ellie's apartment, a hotel that also has a first-floor room?

I saw my husband as he paced back and forth in the kitchen this morning, his phone pressed against his ear. *Yes, that will work*, he said, before he hung up.

What are the chances Alex would pick the exact same place as me? Another crazy coincidence to stack up among all the others? Another deliberate move by my husband? It's frightening how fast I've stopped trusting him.

The footsteps above come to a stop, and a long pause is followed by a flush of water. The water runs down the pipes next.

The person walks back across the room, and I trace their steps, the slow and steady movements, before the creaking finally comes to a stop. They stand very still. This person is directly above.

I hold my breath, as if I'm worried they can actually hear me, as if they can see straight through the floorboard to where I am sitting below. They will know that I'm on the edge of the bed, my heart in my throat, my eyes locked to the ceiling as they stare right back.

It's another face-off, I realize, another stand-off of sorts, and it reminds me of the way Alex and I glared at each other as I held the pictures.

The squeak of a mattress against a bed frame, the gentle sag of metal springs above me, and then nothing. Silence. They must be going back to sleep. I wait a few more seconds before my shoulders relax.

They can't hear me. This person can't see me. No one knows that I'm here, and I'm getting myself worked up for no reason. I'm frightening myself, spooking myself the way Ellie used to do with her ghost stories, my sister holding a flashlight up to her face, her wide, frightful eyes in mock horror in the dark.

So many nights, we climbed to the top of the treehouse, both of us refusing to come down, even if sometimes Ellie had to coax me up in the first place, despite Mom and Dad's repeated calls for us to climb down for dinner or get ready for bed.

I find my purse and dig around until I find my phone, my screen lighting up with new messages, but they're not from the detective. Each one is from Alex.

It was after 1 a.m. when he reached out.

I'm here.

And my eyes shoot again to the ceiling.

I just landed.

I relax—he means he's in New Orleans, and not this same hotel, not the room above.

I can't keep jumping to conclusions. Alex took a late flight and wanted to notify me when he arrived.

I love you. Please know that I love you.

I bite down hard to keep from crying.
Alex sent a follow-up note:

I have a meeting with Detective Rayburn in the morning. Can you meet me there?

I let out a bitter cough and drop my phone to the mattress. I will absolutely not be there. I've done my part. Like me, he needs to sit and talk to the detective on his own.

Because I know there is something else I must do. There is something I need to see first. I will wait until daylight when I make my move.

THIRTEEN

I'm showered and dressed, a to-go cup of coffee in my hands, as I wait outside the bed-and-breakfast for a cab to pick me up. It took forever to fall back asleep, and I'm not sure if I ever did, but I lay there, my thoughts suspended and foggy, my worries drifting, then rising about another phone call, another text message. A knocked fist against my door.

I kept waiting for the person above me to get up and move again, for a hard rap of their knuckles to sound, with Alex announcing he was waiting for me outside. *We need to talk*, he would say. *Come out now*, he would warn.

Shortly after dawn, I couldn't take it any longer, the deep, needed sleep evading me and slipping away like smoke, and I threw back the covers and showered. I kept listening for sounds as I got dressed, my paranoia ready, my ears perked.

Stepping into the hall, I looked up and down, holding my breath. I waited to see Alex.

Would he hurt me? Get me? Drag me back into my room? Force me to stay behind a locked door until I believed him?

The lobby was at the end of the hallway, but it didn't seem close enough, and every step felt like an eternity. I kept looking for a flash of Alex's dark hair, for his hand to reach out and spin me around, for his eyes to tell me I wasn't going anywhere.

Placing my hand on the wall, I tried to steady myself. I knew I was working myself up again.

I found a breakfast room on the other side of the lobby with carafes of hot water and tea, large thermoses with various medium- and dark-roast coffees. A staff member announced that a cooked breakfast would be served later, but I didn't acknowledge them. I wouldn't be sticking around for that.

It's early, but the air outside is already warm, it's languid, the humidity of a New Orleans spring already taking shape by morning. Waiting for the cab, I look down, rubbing the toe of my shoe back and forth across a patch of weeds that rises through a crack in the sidewalk. Dandelion puffs spread out in front of the fence with a wind chime tinkling somewhere in the breeze.

New Orleans and the Garden District, and all of its old-city charm: Ellie was right about this place. It's unlike any other city in the world. The roads are in constant need of repair, potholes sagging with chunks of asphalt, flood waters seeping in from the gutters after sometimes only a half a day of rain, with so many parts of New Orleans below sea level, but the city is indeed wonderful. Magical, its history filled with secrets, voodoo, and charm.

New Orleans has its own heartbeat, its own soul, a rhythm to the communities and the people who live here, the people who thrive in this place and make it home. Bright smiles on their faces for when they're having fun. Mischievous winks for when they're up to no good. Sweat along their brows from working hard also.

The roots of a nearby oak tree break through the soil and push against the pavement, causing the sidewalk to rise crookedly. Nature is like this, I realize, always finding a way to break through. Bodies are eventually discovered.

I trace the shadows, the moss from the oak trees drifting above, the shadows gliding back and forth across the pavement, the movements listless and carefree, just like this humid weather.

For the first time in years, I am awake and ready so early in the morning. With my own coffee in hand, I will make things happen for my sister. I will make things happen for myself. I no longer need to depend on Alex.

The cab rounds the corner, and as the driver approaches, he rolls down his window. He greets me with a pair of sunken eyes that tells me he's either just started his shift and isn't fully awake yet, or he's been driving all night and is counting down the time until he can go home.

Either way, we don't have too far to go, and I climb in, saying, "The French Quarter. Jackson Square."

He nods, then pulls away without saying a word.

We rumble down the tree-lined street until we reach St. Charles Avenue, and it's quiet. At this hour, the city is slowly waking up and brushing itself off from the night before. A woman walks her dog on a purple leash. An older gentleman emerges onto his front porch.

We pass a series of row houses, the properties eventually giving way to classic revival mansions with their large white columns and peaked roofs, each estate becoming larger and statelier than the next, their majestic front gardens shadowed by hundred-year-old oaks.

So many of the restaurants are closed, but a sole donut shop is open, as is a local grocery advertising: *Ice, milk, and beer twenty-four hours.*

We loop around Harmony Circle before passing blocks of office buildings and renovated apartments that are adorned with their wrought-iron entrances. On either side of the road, delivery vans are parked, their hazard lights flashing, and the cab driver must maneuver around each one.

The last time I was in New Orleans was four years ago, and I can't believe it's been that long. My search the last few years shifted toward online chat rooms and Facebook messages that I could easily take care of from Chicago. Once Dad moved into the senior center and I no longer traveled as often, and with the detective retiring also, my number of trips to this city lessened.

But New Orleans still looks the same, the streets still sound the same, and I crack open the window to let in some fresh air. We're on Canal Street next, the downtown thoroughfare that brings visitors to the Riverwalk, a shopping mall that overlooks the Mississippi River. The street is filled with clothing stores and liquor shops, window displays showing off jewelry and every kind of Nola souvenir imaginable. The fleur-de-lis symbol is everywhere.

The bright lights of Harrah's Casino flash are along here too with some of the more die-hard, all-night gamblers walking ashen-faced from the revolving glass doors. They stumble down the steps, presumably toward their hotel rooms and beds. More money lost as they will defiantly, and carelessly, return later and try again.

Canal Street is lined with larger hotels, the Marriott and the Sheraton, their floors towering above, but I don't look up. I don't need to because somewhere along this street is where Alex stayed with his brother. Out of one of those brightly lit lobbies, the two of them left in search of a day of fun, of great food and music. At some point, Alex and Clive walked deeper into the French Quarter to meet my sister.

The cab turns onto Decatur Street, the blocks becoming shorter with the buildings crowded together, the Creole-style structures that were inspired by French and Spanish architecture, a Caribbean influence to the buildings also. Leftover Mardi Gras beads dangle from the railings with potted ferns pushed against the balconies.

The oyster bars are not yet open, and neither are the Cajun

markets and gift shops, but Café Du Monde is available, the café and its outdoor space already serving a small number of early risers and tourists. These early-bird, eager souls sit fanning themselves beneath the café's iconic green-and-white awning. They sit, ready for their caffeine.

I pay the cab driver, and he pulls away with a tired wave of his hand. My to-go cup from the hotel is now empty, but I will find a table at Café Du Monde that faces the rest of the French Quarter. I will order another coffee, and from here, I will call my dad.

After that, I will find the restaurant from those photographs, that same balcony. The place where my husband first met my sister.

A ceramic mug is dropped off on my table. It's filled to the brim with dark chicory coffee, a Café Du Monde specialty, and I take a sip. The flavor is intense, woody and earthy, and somewhat bitter, but the caffeine is what I need. It's what will help sustain me. That, and the need to find the truth.

I call the senior center and am relieved that it's Nurse Sheryl who answers.

"Lauren, are you okay?" she asks.

"I'm okay." But I begin to cry at once. Something in her tone, in her genuine love and care, breaks the floodgates open. "It's a lot to handle," I say. "It's awful."

"We're so worried about you."

"Thank you. That's very kind." I inhale deeply. "I met with the detective last night and they're still running tests. There's a lot to determine. I'm not sure when I'll be able to bring Ellie home."

"We're so sorry," Sheryl repeats. "Please know that everyone here is so sorry. We're thinking of you."

More tears fall. "And how's my dad?"

"He's okay. We keep checking on him and monitoring him. But I'm told it took a while to get him settled last night for bed. He eventually relaxed."

I trace the coffee mug with my finger. "And today? How is he?"

"He ate a little bit of his breakfast, but he's quiet. Then again, he's usually quiet unless he's talking about Ellie."

A bittersweet smile crosses my face. Dad will talk to anyone at any time about Ellie.

Sheryl's voice muffles. She says something to another staff member, something about checking on another patient, before she returns. "By the way, Alex stopped by yesterday, I thought you'd want to know. He asked to see your dad, to make sure that he's okay. He said he was flying out to join you."

My breath holds. "What time was that?"

"Around three or four." She pauses. "I think it was four. I'm pretty sure since I was finishing up my paperwork around then. Did he arrive okay? Is he with you now?"

I scan the café, the tables and sidewalk beyond, my eyes locking in on every person, every tourist, as if my husband could appear at any second, he could materialize right beside me at my table, his hand reaching for mine. I will either sit tight or run.

One of the waitstaff from Café Du Monde strolls past with his white paper hat and long white apron. He carries a tray with plates of beignets loaded with powdered sugar, and a customer at a nearby table lifts his hand to request his order. There is no sign of Alex, and I breathe out again.

"Lauren?" the nurse asks. "Are you still there?"

"I'm here." But I watch as a man steps away from the café. He crosses the street. He's wearing a suit and tie, the back of his balding head glistening with sweat. Not my husband. "How did he seem?" I ask. "Did you talk to Alex?"

"He was pretty upset. He's worried about you, Lauren.

About your dad too. It was so good of him to stop by. They sat together for some time."

My eyes lift. "Just the two of them?"

"Yes."

"Do you know what they talked about?"

"I'm not sure. Maybe your dad—"

"Sheryl, can I please talk to him?"

Sheryl puts me on hold, and a few minutes later, the receiver lifts. I hear her gentle voice. She must be in his room helping him get situated in his wheelchair before she moves him closer to the bedside table and the phone.

"Lauren?" he says. His voice is throaty and raw, and it crushes me.

"*Dad.*" I immediately start sobbing. My emotions are too much. Everything that is happening in my life is too much, and hearing his voice, how frightened he is, how far away, he's fragile and hurting, and I find myself crumbling again.

"Lauren...?" he says.

"I'm here, Dad." I gulp back my tears. "Everything is going to be okay."

"And Ellie?"

"I'm bringing her home, just like I said I would."

Dad is quiet for such a long time that I wonder if he's still listening, if he's not drifting in and out instead as he does sometimes, if he's confused, the grief possibly making everything in his mind worse.

But no. My dad remembers painfully well.

"I woke up this morning, and I thought it was a dream. I wanted all of it to be a bad dream." Dad cries softly.

"I'm so sorry."

"Your mom," he whimpers. "Do you think they've been together all this time? And that's why she left us so soon, so she could be with Ellie? Your mom left us to take care of her?"

I pull several napkins from the metal dispenser and press

them against my face. The thought of Mom's heart giving out so she could be with Ellie crushes me, pains me, but there is some peace in there too. Maybe she felt like Ellie needed her, that Ellie needed her desperately. She knew her youngest daughter was alone and was waiting for her. She had to go.

But we miss you too, Mom. We need you here with us also.

"They're together," I agree with him. "They're together, Dad. I'm so sorry I'm not there with you." I sniffle. "I should be with you."

"It's okay. You stay strong, Lauren. You need to be strong for all of us."

"I'm trying."

I settle the napkins against the table. My gaze drifts to a pair of women strolling by. Behind them, a man jogs with his earbuds in, his white tennis shoes slapping against the pavement.

"Dad? Nurse Sheryl told me that Alex came to see you yesterday."

"Did he? Alex?" Nurse Sheryl murmurs something to him in the background and he makes a sound. "Yes, that's right. Alex was here. But why wasn't he there with you? Why aren't you together?"

"I caught an earlier flight. Dad... does he often come by and see you? Does he visit you by himself?"

He doesn't speak, and I worry that I might have confused him, that he won't understand why we're talking about my husband and not about Ellie.

"Alex?" he repeats, and Nurse Sheryl murmurs something else. "Yes. He's here. I mean, he was here before. Other times too."

Other times too.

"What do you guys talk about?"

"So many things," he says. Dad's voice is light, almost wistful. "He does most of the talking."

"About what?"

"About Ellie... so much about Ellie." He lets out a gentle sigh. "One time, he talked about you too. He asked what you girls were like as kids, about the two of you growing up. About that day."

My pulse beats at my throat. "Which day?"

"You know which one. About the day that boy fell. You remember that, don't you?"

Despite the heat, a chill hits my neck. "What does he say?"

"All kinds of things," he says. "And it's so nice to hear him talk about her. It's almost like he knew her. Isn't that strange?"

FOURTEEN

"Come on, Lauren. Climb higher! Check it out with me."

I have to crane my neck, Ellie having climbed on top of the treehouse and onto the roof, stepping on the railing and hoisting herself up like an acrobat, no fear. There's never any fear when it comes to Ellie.

I look for our mom and dad, but they must be inside. A week after Dad finished the treehouse and they no longer feel the need to watch our every move.

"Ellie, get down!" I hiss. "It's not safe."

"Don't be such a scaredy-cat," Ellie says, grinning. "You can see so much from up here. Come on, Lauren. You're missing out."

"I am not."

"Yes, you are."

"You're going to get hurt."

"No, I won't." And as if to prove herself, she drags her hips and scoots higher until she is at the roof's peak. She looks out. "This is so cool," she says.

I'm halfway up the ladder, thinking I can coax her down better this way, my hands clutching the railing, when

Ellie's mischievous smile peers at me over the edge of the rooftop.

"You can do it, Lauren," she begs. "Don't be scared. Come up here with me. You won't fall. I won't let you."

"But you could," I tell her.

Her grin gets brighter. "I never fall."

A burst of noise at the fence, and it's the kids from down the street. They swing the gate open.

"No way!" Jacob says when he sees Ellie on top of the tree-house. He pushes his unruly, blond hair from his eyes.

His friend Aaron is right on his heels. Wherever Jacob goes, that kid always follows. My heart beats double-time to see Jacob standing there. I've had a crush on him for so long.

The boys gather at the bottom of the ladder beneath me, but they pay me no attention. Instead, they stare at the top, the boys whistling at how high Ellie has climbed, her dare to reach even higher to the roof.

Another girl, Brooke, runs into the yard next, and she joins the boys at the ladder. She gasps, her eyes open wide with awe, which only makes Ellie beam prouder.

Jacob says, "I'm going up," and he grips the ladder.

"Wait until my sister gets up here first," Ellie shouts.

Jacob gives me a look and scoffs. "Doesn't look like it. It's like she's frozen halfway."

"No, I'm not." My face burns.

"Just give her a second," Ellie says.

Jacob ignores me, he always ignores me. And once again, I'm in the shadow of Ellie's light.

Jacob digs his tennis shoes into each foothold and clambers up. With him approaching, I get out of the way and finish climbing the ladder to the landing.

"This is so cool," he says.

Below, Aaron and Brooke tent their eyes to watch him.

He looks up to the roof, to where Ellie is perched, for a

place for him to hoist himself up next. "You can't go up there," I say. "It's only for me and Ellie."

Jacob shoves me aside. "As if you're going up there, Lauren."

"We don't want you up here," Ellie warns him.

I try to block him, but he pushes at me again, placing one hand on the edge of the roof and lifting his leg to the railing to pull himself up. He's on the roof in seconds.

Ellie scoots away. "Get away from me," she says.

"I just want to see."

"This is my spot—mine and my sister's."

From below, Aaron and Brooke holler their excitement, and Jacob laughs. He shoots me a look. "Lauren is never going to come up here and you know that. She's too much of a chicken."

The heat spreads from my neck to my ears. "I am not!" I shout.

"Then prove it." Jacob sneers at me. "Come on up here and prove it."

"Prove it!" Brooke shouts.

Ellie shifts her gaze—but there is something different in her eyes when she catches my attention. It's like she's encouraging me too; she wants me to climb. She wants so much for me to stop second-guessing everything I do, to stop being such a worrier, that in front of Jacob and his stupid friends, maybe I can finally challenge myself. I can prove them wrong.

Aaron is climbing up the ladder next, followed by Brooke. "Don't be such a chicken," Aaron teases.

Jacob laughs again, and I can see how my sister winces. I think she knows about my crush on Jacob, despite the obvious disregard he has for me in front of everybody. And for a second, my baby sister looks embarrassed. She is embarrassed for me. Another wave of shame rises quickly to my cheeks. I want nothing more than to run and hide.

"Your little sister can do it," Jacob calls, "so why can't you?"

Brooke ignores me, leaving the taunting to the boys. She leans against the railing. "Wow, you can see the playground from up here."

Aaron turns. "Hey, there's my house! You can almost see the school from here."

But Jacob doesn't look. Instead, he lowers himself on the roof, his legs scooting closer to the edge, close enough that his body is nearing mine and I can see his tongue stick out, his lower lip wet where he has licked.

He reaches out his arm toward me—and I freeze. He isn't going to pull me up, *is he*?

I look down, my head spinning. I should climb down the ladder, go inside the house. The shame of Jacob treating me this way, my sister who is always so much braver, and I blink back my tears, not wanting them to see.

I peer again at my sister. But she is no longer cringing with that embarrassed look from moments before. Now, she is angry. Furious at how Jacob is treating me, a pinched disappointment that I'm not going to prove him wrong after all, and the redness in her cheeks settles around her eyes, her hands balling into fists.

"Look!" Brooke cries. "There's Hannah's backyard and her dog!"

But Jacob doesn't care. He doesn't look. He keeps his face close to mine. "Chicken," he whispers.

And from behind him, my sister lowers herself another inch.

"Why are you always such a wimp?" Jacob teases.

The first tears nearly drop from my eyes. I quickly scrub them away, my chest tightening. Fortifying.

I've had enough. I might not be able to climb onto the roof, but I can do something else. I can stand up for myself finally. Teach Jacob not to mess with me, not to tease me.

And I reach out my hands just as Ellie holds her palms out

too, her hands hovering behind his back, ready to push. And I'm ready to pull.

Jacob's scream comes next, and it cuts through me like a knife. The sound of my heavy breath, my sister's and my hands extended. But I am the only one who made contact. I am the only one who followed through and snapped. Ellie and I thought the same thing, but I got to Jacob first.

FIFTEEN

Last night, Detective Rayburn told me the name of the restaurant where the photos of my sister and the two brothers were taken. The police had already determined the location by the wrought-iron balcony and white-plastered corner of St. Louis Cathedral that is visible in the background. Even with the poor picture quality, the gray flagstone paving of Jackson Square is easily spotted. It's unmistakable.

I pay for my coffee, half a beignet eaten, since I really couldn't stomach much more, and walk across the street to Jackson Square. The park is surrounded by a tall iron fence with a neatly manicured lawn beyond, its row of hedges lining a path and encircling a massive statue.

Closed off to traffic, tourists can walk freely around Jackson Square and shop and have drinks. A Creole candy store is closed for now, and so is a Tabasco country shop, but signs on the doors announce they will be open at 10 a.m. Not that many people are out and about just yet. Much of the French Quarter is fast asleep.

I walk steadily until I'm on the other side of the square, and to the right of St. Louis Cathedral I find the red-painted walls of Muriel's Restaurant. That balcony.

It's stunning, this nineteenth-century building that was once a private home and was then turned into a popular restaurant and tourist attraction. Its location is prime, and so are the reviews about its food and its ambience, the old-world elegant décor that attracts diners. I checked the website earlier, the images of the main dining area that is within an enclosed courtyard, the room that is filled with natural light from the glass ceiling above, the look resembling a type of greenhouse with its abundance of flowers and lush plants. It's the kind of place Alex would love.

But on the second floor, the atmosphere is darker, as if the upstairs area is inhabited by completely separate guests. A separate entity. And as the stories go, maybe it is.

The walls are painted a deep maroon, the lights lowered, with one corner of the room displaying an honest-to-goodness séance lounge, where tales of former residents and ghosts are shared. Those who are said to be lucky enough to experience the phenomenon will climb the steps and feel the chills running up and down their spines. They might feel that someone is standing behind them.

A table is roped off in the corner and reserved. It waits for its guest, the table that is always set with wine and bread, an offering to the original homeowner and in honor of his ghost.

Pictures of the restaurant took my breath away, but mostly because I imagined Ellie walking past those same tables, my sister standing at the bar, her climb to the staircase with her hand gliding along the banister. The moment she stepped onto the balcony and found their table, the brothers greeting her, my sister sitting next to the man who would eventually become my husband.

I reopen Ellie's images on my phone, and from the curve of the balcony behind her head, the slate flagstones behind Alex's and Clive's profiles also, I'm able to follow the second-floor railing until I'm confident I've found their table. That's where they sat, the table that is pushed against the railing with its wrought-iron black chairs.

From there, my sister would have had quite the view. When the server stood back and took their photo, the corner of St. Louis Cathedral would have lined up perfectly.

I stare at that space, the empty table, for such a long time that my body grows stiff. But my breathing never slows.

I imagine my sister smiling and laughing, Ellie flipping her hair over her shoulders as she enjoyed their company. Did Clive tell her a funny story? Is that something he would do?

Up there, my sister sat with a bouquet of pink camellias in front of her, glasses of Bloody Mary that were nearly empty. Twenty years old, and the world should have been hers for the taking. She had so much promise, so much to live for, but someone cut that down.

How long did they sit together? Who paid? Such minor questions, I know, but it's these details, these bits of information, that I can stack together to tell a story, that could add up to explain everything. I want each of these details revealed.

What did Alex think of my sister? Was he pleased that Clive had met someone, someone who loved music as much as he did?

Alex said that Ellie joined them at the last minute, that he didn't know she was coming until Clive mentioned having a guest. Were they already sitting at the table, the gray November sky above them, when she arrived? Did they order a drink for her as they waited at the table?

Did Alex have feelings for her also?—and I stumble where I stand, not knowing where that thought came from, but it's there, the white-hot fear pulsing quickly and steadily in my mind.

My husband and Ellie... those flowers.

Is that what it is—the pink camellias? Is that another reason to suspect my husband?

I stare at my feet, trying to ground myself. Running a finger along the letters of Ellie's name on my skin, I beg for my sister to give me a clue, to tell me something. *Ellie, I need to know who did this to you... If it's Alex, even if it is Alex, I want to know. God help me, I just want to know and bring you home.*

I feel it—the acute awareness of a pair of eyes on me. A feeling so sharp to know that someone is watching me.

There he is. A man at the edge of the cathedral. He hides behind a pair of street sweepers. I can just make out his looming shape.

But the man halts. He moves back. And it's his stepping back that truly gets my attention.

Alleys run along either side of the cathedral, and I remember this from when Ellie showed us around years ago. *Down here is Pirate's Alley*, she pointed out. *And over there is an old bookstore.*

The man emerges, a tentative, cautious step forward, and the front of his baseball cap appears. He's watching me. He doesn't step any closer.

Alex?

But I can't be sure if it's him, and the baseball cap hides most of his face, dropping his features and eyes into shadow. The sun is bright, the glare of the sky making everything hazy. He steps back.

I move—I don't think but snap into action, an anger so fierce that shoots into my legs as I pump my arms. If it really is Alex, if that is in fact my husband, I am ready to confront him. If he's following me, if he's ducking behind corners and taunting me, I will tell myself to no longer be frightened. I will face him head-on and question him.

But when I round the corner of the cathedral, the alley is empty. The doors to the other buildings are closed too.

Where did he go? How did he hide so quickly?

To my left is the Cabildo building, the large historic museum that sits adjacent to the cathedral, but it isn't open for visitors yet. The covered walkway with its ornate arches remains vacant too.

I peer down to where the alley dead-ends at Royal Street, a row of antique shops and art galleries beyond. But halfway there, I spot another cut-through, another alley. It's narrow.

If Alex has followed me to the French Quarter, it's strange, his actions maddening—but sneaking around the corner like that, then running away to hide, is downright creepy. My fury builds at him wanting to frighten me.

I run into the narrow alley and a group of pigeons bursts into flight, their wings flapping noisily to get out of my way. I find myself directly behind the Cabildo building, the gray pavestone extending to a deeper section of the French Quarter.

It's much quieter here and more secluded. No one would hear me if I cried out, and it would be a while before someone would walk by and come to my aid. I lower my hands to my knees to catch my breath.

A storefront to my right boasts haunted ghost tours and aboveground cemeteries, but the place is closed, the windows locked down with heavy green shutters that run the length of the wall to the ground. *The ghosts come out at night*, a sign proclaims. *Don't be scared*. But that does little to calm my nerves.

Alex shouldn't be here. He should be meeting with the detective—that's what he said to me in his text message. They're supposed to be meeting first thing this morning.

But if Alex is in the French Quarter, if he is indeed following me around, how did he know where I'd be? How would he know where to look?

I take out my phone, remembering the Life360 app that Alex suggested we download several years ago. He thought it would be a good idea for us to know where the other was in case of an emergency. But I laughed and asked him what was the point when we were mostly at home anyway, sitting in front of our computers, and there weren't that many other places that we went besides the grocery store and back. Tracing our paths wouldn't be very exciting.

But with our family history, Alex said, *and the missing people in our lives, we need to be safe.* He reasoned we should want to be able to find each other.

I'd forgotten about the app until now.

I scroll to Life360 and kick myself that I didn't check it sooner—not just today, but weeks ago. Months even. I might have known about Alex's visits to my dad. I might have known what else he's been up to, the other locations that he may not have told me about.

His past trips to Houston are coming into question now, all those times he left, the instances when he said he was searching for his brother—is that what he was really doing? Or was he driving to the outskirts of town and stopping at some apartment complex somewhere, or a house on a desolate road, all the time knowing that's exactly where Clive was hiding, knowing his brother was safe and sound.

No social media accounts. No credit cards. *Clive Capshaw has gone off the grid,* the detective said.

Has my husband been helping him? Has he been sending him money and checking on him? That's what a good brother would do. That's the kind of help my husband would give him.

No one suspects a thing, Alex might say. *They haven't found her body. We're still in the clear.*

In the last twenty-four hours, has Alex sent Clive a warning about the reopened case? Is that another reason why he feels the need to keep an eye on me?

I open the app, and the screen zooms in to show my location. My profile picture appears hovering right over this spot.

My exact location behind the Cabildo building is displayed. I'm a sitting target.

I whip around, but no one is there. Turning in the other direction, I don't see Alex.

The light is faded, the shadows of the buildings hanging over my head with the sun blocked out. I look again at the tracking app, but Alex's photo doesn't appear anywhere on the map. I zoom out, and it's strange: I can't find his position anywhere in the city. I see that his location settings are paused.

According to Life360, Alex disabled his location sometime yesterday afternoon.

I walk down Royal Street, my anger and fear pounding in my chest.

I pass one antique shop after another, their windows glistening with priceless chandeliers and works of art in oversized gilded frames. Someone wearing a black cloak and flowers sewn along the brim of her hat sprays down the sidewalk in front of her shop with a hose. I step around the water as it runs into the drain. A delivery van parks, and the driver hops out and unloads a package. Jazz music plays from someone's speakers.

I don't pay attention to the window displays but stare straight ahead, keeping my hand wrapped around my phone. This lifeline I need for making calls, for finding out information, also shows a pulse point of what I'm doing, where I'm going. Alex can follow me easily. He can track me.

I should disable my location settings the same way he did. I will do this soon enough.

It feels good to move, and for every step, I feel as if I'm purging some of this violent storm from my body. If I walk quickly enough, I can rid myself of some of this wound-up energy and clear my head. I can plan what needs to be done next.

I will take the streetcar and head back to the Garden District, that's what I'll do. It's time for me to make another call. Heartbreakingly, it's time to shatter someone else's world.

* * *

I'm heading back to my dorm and in my car when my phone vibrates in the cupholder in the center console. It's Carmen's number, and I sense a twitch of something unsettling along my chest, the first indication that something could be wrong. The pitch of Carmen's voice tells me the rest.

"She's not here," Carmen says. "She hasn't come home."

She's trying not to rush her words, wants to remain calm. Rational. Informative, is how Carmen will explain it later. But it doesn't take long before she releases the first wave of tears.

"I'm not panicking for no reason, right?" she says. "I should be worried. This isn't like her. You know it isn't."

Ellie not turning up, not leaving a message? No, this isn't like her at all.

"Did you try calling her?" I ask, which is an unnecessary question. But in my haze, in those first seconds of incomprehension, I tell myself we should go over the obvious first steps. We should do what we can before sounding the full alarm.

But Carmen has already called, of course she has. Numerous times, she tells me, and Ellie isn't answering.

The silence is excruciating, my sister's phone ringing out as we keep hoping and thinking the same thing, that Ellie will have stayed at a friend's place and forgotten to let Carmen know. It's her mistake as Ellie lost track of time and she slept in late. She'll apologize and will let Carmen know in the future.

She'll show up at the apartment and ask, *Why is my phone blowing up with calls from you and my sister? What's going on?*

And Carmen will hug her. *You should have called me*, she'll say. *You should give me a heads-up next time.*

The group of us will breathe out our relief, our moment of panic quickly over, and Carmen might flush pink on the other end of the line, apologizing to me for bothering me, for worrying me. Ellie will sit back on the sofa as she tells Carmen that it's sweet of her to care.

And I'll tell Carmen the same, that she can call anytime, that it's comforting to know my sister has a roommate who looks out for her. We'll end the conversation, a trickle of nervous laughter escaping our lips, the crisis averted. And thank goodness for that.

I will walk the rest of the way to class, and Carmen will go about her day too. Ellie will flip open her laptop and finish her write-up about the band. She'll come home to see us for Christmas. She'll wander out to the backyard and stare up at the treehouse.

Except that is not what happens. An hour later, there is still no word from my sister, and her voicemail has filled up between my phone call attempts and Carmen's too. All we can do is call her repeatedly, her phone ringing out, the interminable wait for Ellie to pick up, and that sound, that endless dialing, is what never leaves my mind. The ringing and waiting for Ellie to pick up.

Another hour passes by the time Carmen says she's contacted a bunch of Ellie's friends and co-workers, but no one has seen her. No one has talked to her. She didn't go into the office to catch up on work either.

When I tell my parents, my mom immediately cries out, like she suspected something bad could happen, like she worried that with one of her daughters living so far away, we would hear about something like this happening one day. I talk to my dad, and he immediately calls the New Orleans Police.

We're on a flight the next morning, and I take the aisle seat, my parents each making their own frantic calls until the flight attendant asks them to switch off their devices. I refuse to look out the window but keep my eyes glued to the tray table, my stomach twisting into knots. Who was last with my sister? Did anyone see where she went?

When we land, I'm so relieved to be off that plane, to be out of that vast, empty nothingness and safely on solid ground again, that I rush from the terminal, my parents struggling to keep up.

I tell myself that I'm running toward Ellie, that she's waiting for us. But she isn't. She's not there. The nightmare for my family is only just beginning.

SIXTEEN

Carmen stands outside the apartment. Her hair is shorter than I remember, a dirty blond with highlights that are growing out and losing their shine. Her eyes are swollen from crying, her purse lowered at her feet.

She wraps her arms around me. "I can't believe it," she sobs. "I just can't believe it."

Calling Carmen was difficult, and it's made our loss more horribly real. She trembles, her shock reminding me of the state I was in yesterday. I'm still in that state now.

"What was she doing there?" she says. "Do the police know? Do they know who did this?"

I shake my head. I haven't told her about the pictures of Alex and Clive yet, but I will. I'm working my way up to it.

Carmen likes Alex. She's always looked up to him. Like me, she was relieved to have someone new in the picture to ask questions. A year later and we needed a new perspective, someone who knew what it was like to search for a loved one, the empathy and knowledge Alex brought to our family and friends.

Carmen turns to the apartment now and shudders. She

hasn't been back since my sister disappeared, she tells me, as she lives in River Ridge now and works at a hiring agency. She's engaged to a man named Jacques, whom we met the one time several years ago. He's quiet and bookish with his wire-rimmed glasses and soft-spoken voice, and they have yet to set a wedding date. Carmen said there's no rush. They already live together. They share everything.

The tree-lined street where Carmen and Ellie's former apartment is located is only a few blocks from St. Charles Avenue. It's not part of a large apartment complex but the lower level of someone's house, the main entrance for the owners located at the top of the brick steps, and that's where the Broussards live. On the ground level is the separate entrance to the rental, the window where Carmen waited for my sister.

When I look at the apartment, I can't help the shudder that runs through my body also. Ellie should have come home that night. She should have walked this very path to the front door. Someone hit pause on my sister's life and it remains unfinished.

The Broussards are an older couple who have lived here for years. After their children grew up and moved away, they rented out the lower level, a basic ground floor which they outfitted to include a kitchen and two bedrooms. It's been a great source of income for them.

The Broussards stand at the top of the brick steps waiting to greet us. Carmen said that she called ahead to let them know we were on our way, which also meant she was the one who had to break the horrible news. At least, for me, it was one less awful explanation I had to make.

The Broussards are in their late seventies now, and they move slowly, their hands clutched to the metal banister to keep their balance. Tears fill Mrs. Broussard's eyes as soon as she approaches, and she hugs me tight. My body relaxes against her soft, warm skin, her neck lightly touched with Pond's cold cream.

Mr. Broussard rests his hand on my shoulder next. He keeps his gaze pinned to the ground while Carmen leans against him. We huddle together like this for quite some time.

This group of people I hardly knew before and only through my sister, and we're forever bonded by this tragedy, by our years of hoping and searching, and now, this crushing loss. It's a relationship that is fragile and bruised and unlike anything I've ever experienced. These are some of the most important relationships of my life.

"*Mais, cher*," Mrs. Broussard says to me, crying softly. *Hello, sweet girl.*

It's what she used to say to Ellie too, which is another reminder, another reason why my sister loved New Orleans so much, the French-Creole sentiments that have remained throughout the generations.

Mrs. Broussard wraps her arms around Carmen also. She kisses her forehead and cradles her head against her chest. In Mrs. Broussard's eyes, Carmen and Ellie must remain those same twenty-year-old girls who lived below them. They must see me as that young college student who came to visit. They treat their tenants like their own children.

"She's with the angels now," Mrs. Broussard tells me, and she holds my hand. "She was always meant to be with the angels."

I stiffen. Her intentions are kind, I know they are, the platitudes that are to be expected, the sentiments she wants to share. But it's heartbreaking, and I tell myself to calm down. In the days to come, I will need to prepare myself to hear more of these emotions, especially at the funeral and in the weeks and months after. It's what people say when they don't know how else to comfort you. It's what they tell themselves to heal their own hurt.

And as much as I want to tell Mrs. Broussard that, *no*, Ellie shouldn't be with the angels—she should be here with us, *with me*—I nod and thank her. I tell her that I appreciate her words since there's no sense in correcting someone whose intentions are kind. They're at a loss for what to say too.

Mr. Broussard leads us toward the apartment. "We're in between tenants," he explains, holding up a set of keys. "We can take a look."

I check in with Carmen, and she hesitates, her face paling before she gives a faint nod. We must be thinking the same thing, that moment in time before the door opens and the memories come rushing back.

I've already explained to Carmen why I wanted to meet here, how this is my grieving tour of sorts, my way of remembering my sister. Later, I will face the concert hall. I will visit the magazine where she worked. *My desk is close to the break room*, Ellie told us. *This guy, I think, has a crush on me.*

Mr. Broussard steps inside, and he turns on the lights, gazing about the room in case there is something he needs to clear, something that was left behind. He reaches for another switch and the ceiling fan sputters to life above and helps to circulate the air.

Carmen sucks in her breath, and so do I. The apartment is just like I remember, except the living room is no longer a pale blue but painted white. The linoleum floor with its unusual burgundy diamond pattern has been replaced with carpet. The same narrow archway leads to the kitchen with its casement window overlooking the garden. The kitchen has been coated with fresh paint.

In the living room against the wall is where the sofa used to be, where Ellie would kick up her feet to study. During one of my visits, we pushed the coffee table out of the way for a party. Her friends and co-workers filled the kitchen with cases of beer and cheap wine.

I sat on the counter for what felt like forever, talking to someone who worked with my sister, someone from *Nola*

Magazine. What was his name—Peter? Connor? I can no longer remember. But we struck up enough of a conversation until Carmen announced it was getting late, that we shouldn't upset the Broussards, who were trying to sleep upstairs.

Ellie suggested we find another bar, and the group of us stumbled down the street before we had a few more drinks, the evening landing us at an all-night diner.

Ellie looped her arm through mine, the young man from the magazine long forgotten and trailing somewhere behind us. She said, *I miss you. I wish you lived here too.*

Ellie begged me to stay longer. She also begged me to transfer schools. But I loved Northwestern and I wanted to finish my degree there before contemplating my next steps. After graduation, Ellie said she was thinking about living in New Orleans full-time. This was her home. She'd found her people.

A set of white curtains hangs from the window, but the rest of the apartment is empty, posters removed from the walls, the previous tenants having collected their furniture and taken their belongings. An empty cardboard box rests on its side. It's been tossed in the corner.

Carmen enters the hall and she stops in front of one of the bedrooms. It was Ellie's room, and she traces her hand slowly along the doorframe. "It feels like just yesterday, you know? When we were just here, and everything was fine. Everything should have been fine," she cries.

"Oh, sweetheart," Mrs. Broussard says, and is at once by Carmen's side.

I move to the bedroom also, the tug of that space, the pull of those memories that have me stepping inside.

I can still hear my sister, her raspy laugh, the way Ellie's voice would echo off the walls. I can still picture her springing from the bed and rummaging through her closet, her insistence that we dress up for the party and decorate. She would stand at the window sometimes and eat her bowl of cereal. She would lie in the middle of the floor while she listened to music, the bass beating through the floors.

But Ellie isn't here anymore. The floor is swept clean, the apartment clear of dust, and my heart drops lower in my chest. So many other people have lived here since, and by the looks of things, the Broussards are ready for the next group to sign their lease. These people, a young couple, new students, will move in soon. They'll be excited and hopeful just like my sister.

Azaleas bloom in clusters of red and white along the driveway. A postal truck rattles down the street with the creak and slamming shut of the Broussards' mailbox coming. Life keeps moving on for everybody else.

Mr. Broussard joins us. He's quiet, thoughtful, his own memories possibly taking shape as he thinks about my sister.

"This should never have happened," he says. "I still don't understand why this had to happen."

"The students who rent from us"—Mrs. Broussard looks at me—"we try our best to prepare them. It's safe enough, but we tell them to look out for themselves just in case, to walk in pairs if they can, especially at night. Especially the female students."

"But Ellie didn't have any problems here," I remind her. "She was happy. She was safe. You too, Carmen."

"But we were so young," Carmen says. "And we felt so invincible. Everywhere we went, leaving bars at night, walking home, and we thought nothing bad could ever happen to us. Ellie went to the concert, and she should have had nothing to worry about it. She should have been able to come home."

Mr. Broussard shakes his head. "But I always worried about her. I worried about you girls all the time."

I lift my eyes. It's the same sentiment he shared when Ellie first went missing, the comments he repeated to my parents after weeks of searching stretched to months, then years.

"The two of you going out," he says, "and so often at night and alone, and Ellie would go to those shows. She was in so many different parts of town and I couldn't help but worry. I would wait up for her sometimes."

I breathe out slowly. I've never heard him share this detail before.

"He used to wait up for both of us," Carmen says, looking at me.

"Raising kids, you never stop worrying," Mr. Broussard explains. "It's hard for me to sleep until I hear that downstairs door click and I know that everyone is accounted for. I used to do the same when our kids lived here, didn't I?" And his wife nods. "I tried to do the same for Ellie, for you too, Carmen. But that night, I failed her. I failed both of you."

His wife reaches for him. "Joseph, you can't blame yourself. There's nothing you could have done. We've talked about this so many times. What happened to Ellie was miles away, and so many hours had passed by then, before we thought to worry. You couldn't have known."

"But it happened before," he says. "Remember? She was nervous that time. We should have taken her more seriously. We shouldn't have let Ellie say we shouldn't worry, and maybe it was..." His shoulders sag. "Maybe it was something."

"It wasn't, Joseph. It was nothing." She passes me a cautious glance as if to say, *There's nothing here, he's getting worked up.*

I look at them both. "What was Ellie nervous about?"

"She spooked herself sometimes," Carmen says. "Remember that, Mr. B? How we laughed about it later, and Ellie did too. She would tell us these ghost stories." She continues, "She got it into her head. She'd be walking home, and she'd think there was someone behind her. Like someone was right up against her."

My stomach churns, remembering Ellie's words. *An apparition. Like a ghost.*

"But was there someone?" I ask.

"No." Carmen shakes her head. "We would have told the
police if there was anything serious. I promise, Lauren. Ellie
said it felt real, but then she realized it was nothing. It was just
her imagination."

Nothing.

That's what my sister said to me too. Ellie had a feeling
about someone following her, watching her, and she down-
played her fears to Carmen and the Broussards too.

"This is a lot to handle." Mrs. Broussard takes hold of her
husband's arm. "We should go back upstairs and rest. We'll let
you girls stay here and talk some more." She passes me a sad
smile, and one for Carmen also.

It pains me to see them go, their devastation with their grief
for my sister. The Broussards loved her, I know they did, and
they looked out for her the best they could, far more than what
was required as landlords. Her death will be hitting them hard.

As they step outside, Mrs. Broussard says, "Do you know
how much longer you'll be in town?"

And I lift my eyes. "I'm not sure. A few more days, I think.
I'll call you. I'll let you know what else we find."

"Please do," she says, and she hugs me. It's followed by a
hug from Mr. Broussard, who tells us he'll come back later to
lock up the apartment, to take our time. "Stay as long as you
like." He gives Carmen's shoulder a gentle squeeze.

They walk slowly up the steps as Carmen and I stand
together in the doorway, watching them go. The click of their
own front door sounds from above and I finally turn to Carmen.

"Did Ellie ever mention meeting someone named Clive?"

Carmen is still crying, and she wipes her tears with the back
of her hand. She gives me a puzzled look. "Clive? Like the same
name as Alex's brother?"

My stomach churns. "Not the same name, but actually Clive. Like as in Ellie met Alex's brother."

Her eyebrows lift. "What?"

"I know you told us she wasn't dating anyone, that Ellie didn't mention meeting up with anyone after the show. But did she talk about a guy she'd met, someone she might have gone to a couple of concerts with? Someone she hung out with earlier that day?"

"Earlier that day?" She shakes her head. "I don't understand... Ellie knew Clive? How?"

I brace myself. Carmen will be the first person besides my husband that I show these images to, and I pull up the pictures on my phone. The blood beats steadily in my ears as I show her the first one, where Clive looks directly into the camera, same as Ellie.

She stares at the screen. "Wait... that's Alex's brother?" She points. "That guy?"

I nod. My breath is tight. It feels as if I'm wheezing.

"When?" she says. "When was this taken?"

"It's from the same day Ellie died. They had brunch that day." I regard her closely, watching as the skin tightens around her mouth. "She never mentioned him to you?"

"No," Carmen says. "I mean, I would have said something to you before." Her eyes widen. "You know I would have said something, Lauren. I swear. She told me she was going to work, she didn't say she was stopping somewhere first." Her voice rises. "I promise you I had no idea. None at all. And that night, I saw her for a little while before she went out, but I left for my boyfriend's. I stayed the night. When I came back, she wasn't home in the morning." Her eyes widen a little bit more. "That's all I know."

"It's okay," I tell her. "I believe you."

She stares at the picture. She pulls my phone closer to her face. "Where did this come from?"

"Her pocket. It's from when they found her body. The photos..." I swallow. "She had them on her."

Carmen staggers. "Oh my God." She covers her mouth. "Oh my God, Lauren. Does Alex know about this? Does he know about his brother?"

I open the next image, and the nausea rolls through my stomach.

Carmen leaps back as if physically sick. She wants to get as far away from my phone, from the truth, as possible.

"Holy shit." She stares at me, her eyes searching mine. "Alex lied to all of us." She shakes her head. "I can't believe it. He lied to me too."

SEVENTEEN

Carmen is quickly walking out the door and heading for her car.

I chase after her. "What do you mean he lied to you too?"

She doesn't look back. She doesn't wait for me to catch up either.

"Carmen!" I shout.

"I just need to think," she says. "I need to..." Her voice trails. She lifts her purse to the top of her car, her eyes darting up and down the street.

"Carmen, what's going on?"

"How could Alex not tell you anything?" she says. "How could he lie to all of us? To your parents? I wondered why he wasn't with you, you know. When I saw you walking up the street, and he wasn't at your side. I didn't want to ask before... but now... oh my God, Lauren. How could he do this? How could he keep this from everyone?"

I shake my head. It's the million-dollar question about my spouse and all his secrets.

"And why didn't Ellie tell me about Clive?" she says.

"I guess it was new. She thought it was nothing serious. He was leaving town anyway."

"But then your husband?" The tears are in her eyes.

"Carmen, is there something you're not telling me?"

"I'm telling you everything." But she can't help but peer once more up and down the street. "I'll drive you to the office," she says. "I'll take you to the magazine. We'll do this next. I'm just shocked that he lied to all of us."

"Carmen—"

"I'm telling you I had no idea about Alex," she says, and her voice is sharp. I rear back.

She tosses her purse into the backseat of her car. "You should stay at our place, with me and Jacques. Once the reporters find out, you shouldn't be at the hotel. Things are going to get intense just like last time. You don't want to be around that again."

"They're going to want to talk to you too," I remind her. "And Detective Rayburn said he'll call you."

"I will talk to him, I will help him, absolutely. But honestly, I don't know what else to say. It's what I told the cops before: Ellie went out, I went to my boyfriend's, and she wasn't there the next morning. I didn't go with her to the show."

She shudders, then brings her hands to her face. "If I'd gone, I would have seen them, wouldn't I? I might have seen Alex or Clive, and I would have known about them. From before. And when you met Alex... he wouldn't have been able to do that. He wouldn't have been able to..." she sucks in her breath, "... fool you."

Fool me. My neck heats with shame.

"He did fool me."

"I thought he cared," she says. "I mean, I really thought he wanted to help. He did those interviews and then he helped you set up that Facebook page. He would send me messages sometimes too. He'd check on me."

The unease ripples in my belly. "What messages?"

"Text messages, stuff like, *I'm thinking about you. Hang in there*. He would tell me about you too, if you were having good days or bad. He worried about you so much, Lauren. He knew how much you missed Ellie."

Of course I missed Ellie.

The churning in my stomach doesn't stop. "I need you to go through every one of those messages, Carmen. If there's anything he said, something about that night, about his brother, about knowing Ellie, and you didn't pick up on it before, you need to tell the police. Please tell me too."

"But that's the thing," Carmen says, her hands trembling. "He never talked about Clive. It was always about Ellie. He said that he wished he could have met her."

The *Nola Magazine* office is in the same building as when Ellie worked there, a one-story brick structure on State Street that's close to Loyola University. Like the other student staff writers, Ellie was able to walk here after class.

Carmen pulls into the parking lot, and she's nervous; she's tapping the steering wheel even after the car is in park, her thoughts about Alex, then Ellie and Clive, tumbling from her mouth from the moment we drove away from the apartment.

"I'll go through every one of those messages tonight," she says. "I'll send them to the detective as soon as I can."

I thank her and hit share on Detective Rayburn's contact information so she can have his number.

"Has Alex texted you recently?" I ask. "Has he sent you anything new?"

She looks at her phone as if there could be a message pinging her now, and the screen lights up, the phone jostling awake in her hand, but there are no missed calls, no unread messages. "I still can't believe this," she says.

"It's going to be okay," I tell her, but I can't promise her that. I can't promise anyone that, and I sink against my seat.

Carmen's best friend is dead. She will never see my sister again, and neither will I. And my marriage... I have no idea what remains of my marriage.

I stare at the teal-painted front doors of the building with the name *Nola Magazine* mounted in steel letters against the roof. It's the same sign Ellie proudly posed in front of when she first landed the job.

The magazine was mostly in print back then, but when my sister and a few other reporters recognized the importance of an online presence, they encouraged the editors to feature weekly blogs, then daily write-ups. The blogs became a major hit, and so did the welcomed additional advertising revenue.

The magazine is entirely online now, with their write-ups branching out to not only include reviews about bands, but restaurants, tourist attractions, and creators and performers of all kinds. Last month's issue featured the history of hip-hop and breakdancing in New Orleans, and it's one of my favorites.

Over the years, I've kept up with the magazine, pulling up articles and bookmarking them the way I used to save my sister's. Everything that Ellie wrote is archived, and for the days when I'm emotionally strong enough, when I'm missing Ellie more than ever, I'll pull up one of her past reviews. It's like hearing my sister's voice all over again.

Keep an eye out for these guys! The electro revival sound will keep everyone on their feet with their beats of soul, house, and bounce. Groove Funk is back next month at Crossroads. Don't miss it!

How many bands did she cover during her brief time working here? How many more articles would she have written if she was still alive? Would she have risen through the ranks and become a senior editor one day? The sky was the limit for Ellie. Her job had meant so much.

The front doors open, and two women walk out, students by the looks of them, their backpacks looped over their shoulders. The one with blond hair flowing halfway to her waist sips an iced latte while her colleague walks alongside her, scrolling through her phone.

A lump catches in my throat. That would have been Ellie back then. She would have been returning to class. She would have been making plans for the rest of her day.

The women stroll past a row of hedges and a low, weathered fence that separates the magazine from the office next door. The woman sipping the iced latte steps to her right, her movement sudden, and she nudges her colleague to move out of the way too. They don't look back. They don't check on who it is either.

But I do. There is someone standing there watching, waiting. But the man isn't looking at the students. He's lurking and staring at our car in the parking lot. He quickly ducks behind the hedges.

That black hair and those squared-off shoulders. No baseball cap this time.

Carmen rolls down her window and leans forward. "Wait... is that *Alex*?"

I stare at him, but can now only make out his shape that is tucked behind the bushes. Through a crisscross of branches, I spot his outline.

"How would Alex know that we're here?" Carmen says.

I check my phone, and I should have known. The Life360 app shows exactly where I am: along State Street and at *Nola Magazine*, practically a beacon of light that has tracked my path from Ellie's old apartment. I should have turned off my location settings already, but maybe this was a subconscious test to see Alex's next move.

He followed me.

And my husband's location? It's still paused since yesterday.

A foot appears, a scruffy tennis shoe that steps onto the sidewalk, then another. The ragged hem of a pair of blue jeans appears next.

And I frown. That's nothing like what Alex would wear. My husband takes great care of his appearance, and he prides himself on the latest running shoes. Whoever this is, it isn't Alex, and my skin prickles.

The man takes off, and before I know it, my hand flies to the door handle and I launch out of the car. Carmen shouts my name, but I ignore her. I'm sprinting across the parking lot to catch up.

I'm winded—I'm not a runner, I will never be a runner—as I throw myself around the hedges. I cut around the fence.

But he's fast. He's gotten a head start, and I'm panting by the time I make it to the back of the building next door. An air-conditioning unit splutters to life. Several cars are parked beside a dumpster. A couple of bicycles are chained to a rack.

He isn't here.

And then a flash—a sudden burst of movement out of the corner of my eye—and he's made it to the next block. He's sprinting, and I'm wishing I'd stayed in the car and shouted at Carmen to follow.

He rounds the corner, his hair streaking past his ears, his windbreaker flapping as his worn shoes kick up the grass.

His dark hair... and I stop. It's too long. It's not the cropped hairstyle that Alex has worn for years.

But there is a similarity to my husband—I saw it. I felt it as soon as he ducked behind those hedges. Carmen spotted him for a split-second and wondered if it was my husband too, the fact that Alex is already in New Orleans, our suspicions about my husband quickly heightening from the last few hours.

This is someone who looks like him. Someone who hasn't been seen in a very long time. And I stare into the distance.

I think I just saw Clive.

EIGHTEEN

Carmen waits for me outside her car, her relief palpable, her hands twitching when I return.

"Was that him? Was it Alex?"

I try catching my breath. "No."

"Who was it then?"

I lift my hand to my chest. What do I tell her? How do I stop her from becoming more frightened?

And do I tell Detective Rayburn about this, that someone might be following me? That there's a chance Clive is in New Orleans?

Or maybe Clive has always been here. He never left.

Or he's returned because Alex told him about the body. *They found her*, Alex might have said, the phone pressed against his mouth.

But why would Clive risk coming back to the city, where he could be spotted and questioned? Why would he follow me to the office?

Someone steps out of the building, the teal doors swinging behind him.

"Are you okay?" he says. "We heard shouting. We saw you

taking off after someone." He spins around to check the sidewalk before he turns around to face us again. "Is everything all right?"

"I'm okay." I'm still panting.

"Are you sure?"

I nod faintly.

He takes a step forward. "Wait... are you?" His eyes narrow. "Are you Ellie's sister?"

I don't look at him.

"Lauren?" he says, and he lifts his hand to his chest. "It's me, Connor."

I lift my eyes to his. *Connor?* With his light brown hair and trendy blue frames, he's different from the last time I saw him. He wasn't wearing glasses back then.

Connor, my sister's co-worker who I talked to in the kitchen the night of that party. He followed the group when we left, everyone walking to the bar, then crowding into a couple of booths at the all-night diner. It was so long ago. I'm surprised he still works here.

He acknowledges Carmen with a small wave, but it's awkward. She doesn't reciprocate and launches into a stream of questions instead.

"Did you get a good look at that guy? Do you know who he is?" Carmen says.

Connor peers again at the sidewalk. "No, he was pretty fast. I mostly saw you running." He says to me, "It's not often I'm at work and see someone chasing someone else."

"I'm sorry about that. I just thought..." I shake my head. I don't know what I think anymore.

He hooks his thumb over his shoulder. "Do you want to come inside? Get some water? Maybe take a minute and sit down?"

I swallow. I must look as winded, sweaty, and panicked as I feel. "Thank you," I tell him. "That's probably a good idea."

"Lauren, I can't stick around. I've got to head back to the office," Carmen says as she backs toward the car. "But I'll call you later, okay? We should talk more. Figure this out." She pauses before she looks at Connor, her eyes sliding back to my own. "Are you okay to get back to the hotel?"

"There's always the streetcar," I tell her. Then I add, "Don't worry about me. Seriously. I'll be fine." As soon as the words leave my mouth, I think of how thin they sound, how confident I am that nothing bad could happen. Did my sister feel the same way the night she vanished?

"Let's get you inside," Connor says, and he holds out his arm as if I'm wounded, as if I've been in a terrible storm and need shelter.

But I have been in a storm. I'm in an ongoing storm that's still whipping around my head.

The last time I visited the magazine was soon after Ellie went missing, when we spoke to several of her co-workers, including her boss at the time. They talked about the article she'd prepped. By the next day, she would meet with Alex and Clive in the French Quarter.

Connor hands me a bottle of water from the reception desk, but there is no receptionist and the area is clear, the computer powered down with the chair pushed in.

"Budget cuts," Connor says, noticing my gaze. "But we manage. We go out of the office for most of our interviews these days anyway."

I crack open the bottle and take a sip, the water cool and welcomed against my throat.

"I'm really sorry about your sister," he says.

I lower the bottle. "You already know about that? That they found her?"

"The police came by earlier. The detective. I can't remember his name..."

"Rayburn."

"Yes, Rayburn. He told us what happened, but I only wanted the management team and two of our staff members who used to work with Ellie to be in the room. The detective described finding her at that house..." He grimaces. "It's terrible. I can't believe it." He glances at the hall as if to be sure no one is walking by.

"He asked if we knew anything about the place, if Ellie ever talked about the house. But we don't know anything. No one knows. And Ellie didn't talk to me a lot back then, you know? Outside of work and all, she was nice, and a bunch of us would go out sometimes for drinks. I went to her party. But I wasn't always in her circle if that makes sense. I wouldn't know what she got up to on the weekends." For this, Connor looks disappointed, maybe even hurt.

"So she never mentioned the house to any of you?" I ask. "Or talk about some guy she was hanging out with?"

"She never talked to me about boyfriends, no." His expression changes. "But you remember Rachel? She doesn't work here anymore—she works in hotel management somewhere downtown—but the detective said he spoke to her too. He asked her the same questions about Ellie taking off from the concert. But Rachel said that Ellie didn't mention checking out some creepy house either."

Rachel, Ellie's co-worker, and I tell myself I should reach out to her at some point too. She'll be hurting to find out about Ellie.

"Why do you think she was there?" Connor asks. "At that house?"

I shake my head. "It could have been the balcony. She wanted to see the view."

"Even though the house was closed off?"

I smile, sadly. "Even more so because the house was closed off."

"The detective pointed out that balcony in the photos. The cupola was pretty unique. It was pretty high. Not a lot of houses around there would have something like that."

The water sloshes around my stomach. "You saw pictures of it?"

"Pictures of the house, yeah. What it used to look like, and then from last week when the construction crew started. The house falling apart like that... How she was hidden all that time..." He makes another face. "It's awful."

My throat tightens. Connor has seen photos of the house, and so has Rachel, but I have yet to do so. The detective didn't slide them across the table to me last night. He didn't pull them out from his folder.

Connor has already seen the home where Ellie's body was found. He laid his eyes on where she was abandoned, her hidden resting place. And I shudder, because the truth is, I don't know when I'll be ready to view those photos myself, let alone stand in front of the property that is now a crime scene, the cops digging through the debris where my sister's body once lay.

The detective has been busy, and that in itself should be reassuring. He's taking the case seriously, just like I thought, just as I wanted. He's already met with Connor and several staff members, plus a separate visit to Rachel. His team is making house calls while they work through the concert attendee list. They will pick through everyone's memories. They will venture closer to the truth.

But the detective has yet to contact Carmen, and that gives me pause. The way Carmen acted earlier, it was as if she hadn't spoken to Detective Rayburn.

I will talk to him, I will help him, is what she said. I sent her Detective Rayburn's number because I didn't think she had it.

I would have thought Carmen would be one of the first people the detective spoke to. Surely, he would have reached out to the roommate shortly after contacting me: the natural progression of things.

And if that's the case, if he's already called, why didn't Carmen tell me anything?

NINETEEN

Ellie used to work at the back of the office. When we visited, she showed us around, taking me and our parents on a mini tour and pointing to different department areas. She introduced us to some of her co-workers.

Here's where the boss sits, she said. *And the art department is down the hall, so is the sales team. The meeting rooms are right along here*, and her face brightened at this. She loved it when the staff gathered around to pitch their ideas.

My sister eventually stopped at her desk, beaming at the colleague sitting across from her.

And this is Rachel. If it weren't for Rachel showing me the ropes, I'm not sure what I would have done.

Rachel stood up to shake our hands, and I remember the top part of her ear was pierced just like my sister's, a similar hoop. She was also a student, but older by a few years. *Don't listen to her*, Rachel said. *Ellie is a talented writer. She doesn't need my help. She's got so much passion.*

My sister smiled, and so did our parents. We were thrilled she was finding a career path to follow, something she loved. Ellie sat down and swiveled in her office chair to show us her setup. On her desk was a half-eaten apple, a crumpled bag of pretzels, and a ceramic pot that instead of flowers was filled with pens and highlighters. On Rachel's desk was a similar ceramic pot crammed with pencils. They had the same notebook with a stack of sticky notes piled on top, the items possibly raided from the supply room.

Now, Connor points out to me the student staff area. Several of the writers lift their heads, and they glance at us with a polite smile or an obligatory wave—after all, the boss stands less than ten feet away. But many of the students keep their earbuds in, their gaze focused on their keyboards.

"We've rearranged the space a couple of times," Connor says. "But this is where Ellie used to work, if you remember. The bullpen where the students and interns complete their assignments. As you can see, they ransack the break room just like we did. Nothing like free snacks when you're a broke college kid." He smiles at the packets of trail mix that litter the desks and trash cans.

"But I'm proud of these guys," Connor says. "Everyone here works really hard. They do a great job."

The desks are grouped together in pods, similar to how it's set up at the police station, but the furniture here is made of that cheap particleboard, the surface of the desks topped with a synthetic, high-gloss resin to make the furniture appear nicer. The chairs look like they've been in use for quite some time too, the seats upholstered in a standard cloth material, gray and maroon in color and tattered in a few places. Where Ellie and Rachel once sat is now a long table with an antiquated fax machine.

"You'll never believe how many people still fax," Connor says. "Especially for invoices. We have the interns go through everything since we all have to start somewhere, right? Ellie and I did too."

"It's great that you've done so well," I tell him. "You've risen through the ranks, Connor. Congratulations."

Connor lowers his head as if bashful, as if he doesn't often receive compliments and doesn't know what to do.

"I could never leave this place," he says. "It's all I've ever known with so many great memories too. Ellie was with us during that golden age, you know? When people were still reading print, then hopping online to learn more about the bands. She was so good at capturing what the musicians thought, what inspired their lyrics and sounds, and the readers ate it up. They loved everything she wrote. She was one of our best."

He pauses, his voice softening. "Ellie would have taken over one day, I'm sure of it. She would have been so good at figuring out the magazine's direction. She would have been a lot better than me, at least."

"Don't say that," I offer, but I really don't know much about Connor or what it's like to be the editor-in-chief of an arts and entertainment site.

While I've kept up with the magazine over the years, I haven't paid much attention to the management and who's left, who's been promoted. What I wanted most was to read the articles and discover other writers who had the same passion and love for music as my sister. I wanted to hear her voice carry on.

Connor motions toward the break room. "Can I offer you something? A coffee, perhaps? At least more than a bottle of water."

I tell him that I'm fine, that it's not necessary, but he's already opening kitchen drawers and showing me granola bars and peanut butter crackers. I look them over. I haven't eaten much today, not since that half-eaten beignet.

Connor offers me a blueberry muffin that is wrapped in plastic. He looks eager to please as if he wants nothing more than to cater to me in my time of grief.

A box of donuts is left on the counter, and he lifts the lid, taking one, his fingertips covered in a thin layer of powdered sugar. I tell him no, thanks, and accept a protein bar instead, a cup of coffee.

"Cream? Sugar? We have that awful creamer stuff if that's okay."

"That's fine," I tell him.

He pours coffee into a mug that he lifts from the drain rack beside the sink, then adds the sugar and creamer, stirring carefully.

I start remembering more about Connor from the night of the party, his eagerness to talk, his relief to have someone paying attention to him. I didn't know many of Ellie's co-workers back then. Rachel was around somewhere, but she might have been outside having a smoke. Carmen and Ellie were in the living room playing beer pong with friends. I'm pretty sure Carmen won.

Connor talked a lot that night, I remember this also. He'd been so willing to fetch me a beer, then another, and I must have told him about Northwestern at some point, my graphic design studies, because he said something about the two of us being so creative. *Both you and your sister*, he said.

I sip the coffee now, the words *Nola Magazine* branded across the mug. The brew isn't as strong as the dark chicory from Café Du Monde, but it will do the trick. With the past two days and a horrible night's sleep, I'm in desperate need of the caffeine boost. In this state, I need every bit of caffeine in the world.

A staff member walks into the break room, oblivious to us being there as he stares at his phone. His hand reaches for the coffee pot before he looks up.

"Oh, hello," he says, then glances between us in case he might be interrupting.

Connor nods as the co-worker proceeds to fill his mug.

Then he turns around to study me, the registration sparking in his eyes. "You were outside," he says. "Earlier. I thought I saw you running, chasing after someone." He casts a glance at Connor. "Is everything okay?"

"It's fine," Connor says. Then he adds, "Riley, meet Lauren Duncan—"

"Capshaw," I tell him.

"That's right. Capshaw. This is Lauren, Ellie Duncan's sister."

His eyes widen. "Oh, I'm so sorry. We just learned about what happened."

Riley is tall, maybe six three, six four, and I have to look up at him as I murmur my response, a *thank you* of sorts for his condolences, the protein bar I'm chewing suddenly tasting like sawdust in my mouth. Nothing, I fear, will ever taste good again.

"We haven't told the rest of the staff, right?" Riley asks.

"No," Connor says. "Not yet." He looks at me. "Riley worked here when Ellie was here. He was in the staff meeting this morning with the police. He leads the Culture and Arts section now."

Riley tilts his head. "That guy you were chasing, was he bothering you? Did he ask you for money or something? He does that sometimes. We see him hanging around."

"You know him?" I ask.

"If it's who I'm thinking of, he's harmless. But then he bothers the students, thinking they'll be nice and toss him some cash. I give him a few bucks now and again just to help out. It looks like he might have come back."

The scruffy shoes and ragged hem of the blue jeans. The dark hair that streaked past his ears... it could still be Clive.

"I didn't get a good look at the guy," Connor says. "I'm not sure if that was him."

"If it was"—Riley smiles—"I've never seen anyone chase after him like that before. You might have scared him off."

"But this guy didn't ask for money," I tell him. "He just stared at me, then jumped back. There were these two students, I think they work here, and they walked right past him. He didn't ask them for money either."

Riley frowns. "Well, either way, I'm really sorry that happened. We shouldn't have someone hanging outside the office like that." He glances at Connor. "We should call the cops again, see if there's something they can do."

"I will," Connor says. "I'll definitely let them know. I don't want this guy hanging around, especially not after today." He looks across to the main area that's filled with staff writer cubicles. "It's about to get really busy around here and the reporters will start calling again. They'll be parking outside. The detective said a formal statement will go out later so there will be all kinds of new people hanging around, wanting a comment. I need to get with security."

Connor nods at us, his plan setting into motion. "I'll ask Stacey to draft an official statement and tell her I need to be the main point person from this office. The reporters will want sound bites, exterior shots of the building. All that B-roll from before, and they'll want something new. I'll call a staff meeting later today and loop everyone in."

Connor says to me, "We'll include a write-up about Ellie. I promise. We'll honor her memory, don't worry. She's one of us. She will always be one of us."

My eyes sting with tears. Connor's predecessor had repeated the same sentiment to us years ago about Ellie being one of their own, how they would help when it came to searching for my sister, and they did. They ran full-page spreads about finding Ellie, with several more articles posted online.

The magazine staff sent any leads that came into the office to the detective while Ellie's co-workers joined the search teams too. Connor and Riley must have been among the groups of volunteers combing the streets, but I can't remember. There were so many people back then. Everything was a hazy, chaotic whirlwind.

"Do you remember when that reporter asked us for things that belonged to Ellie?" Riley asks. "Stuff from her desk, her workspace, so they could try to personalize her better?"

Connor says, "They asked her roommate for some things too."

I remember Carmen calling my parents and asking for their permission, Ellie's boss phoning to also make sure it was okay. My parents told them that it was fine. Anything for the media attention to help us find Ellie.

Carmen allowed the reporters inside the apartment, and they spotlighted pictures of my sister, the guitar she loved to play when she took breaks from her studies. The media snapped photos of her empty bedroom, her empty bed.

The magazine allowed the news teams to shoot video of her workspace also, the ceramic pot that was filled with pens and markers, the desk that was left waiting for her.

Someone had pushed in her chair and powered down her computer, the screen lifeless and blank. And of all the images, that's one of the ones that hurts the most. It has stayed with me the longest—I hate the implied finality of it all.

But she's coming back, I wanted to scream. *She'll be back in this office soon doing what she loves.*

A lot of the coverage at the time was focused on the music hall, the sidewalk where she was last seen, the Broussards' home to where Ellie failed to return. But the media also included exterior shots of the *Nola* office. Views of her blog went up and had tons of new clicks.

Connor thinks it over. "I think we gave everything to your parents. We packed up Ellie's stuff and had it shipped to Evanston. I hated doing that," he tells me. "I thought we should have kept her desk the way it was, but the bosses thought otherwise. It was upsetting to a lot of people, the not knowing."

Riley frowns. "Are you sure we don't have anything left?" he asks. "I could have sworn there was some stuff the editors decided to keep. A framed article or something. One of Ellie's write-ups made the front page, remember?"

Connor looks down. "I'm not sure. I think everything's gone. But I can check."

"It's okay," I tell him. "The reporters should have plenty to work with, and I don't want them bothering you too much, not all over again. And with the latest... With her body being found..." My breath hitches, the sting of tears piercing my eyes. "A lot of the attention will be on that run-down house."

I'm crying, and Connor reaches for a box of tissues on the counter and hands one to me.

"Thank you." I take a deep breath. "They're going to be all over that neighborhood soon, the press. It will be horrible. I feel so bad for the people who live around there, around that house. They don't deserve this."

"But neither do you," Connor says. "Remember that, Lauren. Neither did your sister."

"Can I take you back to your hotel?" Connor asks. "Earlier, it sounded like you needed a ride."

I find a trash can and toss the tissue inside. "Yes, I'd appreciate that."

I have no idea what time it is, if I should go back to the hotel, if I should head to the concert hall next, but the truth is, I'm exhausted. The watered-down coffee has done little to help, and I need something stronger. Really, I need to rest. I should try to catch a few hours of sleep or I'll end up pacing my room wondering when Alex will knock on the door and find me.

Riley gives me a hug, and he's shy about it, tentative. Everything about him feels earnest and sweet. "Let us know if there is anything we can do to help."

I smile at him, timidly.

I follow Connor down the hall, past the cubicles to the lobby, where he opens the door. When we get to his car, he digs around in the glove compartment and finds a couple of fast-food napkins that he's stored away. He hands them to me, and I press them against my face. I didn't realize I was sobbing again.

We sit together for a few moments in silence, and I appreciate that Connor doesn't speak, that he lets me take my time.

"We can go," I finally tell him.

I give him the name of the bed-and-breakfast, which Connor enters into his phone, letting Google Maps lead the way. In front of the hotel, he stops, the car idling. We fall silent again as he stares ahead and I search the street for any signs of media, for reporters who might have picked up on my sister's story early and have determined my location.

There is always that one reporter, the one with the inside scoop, the good contacts, who can quickly make the connection from the body that was found to the cold case of a female college student from twelve years ago. That reporter could already be at the hotel. They could be standing on the porch waiting for me, and so could my husband.

I lift my fingers to the door handle, ready to get out.

TWENTY

"Your husband insists that he doesn't know where Clive is," Detective Rayburn tells me.

I'm on the bed, my phone pressed to my ear, not a reporter in sight as I made my way from the lobby to my room. No sign of Alex either, but he's somewhere, I know he is. I can feel him —almost sense him. He's coming. He will want to talk again soon.

"Alex understands that his brother is a person of interest, that we're looking for Clive also," Detective Rayburn says, "but we want to know why your husband didn't come forward about a few things."

"Where is he now?"

"At the hotel." He pauses. "Mrs. Capshaw, you know that he's staying at the same place as you, correct?"

My eyes race to the door, a sharp intake of breath. I knew it. My paranoia is actually the truth. *Alex is here.*

I sit very still, waiting and listening. My eyes peel upwards... Was that him I heard waking in the middle of the night and crossing the room? Was he staring down through the floorboard knowing I was below him?

"I told Mr. Capshaw not to leave town," the detective says. "It's important he sticks around for more questioning."

I get up and move to the window, slowly pulling back the curtains. The courtyard is empty.

"And this morning?" I ask. "What time did you meet?"

"Around ten. He was here for a couple of hours, said that he's being cooperative, which for his sake, I hope he is. The reason he didn't file a missing person's report for Clive is because he kept thinking his brother might return on his own, that the police didn't push him to file one either. He's been searching for Clive by himself, without an investigation, which is not only misleading to you and your family, but to everyone else involved."

The confirmation is tough to swallow, but I can't help but think about something else. My husband only went to the police station at 10 a.m., which means he could have followed me through the French Quarter. He knew when I left the hotel. He could have been hiding from me behind that cathedral wall.

But the man outside the magazine office... was he really a homeless person like Riley suggested? Was it Clive?

"We've spoken to several of the concert attendees," the detective says. "But many of their statements remain the same: they don't specifically recall seeing Ellie that night, there were a lot of people, or it's what they described before, that she stood outside with someone, her co-worker, Rachel Carmichael. Ms. Carmichael returned to the show."

"But Rachel said she doesn't know anything about the house, isn't that correct? I was told you showed her pictures, that the house means nothing to her?"

"She doesn't know why your sister was there, no. Ellie leaving her phone behind didn't help either. There was no way of tracking down your sister's location, as you remember. No way of knowing where she walked or how far she'd gotten. No messages between her and someone about meeting up either.

The last text was from Carmen saying she was sorry she'd gone to her boyfriend's. Ellie didn't respond."

"Detective Henley thought my sister might have left her phone by accident. That it might have been knocked off a table at the bar."

"That could have happened, yes. It's possible your sister didn't realize she had left her phone behind."

We learned this about Ellie after she went missing, and it was infuriating: how she would leave her phone at bars sometimes, either from being distracted and having a good time, or she'd moved closer to the stage, maybe to dance, maybe searching for a band member to interview afterwards.

Carmen said she'd come home and then often return the next day, hoping someone had turned in her phone at the bar. She had a habit of leaving her bar tabs open too, and she'd have no choice but to trudge back in the morning to retrieve her credit card.

It's maddening, this carefree spirit that sometimes enveloped my sister, the forgetfulness Ellie would have at times, her life seemingly moving forward on a whim. But even more frustrating was that by leaving her phone, we had no way of tracking her, no way of narrowing down Ellie's location, where she'd been kept hidden. There could have been a ping to a nearby cell tower. A clue at least.

But Ellie's last known location was the music hall. It was as if she'd never left.

"Mrs. Capshaw," the detective says, "we hosted a press conference a short time ago. We discussed the photographs, but I assure you that your location and your husband's location were not mentioned. However, reporters will be trying to contact you anyway. They'll want to speak to you."

"I know," I say, and I drop away from the window, closing the curtains to hide from the reporters. "I've been preparing for this."

. . .

We end the call, and I'm weary, my limbs heavy as I collapse again against the mattress. The dimness of the room helps somewhat, the quiet hum of the air conditioner with the fountain outside and the water trickling.

I want nothing more than to be suspended in this time, to float in these last few seconds by myself, tucked away and hiding from the media, hiding from the world, from Alex.

My husband is at this same hotel.

Should I leave? Should I take Carmen up on her offer and go to her place?

My phone remains on silent, but I brace myself for the onslaught of media calls. It's funny, but before, we needed the media. In the days and weeks after Ellie went missing, we wanted every bit of their attention in spotlighting her case. Now, I want nothing more than for the reporters to disappear, for all of the press to disappear. For the spotlight to move away from my family.

Alex said he transferred to Northwestern University by chance, that he wanted to relocate to Chicago in order to finish his degree. But is the truth more sinister? By dating me, then marrying me, I'd always be close. He could ensure his connection to Ellie remained hidden.

Instead of avoiding us and staying in a different part of the country—I would have thought someone riddled with guilt and secrets would stay far, far away—Alex put himself front and center instead.

Why would he do that? Why would he risk being so close?

Was this his way of leading me off track? He wanted to keep himself within the fold?

Maybe he thought he could learn something. He could try to lead me in the opposite direction, my dad also. If there was any information, anything new from the investigation, if the police discovered a clue, he could warn his brother.

Keep your friends close, and your enemies closer—isn't that how the saying goes?

Alex put himself right in the middle of our family. He was a wolf in sheep's clothing. Our enemy.

I wonder if he ever feared this day, that my sister's body could be found, that someone could come forward about him and his brother. Was he in a constant state of panic during our marriage to see what would happen? Every time our phone rang, and the Caller ID showed it was the police, would he worry? Would he wonder what was happening?

But with time passing, the years stretching, and still no evidence, no security video, no witnesses connecting him or Clive to my sister, Alex might have begun to relax. He might have thought he and Clive were in the clear, and he settled into our marriage.

But Alex made a mistake, a big one. He forgot about those photos.

Maybe he thought his brother had destroyed them, that he'd also ripped the film from my sister's Nikon camera and torn up the evidence after he stood with Ellie on that balcony. He thought the pictures were lost forever. Her gift to him, he believed, was now erased and unable to prove their meeting.

But the pictures weren't destroyed, and those images lasted alongside Ellie's body. They persisted. Those very photographs could be the brothers' downfall.

Ellie kept the clues to her own killer, and now I don't know whether to be proud or to sob. Because one of those people is responsible for killing her.

I ignore the incoming call and force my eyelids closed, but the buzzing starts up again, and I groan, turning over to one side.

The room is darker than it was before, a heavy thick shadow that falls across the space where night has fallen. Through the window, the flicker from the gas lanterns peeks around the edge of the curtains where I failed to pull them together completely.

My phone continues to buzz, a vibration against the mattress that makes its way to my pillow, then rattles my head.

It's Alex, and I sit straight up.

Several text messages appear on my screen too, but each of those is from Carmen.

I told the detective about Alex's texts. I sent him the screenshots.

I lower my shoulders. That's good. Carmen has finally spoken to the detective.

I ignore Alex's call and text her back.

What do the messages say?

She replies instantly.

Mostly about how I'm doing. About you lighting candles for Ellie's anniversary. He asks about your sister, what she's like.

What she's like, and my throat tightens.

Could you send them to me?

I wait, holding my breath. I need to see these messages immediately.

She's responding, probably looking up those screenshots, when another call comes in—it's Alex again. He's relentless, suffocating to the point of making me want to scream, and now I want to throw my phone across the room. I want it to shatter into a dozen pieces so I can avoid him. My throat aches, the rage pulsing at my fingertips.

For years, Alex has asked about my sister, acting as if he didn't know her. *He lied to me too*, Carmen said.

The ringing stops. Alex has given up on calling because he's sending me a text message.

I need to talk to you, Lauren. Please.

I don't respond.

The detective held a press conference. He announced my brother as a person of interest.

I shiver and wonder when Alex will be implicated too.

I'm coming to your room.

My heart bangs its way into my throat.

Here? To my room? Any minute, Alex will take the stairs, the elevator, a knock on the door that will rattle the doorframe next.

What does he want—for me to comfort him? For us to sit down and talk as if our whole world hasn't been torn apart?

I check the door. The latch is secure. I could pretend that I'm not here. I could text him back and say I'm somewhere else. I don't have to do this. I don't have to see him—

A knock.

It's him.

"Lauren, I know you're in there," he says quietly, a gentle tap against the door, the sound of his knuckles pressed against the wood. "Please talk to me. Open up."

I'm furious. Frightened. I'm trapped.

There is so much about him I don't want to face.

There's so much I need to ask, and with my breath held, I fling open the door.

Alex looks shocked, then relieved, to see me, and I stare at this man, this husband of mine. The skin around his eyes has turned a dull gray. It's as if he's hardly slept, and neither have I.

"Lauren..."

I keep my hand gripped on the edge of the door. "I've asked you before and I need to ask you again. Did Clive have anything to do with Ellie?"

His eyebrows draw upward. "No. I said no."

"Did you?"

He glances up and down the hall, then back to me, registering that he's not coming in, we're doing this here, out in the open. So far, the hall remains empty.

"No, of course not," he says. "We didn't do anything to her."

"Do you know where Clive is?"

"I have no idea—"

"Are you following me?"

"What?"

"Where were you this morning? Before you met with the detective? Were you watching me?"

He narrows his eyes. "Watching you? Lauren, what's going on?"

"Where were you?" I repeat.

"I was here. At this hotel."

"I can't believe you're staying here too."

"It wasn't difficult to figure out this was where you were staying, especially with the other hotel closed down—"

"Did you see me earlier? Did you follow me? Run from me at St. Louis Cathedral and hide?"

"Hide from you?" Alex splutters at the whiplash of my rapid-fire questions. "Lauren, what is happening? Is someone harassing you? Tell me what's happening right now."

I straighten my stance. "I don't have to tell you anything. Not anymore. What did you do to the Life360 app?"

He makes a face. "The tracking app?"

"Yes. Why has your location been paused since yesterday?"

"I... I don't know. I'll check." He pulls out his phone.

"My location is showing up, but not yours," I tell him. "You switched it off. You're tracking me, aren't you? You've been able to see where I go."

He shakes his head then pockets his phone. "Your location isn't showing up either."

"It was showing up before. But I altered my settings the same way you did."

"Altered my settings? Lauren, I didn't alter anything."

A hotel guest enters the hall, and they're either ignoring us or oblivious to our conversation because they swipe their key card and enter their room.

I look again at Alex. "Answer me this: did you see me today? Or do you think it could have been Clive? Was he following me?"

His eyes widen. "Wait, you think you saw *Clive*?"

I rake my hands through my hair. "I thought it was you at first, but I don't know. It might have been him. I'm not sure. There was something familiar in the way he looked. Carmen thought the same thing."

"You saw Carmen?"

"And the Broussards too. I had to see them. I had to tell them."

"Of course," he says, and his voice softens. "Of course you did. I understand."

My chest squeezes. This hurts so much. I miss my husband. Perhaps I miss the idea of him.

I lower my hands. "Alex, in those photos, there are flowers on the table. Pink camellias that were given to Ellie, placed right in front of her. It's just like the ones—"

"I know. Like the ones I give you every year for her anniversary."

And I startle, a sob hitting my throat. "But why? Why would you do that? It's like you've been messing with me all this time, telling me that you knew her—you left a sick clue right in front of my face, and I had no idea. All that stuff about the flowers symbolizing someone you miss, and it meant so much. I bought into it. All of it."

He winces. "It does mean those things."

"Then why did you give them to my sister?"

"I didn't. Clive gave them to her. I told you that he invited her at the last minute, remember? He picked up those flowers on the way, and he was so nervous. They'd only hung out a couple of times and he thought she might like them. She had told him that she missed her family, that she missed her sister. That she missed you."

Ellie... And the tears slip down my cheeks. *I miss you too.*

"So, you *did* know about me." I glare at him. "You knew exactly who I was. All that stuff about randomly meeting at Northwestern."

"I knew that Ellie had an older sister, yes. But I didn't remember which school. I really didn't."

"I don't believe you."

"Lauren, you have to trust me."

"*Trust you?* How can I trust you? And what about my dad?" I ask. "The way you've been visiting my dad and then not telling me about it? These questions you've been asking him, about when Ellie and I were kids."

"I wanted to know more about you, that's all." His simple shrug infuriates me; it concerns me. "I wanted to know about when you were little, how the two of you grew up."

"Why? I could have told you all of that."

"Your dad has his own memories," he says. "His own

wonderful stories. You know I don't have that with my parents anymore." For this, he looks down.

"But you specifically asked him about that day. Why?"

"Which day?"

My heart pounds. "You know exactly which day."

He says, "I wanted to help you, that's all. I wanted to better understand your fear of heights, what really happened. You told me about the treehouse, about your sister, but I knew there had to be something else. Something you were leaving out. I thought that maybe your dad would tell me."

"And did he?"

He eyes me carefully, as if he's wondering if he should tell me. "He did."

It's time to close the door. It's time to end this conversation.

"I thought that if I finally understood the whole story," he says, "I could help you get over your fear of heights. I could talk it through with you."

"I'm fine," I tell him. "I told you that I'm fine. I'm doing better."

"No, you're not." He steps forward. "Look at everything that is happening. All of this with Ellie is bringing it up again. The way she died..."

"It's not..." *It's not related*, is what I want to say.

But the truth is, my sister fell to her death. And one day, long ago, someone else fell too, and I saw it happen. We both did. The boy's screams, the rush of wind at my ears. That forever-dizzying gaze as I climbed down.

"That kid," Alex says. "What he said to you. It's not your fault. You were so young. You didn't know any better."

"I'm fine," I repeat.

"But you're not." Alex looks at me. "You know you're not. Ever since that day, you've never been the same. And neither was Ellie."

TWENTY-ONE
A YEAR AGO

"Your dad seems like he's in good spirits," Alex says.

I smile. "He does, doesn't he?"

We're at the Oak Manor Senior Center, four intense games of checkers with Dad later, when Alex offers to fetch us some drinks. He says he'll head to the cafeteria and be back in a minute.

I remain sitting in front of my dad, the checkers board laid out between us, when a gentle tap sounds at the door. It's Nurse Sheryl, who has come back to check on us. "Everything good in here?"

"He crushed me again," I tell her. "Four games in a row."

Dad chuckles, his eyes lifting to hers. "How hard is it to find good competition these days?"

She smiles. "Keep it up, Mr. Duncan. That's what I like to hear." Sheryl taps the doorframe again before taking off, her blond curls bouncing at her ears.

I set up the checkers board for another game, pushing the red pieces to his side, the black pieces to mine. The board is frayed around the edges after years of wear and tear, with other families shuffling the game from one room to the next, the corners of the box lid torn and flimsy too. I tell myself I'll buy a new game set before our next visit.

Dad watches me set up the pieces. "Lauren," he says. His voice is quiet. "Whatever happened to that kid? Jacob?"

I stop moving the pieces. "Who?"

"Jacob. That boy. What is he up to these days?"

I meet Dad's gaze, one of the checkers pieces still in my hand.

I bite my lip. Where is this coming from? We haven't talked about Jacob in years, nothing about that day when Ellie and I were little. The blood that soaked into the warm summer grass with all that blue sky above us.

"Why are you asking about Jacob?"

"I don't know," he says, and offers me a shrug. "My brain, and these thoughts sometimes will pop up. Maybe someone says something, and it will have me thinking about something else." Another shrug. "But that boy. I've always wondered."

"He's fine," I tell him. "He grew up. He got married I think."

"Did he transfer schools?"

Yes, to get away from me. To get away from Ellie.

"His dad's job changed, and they had to move." I eye him. "What's this about?"

Dad looks at his desk, the picture of my sister, the framed photo of our family where Mom is still smiling, a healthy glow to her cheeks. Ellie is still with us too.

"Do you think the treehouse was a bad idea?" he asks.

I set down the checkers piece. "The treehouse?"

It's been years since my dad has mentioned the treehouse, the treehouse that no longer exists; it was torn down after we sold the place. The new homeowners didn't have children and they wanted to extend the garden and plant a small vegetable patch instead. I always thought Ellie would have been so upset, even as a grown woman, to see the treehouse go. She would have wanted it played on and cherished by so many other kids.

Dad's gaze is wary, and his face pinches, his eyes watering. "It's been so much time now, Lauren," he says to me. "It's okay. We can talk about it now."

But I shake my head. I tell myself I don't know what he means. We don't need to talk about it.

"I always knew you were the one who did it," Dad says. "That day, the lies you girls told. You can own up to it now."

* * *

The grunt is what I hear first, Ellie with her arms held out, her palms facing forward, as she leans forward to give the boy a shove. The next sound is the one in my head, the one that says, *You don't have to take this from him. Defend yourself.*

That thought is followed by another more insistent one: *Make it so he can never talk to you that way again.*

I stretch out my arms and grab hold of his jeans, my fingers crooked into one of his waistband loops as I pull. I give it a strong yank, and he topples forward, off the roof and past my head. His look of horror as he flies past me is followed by a howl, Jacob's blood-curdling shriek escaping his mouth as he plunges over the side. He windmills his arms pointlessly to stop himself as he catapults down.

Down, down he goes... another terrifying scream from that boy who loves to make fun of me, who will never reciprocate my feelings, who is more impressed by my sister instead. This is someone who needs to be taught a lesson. In that moment, I finally found my nerve and fought back.

I peer over the railing to watch. I need to see—horrifyingly —what I've done. Above me, my sister is panting, her shock audible in every breath. Maybe she is disappointed she didn't get to him first.

Jacob has fallen two stories from the treehouse, give or take since he clambered up to the roof, but it feels like it was in slow motion, with nothing to stop him but that hard, unforgiving earth. The heavy thud as his body smacked against the ground. Then silence.

But a shout from Aaron erupts into the air along with Brooke's ear-piercing scream. They throw out their hands, staring at their friend.

Jacob is so still—so frighteningly still—his arms bent at a sickening angle, his legs folded to one side. Blood appears at his nose, then the side of his head, the blood so bright and garish; it trickles into the grass, seeping between the blades, a startling red against green. I think his blood will stain the ground forever.

Aaron and Brooke scramble down the ladder after him and holler their friend's name. But I remain motionless, and my sister does also, until her head peers over the top of the roof and she stares at the ground, then at me. I can't meet her gaze, not while the horror show is taking place below. Aaron and Brooke, and their screams.

Brooke drops to her knees while Aaron hovers uselessly over Jacob. He checks to see if Jacob is breathing, if his friend is making any sounds, but we are only kids. We have no idea what to do, and we need grown-ups.

My parents haven't yet appeared. They must be oblivious with the music turned on high. But one of them will hear the screams soon, and Mom and Dad will have to come out here.

I'm going to be sick.

I did this. I pulled at him.

Jacob fell, and I could have killed him.

I stare at his body... Is he already dead?

If I hadn't done it, would Ellie have pushed him herself?

I crane my neck to look up at my sister, and she meets my gaze, her shocked gasps now turning into a smile at the curve of her lips. She's proud of me, and I shudder. My heartbeat slows.

The consequences are coming—any minute now, as real and as sure as anything—and our parents, the doctors, and nurses will have questions. These last few seconds before we get into trouble bear down on us.

Brooke lets out another high-pitched scream. Finally, the back door flies open, and Mom is there, sprinting from the house, her expression twisted with shock, then all-consuming fear.

She stares wildly at Jacob on the ground, then to the other children, then up at me, at Ellie. My sister remains crouched on the roof.

Dad appears in the doorway next as Mom shouts over her shoulder, "Call nine-one-one!"

I have no choice but to climb down from the treehouse, knowing I will have to answer for this. I will tell them what I've done.

But it feels as if my feet are never going to touch the grass, and the climb down the ladder is interminable, horrifying even, my fears catapulting around inside my head, my body convinced that my own body will fall, my arms and legs will windmill pointlessly and nothing will stop me as I plummet through the air. I will fall and break just like Jacob.

Brooke and Aaron keep whimpering while I force one foot down after the other, the ladder going on forever. I have never wanted so much in my life to touch solid ground, to be away from the treehouse and safely somewhere else. The distance below me warps in my view.

When I touch the ground, I catch my breath, and when I reach Jacob, I see his eyes are open. He looks up at my mom. He is dazed but breathing, and relief washes through my veins that he is alive.

But the shame hits hard. I acted like a monster. Even though he deserved to be punished, I shouldn't have let him push me so far.

Mom rests her hand on Jacob's head. She pulls away her fingers when she sees they are sticky with blood. "What happened?" she cries.

"They pushed him!" Brooke screams.

"Who pushed?" Mom asks, and she swivels her head to me, then up to Ellie.

"I didn't see everything," Aaron says. "But I'm pretty sure Ellie did it." His eyes flare at her. "She pushed him. She was sitting right behind him."

"I did not!" Ellie shrieks. She has yet to climb down from the roof.

"No, Lauren did it!" Brooke says, glaring at me. "She pulled him down. He was being mean to her and—" She cuts herself off, wiping the tears from her eyes.

Mom focuses her attention once again on the injured boy. She pats his shoulder. Not knowing what else to do, she closes her eyes, whispering, "What did you do? Girls, what did you do?"

Jacob moans, and she opens her eyes again. Jacob blinks at her several times, but he is unable to say anything, unable to move his body. Mom tells him to stay still, that it's best for him to keep quiet, to wait for the ambulance. She assures him that help is on the way, that he is going to be okay, that everything—and she stares at me and Ellie—is going to be okay. But her voice wobbles when she says this. I don't think she believes it.

"Don't move," she repeats.

Brooke says, "You did it, Lauren. I saw you. I saw you reach out your hands."

"Why would I?" I screech. In that moment, I have no idea why I lied.

"You were so mad. He was teasing you—" Brooke stops herself again. She waves her hands as if none of that matters, as if people can talk a certain way to one another and not face consequences. She narrows her eyes. "I saw you reach for him."

Ellie starts climbing down from the roof. Soon, her feet land heavily on the platform above us, but she doesn't move down the ladder to the ground.

"He fell," Ellie says. "Didn't you see how he was leaning so far down? He was getting in Lauren's face. Saying those nasty things. He lost his balance—"

"You're lying!" Brooke turns to me. "Both of you are lying!"

Mom keeps her head lowered. She's lost in her own world, mumbling and fussing over Jacob, and ignoring our argument. "We're tearing this whole thing down," she whispers. "I knew this was an accident waiting to happen. I just knew it."

"No, Mom!" I cry, the panic of my consequences setting in. This should be my punishment. My guilt. I can't let the aftermath extend to tearing down the treehouse that Ellie loves so much, the treehouse she begged for and waited so long to have.

Dad appears again at the back door and sprints toward us. "The ambulance is on its way." When he reaches our group, he stands over Jacob's body.

Mom says, "We're tearing the treehouse down." She glares at him. "I told you not to build it. I told you not to let the girls talk you into this."

"No, Mom!" Ellie screams. "It was an accident. You can't do that!"

Dad watches my sister climb down the ladder. He looks at me next. "How did this happen?"

I am ready to confess, ready to tell them everything. "I—"

But Aaron breaks in. "Jacob was up there. He wanted to be on the roof with Ellie, but she pushed him."

"It wasn't Ellie. It was—" I say.

Ellie lands her feet on the ground. "We didn't do anything. He fell. He lost his balance. He doesn't know how to be on the roof like me."

"And what were you doing up there?" Dad says to her.

"How could you be so reckless? Don't you ever go up there again."

"But he slipped," Ellie says. "It's not our fault."

I quickly meet her gaze, bewildered that she is covering for me, that she doesn't want me to confess. She's telling them this to cover us both. It will be neither of our faults. Dad won't have to tear down the treehouse as punishment.

"Is that what happened?" Dad asks Ellie quietly before he gives me a look. "Lauren, is that the truth?"

But the gate swings open and the rush of two paramedics into the backyard causes us to leap back. Dad immediately greets the paramedics and we watch them work on Jacob, assessing him, then carefully fitting him onto the stretcher before lifting it to its wheels.

Mom reports what she can. "He fell."

"We'll call his parents," Dad adds. "We'll meet them at the hospital."

The paramedics roll the stretcher over the uneven grass. Aaron and Brooke chase after Jacob, and so do our parents.

But Ellie remains beside me. We stand in the backyard, both of us riddled with adrenaline. We are processing what just occurred.

"It's not your fault," Ellie says to me. "It's not my fault either."

I don't answer.

She holds my hand. "He had it coming though, don't you think? You did what you had to do. Don't worry."

But I don't believe it. I will regret that day forever, the climb up, the climb down; Jacob's screams will haunt me for years.

TWENTY-TWO

I don't check the news. I refuse to see what is online, the TV reports that are increasing with momentum since Detective Rayburn held the press conference.

I don't look at social media either. The messages will be streaming in by now, and at some point, I know I should leave a post on Ellie's Facebook page so the group can hear directly from me. I will thank them for everything they've done to support us in the past, everything they continue to do, and will ask them to think about our family.

But how do I answer their questions: questions about Alex and Clive?

Did you know, Lauren? How could you not have known about your husband?

How do I explain to them about Alex prodding into my past? What if he talks too and starts sharing his own thoughts?

What he said to me about that day, about me never being the same, Ellie either... I clasp my hands together, squeezing tight. He doesn't know what he's talking about.

Beside me, my phone continues to light up with new notifications. So many people sharing their concern.

Colleagues will be sending me messages, I'm positive, along with the news spreading from one Facebook friend to the next with condolences and pictures reposted of Ellie, alongside dozens of broken heart emojis and sentiments that I will read later, then cry my eyes out. I can't bear to look, to know how many people are hurting right now. They are hurting for my sister.

I don't want to read what they're thinking about the press conference announcement either.

I wonder if Connor and the team at *Nola Magazine* have posted an *In Memoriam* about Ellie yet, perhaps a statement from Loyola University also. Will the article be shared again and again to friends, to Ellie's former colleagues and classmates?

Will Connor and Riley contact me soon too? Total disbelief about the man who has been identified by the police, the connection of Clive Capshaw to my own husband?

Did you know when you came to see us? Connor and Riley might ask. After all, they're journalists too.

Another ping on my phone, and this time, I do look down. I see Carmen's name. She's sending screenshots of her previous messages from Alex.

How are you? Hang in there, Carmen. Stay strong.

The date of this message is shortly after we gathered at Carmen's parents' house.

A few weeks later, he wrote:

We can't stop hoping that Ellie will return. The police are still looking. We should too. We must keep hoping.

The following year:

It will soon be the two-year anniversary and I'm worried. Lauren is a wreck. What should I do? How are you coping?

And months after that:

Did Ellie have a favorite band? Where do you think she would have gone if she actually ran away and left town?

January of this year:

Did Ellie ever tell you about a boyfriend? Do you think she was hiding something from everyone?

A few days later:

I wish I could have known her.

Carmen is right about Alex lying to her too. He played all of us like fools.

I palm my phone, noticing that Carmen's screenshots don't include any of her responses.

The remnants of last night's room service are beside me on the bed, a tray with a half-eaten club sandwich, along with potato chips that are brittle and tasteless, and scattered on the plate.

Before I went to sleep, Nurse Sheryl sent me several updates about my dad.

He's doing okay. The grief counselor will return tomorrow.

Then this morning:

We're doing our best to keep the news away from him.

I'd let out an anguished cry for my sweet, heartbroken father, that he could possibly hear reports about Clive or Alex —he'll be so terribly confused. I pled to Sheryl, asking her to hold off on explaining anything more to him until I had the chance.

The Broussards have left me multiple voicemails also, and I can imagine Mrs. Broussard frantically moving about the house, pacing in her bathrobe, too distraught to get dressed, while Mr. Broussard stands guard at the window trying to decide if he should track Alex down himself. They will want to know what is happening. They will be beside themselves as they worry about me.

Why didn't you tell us? I'm positive Mrs. Broussard's voicemail will say. *What does Alex know?*

I bet she's already called Carmen, and Carmen will have answered. She will have told the Broussards what little she knows, what little she gathered from me; the rest of the story they will have to gather from the news. I wonder if Carmen told them about the photographs, the Broussards' startled expressions.

I cradle my head in my hands; this nightmare situation is only getting worse.

The sound of paper sliding against the carpet—and I look up. The unmistakable smoothness of it sliding against the floor, and I turn my head.

Alex? Has he returned to my room?

He must not want another face-off and he's brought me something instead.

I spot the red folder and step quickly, looking for the shadow of Alex's feet beneath the door, proof that he isn't backing down, that he's waiting for me. There is no shadow, no sound, but I tread carefully anyway. Alex could have easily stepped out of the way, moved to one side.

I check the peephole, preparing to see my husband, for his

eyeball to be glaring right back, his wary smile, as I stifle my scream and jump, but there is nothing. No sign of him.

Quickly, I lift the folder and backtrack for the bed.

The front of the folder is blank: my name hasn't been written on the cover. There is no note from Alex.

There is no reporter's business card asking me to call either, and I'm relieved that the media might not have found me yet.

But then I see photos, dozens of them. Each one of them in full color.

Each one is of my sister.

The photos are 4x6 in size, but unlike the ones found in Ellie's pocket, these are new and undamaged by time. The snapshots are glossy.

My sister sits at her desk at the *Nola Magazine* office staring at her computer screen. On her face is that determined, focused intensity I remember so well from when we were kids, when she was studying or working on something that required her attention, the end of her ballpoint pen chewed between her teeth.

But this is a candid shot: my sister isn't posing for the camera. Something about the angle and how it's been taken— the camera is held low as if the person sat somewhere else. They crouched at another desk or peeked around the corner. They didn't want Ellie to know they were taking her picture.

The next image is of Ellie leaving her apartment, her hair pulled across one shoulder. She looks distracted, like she's in a rush; maybe she overslept and she's worried about getting to class in time. She's late for the office. She has no idea that someone stands outside her apartment watching her.

I pull up the images on my phone, the ones from Detective Rayburn, and hold my screen alongside the new prints I now have in my hand. Ellie isn't wearing the same long-sleeved shirt from when she had brunch with Alex and Clive. She's not wearing the jean jacket from when she went out to the concert either.

This is a different day altogether. She's in a light sweater, which means the weather is cool. It could be mid-November. It could be from around the same time when Ellie went missing.

The azalea bushes in front of the Broussards' home are no longer in full bloom, with the leaves starting to turn. The yard needs to be raked. My sister wears the gold pendant with the letter *E* around her neck, and I can see it dangling at the scoop of her sweater.

These photos could have been taken just weeks before Ellie went missing, days even. Someone stood across the street and waited for her. They watched my sister. They stayed hidden.

That birthday weekend when our parents gave her the necklace, when she talked to me about being afraid. *I'll be walking home and it feels as if someone is right behind me. Like someone is watching from the window.* But then she'd shaken her head. *It's nothing.* She told the Broussards the same. A month later, and she was gone.

I flip through the rest of the prints, and it's a series of progression shots: my sister moving down the drive, the sidewalk. She's heading down the street. She stands beneath the shadow of an oak tree when she reaches the end of the block.

I flip back to the first photo, the one of Ellie sitting at her desk—and my pulse quickens. Someone took her picture from *inside* the *Nola* newsroom.

Anyone could stand across the street, could find out where my sister lived, but how could they gain access to Ellie's office? How could they walk into a newsroom with a camera, and no one asked them why they were there?

This wasn't Alex. Which means...

I run to the front of the hotel room and fling open the door, expecting to see Connor or Riley or someone from the magazine waiting for me. I'll demand to know why they left this folder. I'll accuse them of knowing who stalked my sister—and maybe it's one of them. I'll ask why they didn't show these photographs to the police before.

But the hall is empty, the long expanse of carpet rolling out on either side with no sign of anyone near the lobby.

I lock the door and press the back of my head against it as I breathe in and out.

Are you sure we don't have anything left? Riley asked. *I could have sworn there was some stuff the editors decided to keep.*

I think everything's gone, Connor said.

Did one of them go looking yesterday? After I left, did they search through the storage rooms and stumble upon these photos?

I flip the prints over, looking for a timestamp or a label from where they were developed, a Walgreens pharmacy or a local film shop, the office where Ellie worked herself. But the backs of the prints are blank, and I have no idea what the magazine's in-house processing system looks like, if they would include a marking with the magazine's name.

I can't tell when the photographs were printed either. It could have been years ago. Or the negatives could have been kept hidden and were printed as recently as today.

Ellie had a gut feeling that someone was following her, watching her, and she didn't listen... none of us did.

Did this person behind the camera hurt her? Did they follow her that night too?

"Who else knows where you're staying?" Detective Rayburn asks, and I stare out the window. I'm unable to stop staring and searching.

I've been considering the same thing, that besides Alex and

his visit to my room, I'm pretty sure I mentioned the name of the hotel to Carmen, but I don't think I told the Broussards where I am.

But there is definitely Connor. He dropped me off. He knows exactly where I am.

"The editor-in-chief you spoke with yesterday," I say. "Connor. He would know about photos in the office too."

"I'll talk to him. I'll talk to the hotel front desk also, ask them who they saw in the lobby, if there was anyone spotted in your hall. They might have a description." He pauses. "Any chance you think this could be from Alex?"

I've already told the detective about my conversation with my husband at the entrance to my hotel room, Alex's continued proclamations of innocence.

"I tried calling him to ask, that maybe he spent longer in New Orleans than I thought, that maybe he knew my sister for weeks and lied about that too, but he didn't answer. I don't think this was him anyway." I lift one of the photographs again, staring at the image of my sister standing outside her apartment. "I mean, why would Alex bring these photos to me? Why would he drop them off and implicate himself, give away that he knows more about my sister?"

"I'll definitely ask him," the detective says. "And I'll ask the hotel about security cameras too. We can see who delivered this to you."

I face the window and look outside. Despite the darkness inside my room, my skin that is covered in a cold sweat, the outside world is bright, almost painfully cheerful. The courtyard is layered with sunshine, the water in the fountain sparkling beneath golden shimmers of light. A young couple sits at a table with their little girl, and the small child chews on an apple slice, her feet happily swinging beneath her chair as a bird hops below, hoping to find a crumb.

Besides the family, there is no one else in the courtyard. No sign of Alex. No appearances from Connor either.

The rear door to the lobby remains closed, and I drop the curtain.

I look again at the photographs. "It has to be someone from the magazine," I tell the detective. "Whoever left these doesn't want to get involved. They certainly don't want to get involved with the police. But someone was clearly following my sister, and they want me to know it's someone from the office. Someone they work with."

"I need to collect those from you. I'll have the lab look for fingerprints, where the photos were printed. We'll meet with the rest of the magazine staff too, find out what they know."

I think about Connor, about what he said. *I wasn't always in her circle... I wouldn't know what she got up to.*

But Connor knew exactly where my sister lived. He was at the party. He could have snuck photos of Ellie at work.

And with their *Nola* assignments, Connor a fledgling writer just like my sister, he could have found out which band she was covering that night. He could have learned where Ellie was and followed her. Gone up to that balcony and shoved her to the ground.

Because while Alex is guilty of a lot of things, while my husband knows exactly where my room is and continues to lie through his teeth about that day, about his brother, it's unlikely he's responsible for the photographs. Someone would have remembered him, especially now, with the news out, and they would surely recall him entering the *Nola* office and snapping these pictures of my sister. Unwanted pictures.

Someone at *Nola Magazine* knows something.

TWENTY-THREE

I could call Connor and ask him. I could return to their office right now and ask what he knows, Riley too. But the detective says this should be taken care of by the police, and he's right.

I don't want to leave my room. I don't want to risk bumping into Alex, or anyone else. I don't want to place the folder at the front desk so that one of Detective Rayburn's officers can come by and pick it up. They will walk directly to my room so I don't have to leave. Detective Rayburn assures me that he will be in touch.

I throw on some clothes and brush my hair, my teeth. The small coffee pot brews on the counter and I find a packet of crackers from last night's meal, forcing myself to nibble on a few.

I don't have much time—the police officer could be here any minute—and I lay the photos across the bed. If these were truly taken from the days before my sister went missing, each moment is precious. Each photo is important. Every trace of my sister is something I want to keep. More clues.

The photos of Ellie leaving the apartment, I place in order, along with the progressive shots of her walking down the street. The one of her at work, I place in a separate row.

I take snaps of each of them with my phone, then stack the photos carefully together before sliding them inside the folder.

A knock on the door, and a glance through the peephole assures me it's the police officer. He holds up his badge, and I hand him the evidence. He tips his head without saying a word, turning slowly to walk down the hall, his heavy shoes pressed against the carpet.

I wonder what the detective's next steps will be, what the police could soon learn. Someone at the magazine might recognize a detail, something captured in one of those shots. It could trigger a memory. Connor or Riley could confess.

I lock the hotel door once again and return to the bed, my coffee cup cooling beside me on the nightstand. Grabbing Ellie's blue binder, I slide it onto my lap and finally open the cover. It's been some time since I went through these notes, the information I copied from the original investigation with news articles and updates that are adhered to the pages.

Several emails are printed, along with my dad's scribbled messages with various names and contact details. An article about Ellie includes her picture, and it's the same image we used for her missing person's poster: her happy smile and her bright red hair pulled across one shoulder. Another article features a photograph of my parents sitting side by side in the rented apartment as they give an interview.

Twelve years ago, and my mom is so thin. Dad keeps his arm around her, their faces pulled tight, a haunted weariness to their eyes as they speak to the reporter, begging for someone to step forward, to help them find their daughter. Somewhere in the background, Carmen and I are making phone calls. Carmen is helping us organize another search.

There are a few more articles, but with no sign of my sister, no new leads, the articles become shorter and less frequent; but we returned to New Orleans regardless, year after year, Alex standing alongside me at the concert hall, the latest write-up including a quote from my husband. He talks about how much he misses his brother. *Fate has brought me and Lauren together*, he says. *Lauren knows what I'm going through. It means so much.*

I turn to another page. But where are the articles about Clive?

Was I that wrapped up in my own grief, my own family's despair, that I didn't pay much attention to what my husband was going through, about his search for Clive? I cared, I know I cared. I worried, and I asked Alex questions. But he assured me that I had enough to deal with, that I had enough going on, and my focus should be on Ellie. And every year, while I pushed for more media coverage, I assumed Alex was doing the same for his brother.

How did I not realize he might have been making everything up?

Alex would cry to me about his brother sometimes, his eyes drifting as he recalled some long-ago, bittersweet memory. He would talk to others about his brother too, then post about Clive on the Facebook page.

When I asked Alex for updates or media coverage, he said the publicity was mostly contained around the Houston area. He had his own contacts there, and he was making sure to take care of things. I didn't follow up—I had no reason to. Trust will do that to a person.

Alex didn't file an official missing person's report.

But I've seen Clive's missing person's posters. Alex keeps copies of them in our home office just like I keep a stack of Ellie's. I've watched him bundle up flyers and pack them inside his bag for when he travels to Houston. I've seen details of

Clive's missing person's information that Alex has posted on social media.

The lengths my husband has gone to and how easily he's covered up everything. Because Alex is a graphic designer, same as me. He could have designed Clive's missing poster in minutes. He could have copied Ellie's so easily, and I never questioned a thing.

Alex may not have followed my sister, he may not have taken those photos, but he's guilty of so many things.

A pounding on the door, and my eyes race to the front of the room.

Another sharp rap beats against the wood as I scurry off the bed.

Is it Alex, or the police officer? Did he turn around when he realized he forgot to ask me something? Or it's Detective Rayburn. He's here—that was fast—to say he has information about these latest photographs.

Or it's whoever left the red folder. They have something to say. They're coming back.

The pounding on the door booms again, and it's intense, frightening, the door rattling against the frame.

Neighbors in the hall will start to wonder what's going on if they're not wondering already. They will come out to check. They might even call the front desk to complain. And maybe they should, because whoever this is, I don't want them here. They need to step away.

Another loud knock, and it's more urgent this time. It's threatening, and I hold back.

"Who is it?"

No answer.

"Who's there?"

Another bang, and my fear turns to anger. I grab my phone.

"I'm calling the police! I'll call them right now."

I hold out my thumb: the settings I put in place several years ago mean that if I press the lock button on the side of my iPhone five times in a row, it will send out an emergency alert. When I heard about this feature, I made sure to enable it immediately, and I told Alex to do the same.

I start pressing the button, but the banging stops. The door-frame no longer rattles.

Keeping my phone clutched in my hand, seconds pass before I march across the room and fling open the door. The hall is empty. Whoever it was, they're gone.

One of the doors a few down from me flings open, and it's another guest. He glares in my direction before he stares up and down the corridor. "What's going on?" His tone is accusatory, as if I know who that could have been, that it's my fault someone was practically beating down my door.

"Did you see who it was?" I ask. "Did you see who was banging?"

"No." He shoots me another look. "But they made a hell of a lot of noise." And he eyes me again before he slams the door.

I crane my neck, waiting to see if the person will reappear, if it really is Alex, if I *want* to see if Alex will reappear.

And that's when I notice the pink camellias. I look down, and at my feet, a bouquet has been left outside my door, the flowers tied together with a piece of twine.

My breath is in my ears.

Flowers for me. Flowers for Ellie.

But these flowers are dead. They're wilted, with the petals curling in on themselves in colors of yellow and brown. The scent of dying blooms reaches my nose.

A note is included, a square of cardboard that is tucked among the brown stems. And when I crouch down to see the scrawl of handwriting, the words send a chill.

Only Alex would know about the pink camellias. We just spoke about them.

Not only have I found out that someone was stalking my sister—someone has brought me the proof—but Alex is intent on scaring me. Terrorizing me. He will frighten me into silence.

The card's message is concise and all too clear:

I miss you.

TWENTY-FOUR

I nudge the bouquet inside my room with my shoe, not wanting the flowers to come near but not wanting to leave them out in the hall either. The police will need to take this into evidence next.

The note card falls silently from the stems to the floor.

This can't be Alex—I can't imagine him coming to my room and playing nice, then returning with something as menacing as rotting flowers. Would he really include this reminder about me and my sister, then twist it into something else? Would he really give himself away like this?

I call his phone, and there's no answer. I call again and again, but it goes straight to voicemail. Strange, as he was so insistent on speaking before.

I open the Life360 app and check to see if he's somewhere inside this building, if he's still at the hotel. But his location remains off. Another promise he'd made to fix his settings, and the promise is broken.

I grab my key card and bolt for the lobby, thinking that maybe I can catch up to him, I can chase him down if he only just left these flowers, he only just left my room. Or I'll ask the front desk and find out which room he's in. I can bang on his door and see if he likes the harassment turning around on him.

But I'm not sure if the receptionist working the front desk will give me that information, Alex's room number. We're married, yes, we share the same last name, but we clearly made two different reservations. She will be able to look that up immediately. There will be privacy concerns.

I scan the lobby, but Alex isn't here. Maybe he's in another hall, he's taken the elevator? I start to look when—

I spot Alex. He's outside, standing in front of the hotel, his hand lifted to greet someone as they pull up. He's greeting his rideshare. Alex steps off the curb and holds out his phone as if he's confirming his driver, and my rage builds that his phone is on, he knows I've been calling, and he's ignored me every time.

I burst out of the hotel door. I'm on the porch, yelling his name, but Alex is already in the backseat, and he's closing the door. The car leaves.

Alex doesn't turn his head, doesn't notice me waving frantically from the front steps. My chance to confront him, to demand what the hell he's doing, and he's gone.

A guest arrives at the hotel and they sidestep me, a concerned look flickering across their face as they enter the hotel. I'm breathing loudly, watching dumbfounded as the car disappears around the corner, my husband inside.

Where is he going? Why is he messing with me like this?

Why bother coming to my room to talk, to proclaim his innocence, then pull cheap shots like this? It's alarming.

I shoot him a text.

Was that you? Did you pound on my door and leave me those awful flowers?

There's no response.

My thumbs stab against the screen, each letter I want to press against his skull.

What's wrong with you?? Why are you doing this to me?

Silence, and the minutes tick by painfully.

I've had enough. I refuse to be intimidated, not possibly by him, not by his brother, not by whoever is leaving me these items and running away.

I call the detective.

"What's going on, Mrs. Capshaw?"

"Someone left me a bouquet of dead flowers."

"Dead flowers?"

"Also, I should have told you sooner, but I think Clive is here. He's in New Orleans. He might be trying to scare me."

"No," the detective says. "It can't be Clive Capshaw."

"Why not?" I search up and down the street. Alex has not asked the driver to turn around. "Someone hid from me in the French Quarter, and I think it might have been Alex. He's intimidating me. Also, someone was watching me outside my sister's office, and it might have been Clive. He didn't want to be seen."

"It's not Clive," the detective repeats.

I pause, my frustration mounting. "How can you be so sure?"

"I'm heading to the hotel," the detective says. "I'll explain. I'll be there in a few minutes."

I stare at the empty road, then return to my room. I'm pacing, waiting for Detective Rayburn to arrive, and all the while, I keep calling Alex repeatedly, but my calls continue going to voicemail.

Minutes later, the detective knocks on the door, and it's not the loud boom from before, not the terrifying rattle, but the steady rap of his knuckles against wood. "It's me."

When Detective Rayburn enters, he's wired, a little too keyed up, and I find myself stepping back. This can't be good.

"Mrs. Capshaw, I'm afraid I have some bad news. We found another body."

"What?"

"When they pulled away the Sheetrock, they found additional remains. I held the information back until we knew for sure. Until the remains could be identified. We thought it could have been a homeless person, someone else stuck among that rubble, but it's not."

"Who is it?"

"It's Clive Capshaw."

I lift my hand to my chest. I don't think I've heard him clearly. "Clive? You mean... *Clive* is dead? He just died?"

"No. We estimate the remains are from twelve years ago."

I stagger where I stand. "Clive has been dead this entire time?"

"He had broken bones, just like your sister. The breaks are consistent with someone falling, a similar trauma to Ellie's," he says, and I can finally spot the weariness in his eyes, the weariness that has kicked in following the press conference, the long and possibly sleepless night, the announcement he will now have to make about finding Clive Capshaw, a second body that has been added to his caseload. "Mrs. Capshaw, we have reason to believe Clive died the same night as your sister."

I sink to the edge of the bed. Detective Rayburn pulls a chair from a nearby table and faces me.

"Does Alex know yet?"

"Yes."

"You spoke to him? He's not answering my calls. His phone is going straight to voicemail."

"I talked to him," the detective says. "I already told him."

I cradle my head in my hands, knowing full well the shock and pain this will cause my husband, the devastation Alex will be experiencing from taking in this news. We have both lost our younger siblings.

Clive has not been on the run, in spite of everything I've been considering. Alex hasn't been secretly checking on him and giving him updates. Which means my husband might have actually been looking for his brother. He didn't know what had happened to him.

"We're still trying to determine what took place," the detective says. "There could have been structural damage to the house and part of the balcony collapsed when they were up there. Or there was an argument, and one of them pushed the other as one of them grabbed hold, trying not to fall."

The world, this room, everything is sliding beneath my feet.

Come on, Lauren. Climb higher! Ellie said. *Check it out with me.*

Ellie with her hands held out, mine also, that satisfied grin on her face.

He had it coming, didn't he?

"If it was an accident, they might have panicked," the detective continues. "They fought to keep their balance, and one of them pulled the other. They toppled over." He leans forward. "Or there was a third party involved. Someone could have still pushed them. We haven't counted that out yet."

I lower my head.

"When I talked to Alex, he made it sound as if his brother had left a couple of days after him, that he had taken off for Houston, and Alex stopped hearing from Clive several months after that. But we know he didn't leave New Orleans, that he never traveled to Texas. Why would your husband say otherwise?"

"What did Alex tell you?"

"He claims that when Clive didn't return to the hotel, Alex thought he might have met up with someone, a woman, and it could have been Ellie. His brother wanted to have one more fun night in New Orleans, and he stayed with her. So, Alex packed up his stuff and left for the airport. He figured he'd hear from his brother later. He assumed Clive made it to Houston, and he let the time pass."

"And do you believe him?"

Detective Rayburn lets his eyes wander, to the floor and the carpet, the dying bouquet of camellias. "When did you say those showed up?"

"Just before I called you."

"Right." He gets to his feet, and with a pair of gloves, he gathers the flowers, plus the note card. He slips everything inside an evidence bag, his face grim.

"Mrs. Capshaw," he says, sealing the bag. "I think it's time you moved to another hotel."

Carmen repeats her offer to stay at her house. "I told you before that it's no problem. It's an open invitation."

"But the reporters will be scoping out your place too. They'll want a comment. They'll find me."

"But you've got to check out of that hotel. There's no way you're staying there anymore. I'll pick you up."

I already explained to her about the stack of photographs, the person that was following Ellie. The flowers too.

Letting her know about the discovery of Clive's body left her speechless before she responded, "I'll be there in ten minutes."

I throw my clothes into the suitcase and quickly sweep my toiletries into a bag before I place a phone call to the front desk and notify them I'll be checking out. The detective is still in the hotel, asking about their security footage.

My hands shake, a steady roar of static in my ears.

Clive is dead. He died the same night as Ellie.

My hands reach for my purse, for my wallet that is tucked

inside. I fight the dizziness. There is something I need to see, another photo.

I keep all sorts of things in here, but I find it almost at once. An old photograph of me and Ellie that I cut to fit the wallet-sized pocket, the photo slightly bent at the edges. I'm in New Orleans, and the two of us are standing outside a bar. Ellie wears the jean jacket she loved so much, our arms wrapped around each other as we smile.

A couple of days later, when I was heading back to North-western and to my dorm, my body stiff from the long drive, my visit to Ellie now over, my phone began to ring. It was Carmen telling me that my sister was missing, that she hadn't come home, and I'd asked her questions instead.

No one knew that I'd been in town—not my parents, not even Carmen. It had been a surprise visit for Ellie, a visit that was kept a secret, an unknown factor. It needs to stay that way.

Because as it turns out, I had my own reasons for being in New Orleans that weekend, my own motivations, and it's some-thing I've never told anyone before.

TWENTY-FIVE
TWELVE YEARS AGO

Ellie didn't have a clue I would be in town to visit, and she's still smiling at me, shaking her head.

It's a surprise, a big one, and Ellie keeps buzzing that I drove all this way to see her. I called and asked her to meet me around the corner, a restaurant I picked out that I heard serves the best shrimp po' boys. I've finally done something bold and spontaneous.

Ellie never thought in a million years that I would make such a monumental trip without telling her first, without traveling with our parents either, but things are starting to change. I'm starting to change. It's about time.

My younger sister is my inspiration, with Ellie moving away from home and striking out to live in a brand-new part of the country. Don't get me wrong: I love Northwestern, and I love the familiar neighborhood of Evanston, the urban sprawl of Chicago that is waiting for me whenever I go into town, but I know I should start getting out of the city more often. There's a world out there ready for me to explore.

Ellie is grinning even when she says, "I don't understand. Why aren't you staying with me? You could stay in Carmen's room. She's at her boyfriend's so much these days, and I bet she's there again tonight too."

"It's okay. I've got my own place." And I turn my head, hiding my smile, the upward curl of my lips that I'm trying my best to tamp down. But Ellie sees it. She catches me completely.

"Ohhh," she says, drawing it out. "I get it. You didn't just come to see me, did you?" And her eyes stretch wide with pride. "Look at you. My big sister in town to meet someone special." She nudges me playfully. "So, who is it? How'd you two meet?" She looks excitedly around the restaurant. "Am I going to see him tonight?"

I look around also, double-checking that he hasn't appeared yet. I purposely gave him a later time so I could sit down with my sister first.

"He's on his way. We met online. Some chat forum about music and travel, and we started emailing each other." I shrug nonchalantly, when really, my heart beats double-time with anticipation. "He's traveling through New Orleans—he travels a lot, actually. I thought this would be a good place to meet each other. To see you too," I add.

"Wow, that's a big trip. And so exciting. So adventurous of you." She gives me a wink before she glances once more around the restaurant. "So, you've never met him? What about a picture? Do you know what he looks like?"

"Dark hair. He said I should be able to spot him by what he's wearing, an Arcade Fire T-shirt."

"Good band," she says, nodding her approval. "Very cool." For a second, she looks down at her own clothes, the vintage T-shirt of The Smiths she has on beneath her jean jacket. She's paired it with black leggings. "This guy sounds fun already."

TWENTY-SIX

I tuck the photo of me and my sister inside my wallet and return it to its hiding spot. It's a secret I must keep a little while longer. After all, I've managed to keep it a secret all these years.

I need to do what I can to make sure that Alex and the police don't find out.

A noise outside my hotel window, and I pull back the curtain—but it's an older couple strolling arm in arm through the courtyard. They point to one of the azalea bushes as a bird lands on a branch, the sun casting long shadows on the foliage around them.

My eyes lift to the double doors at the rear entrance of the lobby, and there is movement. Commotion. Through the cleanly wiped glass, a crowd forms, people shuffling equipment and someone holding a news camera over their shoulder, a tripod also. A hotel attendant pushes through the crowd, his arms raised as if he's urging everyone to step forward, to get out.

My shoulders lock. The reporters have discovered where I'm staying. They're here looking for me, for Alex.

I scan the courtyard, checking the garden that extends to the back, the wrought-iron fence. There must be a gate somewhere. I can run and hope that no one notices me fleeing from this place.

I sling my purse over my shoulder, this evidence of me and Ellie from twelve years ago hidden inside. I lift my suitcase next. Searching the back of the garden one last time, I call Carmen and say, frantically, "I have a new plan."

I climb into her car, breathless from my dash from the back of the hotel property, my hip sore from where my suitcase banged against my side as I rushed down the sidewalk.

When I found the gate, it was locked, and I had to beg a hotel staff member to open it. I'd spotted him rolling out a cart of flattened cardboard boxes before he stopped, a puzzled expression to see me standing there before he held up a set of keys. It was my ticket out of here.

I'm in Carmen's passenger seat, thanking her, but she's too busy looking around, the anxiety riddling her face. She parked a couple of blocks away and I'm craning my neck to look too, expecting to see reporters who have come around the building to inspect the property, searching for me. The coast is clear, and we take off.

"Ready to head for my place?" Carmen asks.

But I shake my head. "I need to go to the concert hall first."

She whips her gaze to me. "Are you sure? With everything that's going on? Won't there be media there too?"

"A bunch of them are at the hotel, and they could find Alex. They will hang around. Going now is as good a time as any."

"But don't you want to lie low? Someone is leaving you *stuff*, Lauren. It's weird, and it's scary." She waves her hand. "You can hide out at my place. Stay away from everything."

"But it's time, Carmen." I tighten my hands in my lap. "I need to see that place again. We should go to the house too, get it over with. See it with our own eyes."

Carmen's jaw trembles, the tears appearing at her eyelashes. "I don't know... are you really sure you want to do this?"

I close my eyes. "My dad can't be here with me, and my husband... If I'm going to do this, I need you by my side. I know it's a lot to ask..." And it *is* a lot to ask. I feel terrible about it; I feel terrible about landing this on her when all she wanted to do was give me a ride. But the truth is, I can't go alone; I can't possibly go to these places alone. "It would mean a lot to me. We can help each other."

Carmen drives. She works her jaw side to side. "I haven't been to the house yet. I thought about it, but I couldn't go. I keep reading about it on the news..." She pulls at the steering wheel, blinking back tears. "This is a lot, Lauren."

"I know."

"And Alex's brother is dead too? This is... it's getting dangerous. I'm scared for you."

My guilt sinks like a stone. Carmen has no idea who to be scared of.

"But it's inevitable, isn't it?" Carmen says. She dashes at her tears; her jaw sets. "Seeing where Ellie was all this time, where her body was kept. Okay, we'll go. We can do this for Ellie."

I can't meet her eyes. "Thank you, Carmen."

She doesn't need to be told where to go. She knows this drive by heart, and I do too, the path that leads us directly to Crossroads Music Hall. How many times have we driven this route searching for Ellie? How many times have we parked in front of the concert hall, wishing that fateful November night could have turned out so differently?

Did someone see? Did anybody know I was there that weekend?

Carmen's phone buzzes, and I steal a glance at her screen, but it's a message from Jacques, her fiancé. She tells me that she'll call him back later. "It's okay. He knows I'm with you."

I give her a long, sideways glance. Does Carmen have any idea about me and what I've done?

We head to River Road, and my pulse quickens, and not just because of my anxiety, the walls closing in, my paranoia that someone will soon discover something, but also because we're nearing the place. I recognize the sun-faded awnings outside the storefronts, the vacant lots with their weeds poking through among the crumbled concrete, the row of squat houses with the barbershop and breakfast café around the corner.

The sign in front hangs from two rusted chains, and the words *Crossroads Music Hall* are etched into metal. The venue is still operational, and from all appearances, it's persevering. Through every up and down of the economy, the storm damage and flooding, the wear and tear and repairs, with different bands that have come and gone... even after a young college student went missing, the concert hall still stands.

The exterior is weathered wood, the building painted a pale blue with black trim around the windows. Black bars stretch across the glass.

A van is parked out front, and workers push dolly carts loaded with beer kegs. The men lift the carts over the curb, the metal clang as they hit the concrete, the wheels popping up and over before they roll smoothly across the threshold. The workers push the deliveries inside.

Carmen slows to a crawl. On the other side of the van is a marked SUV, the vehicle branded with one of the local news stations, WWL-TV.

"What do you want to do?" she asks.

I peer through the windshield. The SUV sits empty, but the reporter could be inside. They could be interviewing the manager right now before they step out front and shoot video of the exterior, the sidewalk also. This is where Ellie was last seen.

The reporter could follow the path to the run-down house next. They'll walk the tree-lined streets to retrace my sister's steps, the same steps we tried taking for years, we just didn't know which direction she'd gone. Everyone knows now.

"Lauren?" Carmen says. "Do you want to get out?"

I shake my head. "No." I let out an anguished breath. "I don't know anymore." I stare at the building. "Maybe this is close enough."

Carmen pulls over and parks, making sure to keep enough distance between us and the front entrance. I turn around to look, and the sight of the building always makes me pause, a reverence that I hold that my sister was once here. The bar she and I went to after dinner, the night before she disappeared, is located on the other side of town.

Carmen and I came here with my parents days after she disappeared, with Detective Henley also, standing outside the music hall and circling the block. But here, along this section of concrete, in front of the barred windows, is where Ellie stood. The spot where Rachel said they shared a smoke and leaned against the wall.

Rachel brought us inside also, motioning to the table where Ellie must have left her phone, where it had dropped to the floor, the area in front of the stage where they'd danced. The venue was loud, the music was intense, and she said Ellie had loved it. Rachel then led us back outside.

They hadn't been the only ones standing on the sidewalk, she said. A few others had stood around talking while another group waited for their friend to arrive in a cab. Those same people were questioned in the days following Ellie's disappearance, but there wasn't much to gain from their conversations; they didn't recall anything out of the ordinary. They'd had some drinks, and they didn't recall every single person who was standing out there that night. There were no security cameras.

Rachel said she'd told Ellie she was going back inside, but Ellie had wanted to hang out for a few more minutes. She'd needed to take a breath. It was all that dancing. But had she made plans to go somewhere else?

I was near the stage, Rachel said, *and it was several minutes later before I realized she wasn't back at our table. I should have gone looking for her, but I didn't think she would walk off by herself. I thought maybe she got a ride home and I'd see her later.*

Mom did her best to console her, but Rachel cried and blamed herself, the same way Carmen blamed herself for not going with her, for going to her boyfriend's instead. The same way my parents blamed themselves for letting their high-spirited daughter live so far away.

The delivery workers return to the sidewalk, out into the smoldering heat. Their dolly carts are empty, and the metal once again clangs hard against the concrete while they finish up their work. There will be another concert tonight with new people, many of them students, out here smoking and mingling, the drumbeat bumping up against the windows.

I say to Carmen, "Let's go."

She returns us to River Road, and we drive for a few minutes, both of us silent, both of us in deep thought. But I don't know where we're heading. I don't remember much of this neighborhood anymore.

Alongside is the levee, which runs parallel to the road, the worn patches of grass that lead up and over the embankment to the brown, swirling waters of the Mississippi River. The levee is meant to stop the flooding, to stop the river from drowning the area in mosquito-infested waters, but nature is always finding its way to break through, isn't it? Making its presence known. Like the roots of the oak trees pushing through the sidewalks, weeds popping through each and every crack, debris can be cleared. Bodies can be found.

"I think I know where the house is," Carmen says, quietly. "I saw the street address in the news. It's somewhere in the sixteen-hundred block." She takes an uneasy breath. "Last chance, Lauren." Another sideways look. "Are you sure you want to do this?"

I nod even as my stomach folds in on itself. I face the window to hide my chin, which is trembling.

Somewhere along here is the sidewalk my sister walked, the houses she cut in front of until she found her destination. She crossed one of these street corners too. She had a destination, and none of us had a clue.

Carmen turns off River Road, bringing us into a more residential area. "We should see something soon. Police cars. Crime scene tape." She drives slowly, and it's as if to delay our arrival, as if waiting for me to say, *Stop. I've changed my mind.*

But I don't breathe a word, I don't tell her anything of the sort, and Carmen moves the car forward. "This is closure," she says, nodding. "This will be closure for both of us." I realize she's telling herself this as much as she's assuring me.

Up ahead, we spot the first patrol car, and then another, the dread coiling deep inside my lungs.

Carmen's shoulders tense, and her mouth quivers. She's forcing herself to go through with this, and my guilt washes over me again. It's overwhelming how she's doing this for me.

But I need to see this place, the finality of it all, and the compulsion keeps me looking straight ahead. My need to find answers leading me toward the house like a magnet.

I see it: a stream of crime scene tape that stretches across the front yard. The tape hanging limp without a breeze.

And the house is there. Somehow, it's still standing, dark and decrepit. It's been there all along, waiting for me.

The property is cordoned off just as I knew it would be, as if the home has been lifted straight out of a ghost story, my very worst nightmare coming together in a combination of tumbled brick and stone.

Long gone is the house with the grand cupola and wrap-around balcony that Detective Rayburn described. Long gone is the exterior staircase where the owners' sons said they climbed as kids and peered out over the rooftops. Everything has toppled dramatically.

Half of the home has been bulldozed, and what looks like the original demolition from a couple of weeks ago has since been halted. The other half of the home is in dire shape, paint peeling after years of neglect, many of the roof tiles missing, weeds crisscrossing the yard with several of the windows on the bottom floor boarded up. Other windows are broken too, the boards pulled back where people must have crawled in to hide or take cover. The house is a shamble of derelict pieces.

Carmen parks the car. Both of our breaths are shallow, and the sound fills the silence. Carmen is the first one to let out a cry.

I want to sob too, and I press my hands against the window to stifle a scream.

Where pieces of the house crumbled and fell, white tents have been set in place, the tents surrounded with additional crime scene tape. Members of the forensic team work beneath the tents, while one of them in a white hooded suit walks toward a van holding a tray. A team of police officers stand nearby. They're still looking for clues.

Which pile of rubble is where they found my sister? Where in that crumbled Sheetrock is where they discovered Clive?

I scan the area, looking for signs of that balcony, for a recognizable piece of railing, for any evidence of where they once stood. But the tents are in the way, and half of the house is crumbled to pieces. Most of the Sheetrock has been sorted, however, with some of it cleared already. But it doesn't mean it isn't a mess.

Besides protecting the crime scene, I realize the tents also serve another purpose: they're acting as a shield, a blockade. We're not the only gawkers to line the street.

Neighbors mingle together on the sidewalk, curiosity-seekers too, and a police officer is there to keep them back, her arms lifted when an onlooker gets too close. But that doesn't stop several of them from taking pictures or inching closer when they think the police officer isn't looking.

I wonder if Detective Rayburn is here, if he's returned, especially with the house being the crime scene for, now, two bodies. But I don't see him, and maybe it's because he's returned to Alex. He's seen the hotel security footage and knows who is leaving me photographs and dead flowers.

Carmen cries softly as I reach for her hand. "I'm sorry," I tell her because I don't know what else to say.

"No, *I'm* sorry," she insists, and she gulps down her sobs. "I can't believe Ellie is gone. I can't believe your sister was here this whole time. I'm so sorry, Lauren. I should have tried harder to find her."

I pat her hand. This poor, poor girl. This dedicated friend. She has done so much to help our family with no clue that I was driving back from New Orleans when she first called me about Ellie going missing. I have kept this from her, from everyone.

I am a coward, and I have known this for years.

I look at her, wondering if Carmen has any idea, if Ellie mentioned that she saw me, that I'd surprised her with a visit, but she has yet to say anything. All this time, and I've somehow managed to keep Carmen in the dark too.

"What is that?" Carmen asks, pointing to a chain link fence.

I follow her gaze.

"Oh, Lauren," her voice softens. "It looks like a memorial."

And it is. Behind the crime scene tape, the fence is old and rusted on the edges, perhaps something that was put in place years ago by the original family, to keep trespassers out, and what little that did. But in front of the fence, a small bundle of

items has been left on the ground. A balloon, partially deflated
after who knows how many days since it was left there, is tied to
the chain link, along with several bouquets that are wrapped in
plastic. A memorial for my sister.

But something else is propped in the middle of the arrangement... shiny and golden... a cut-out shape that rests on top of
the deadened grass. I look closely, and the recognition hits me
hard.

Reaching for the door handle, Carmen follows me instantly.
She wants to see it too—she must have recognized it instantly—
and we scramble to the sidewalk. I hadn't planned on getting
out of the car—I didn't think I would set foot on this property—
but I have to see this up close. I have to make sure my eyes aren't
deceiving me.

The police officer motions for us to stand back, but I gesture
at the memorial, the display that is only a few feet away. When
I come to a stop, the pain rises from my chest into my throat.
The surprise too.

It's propped against the fence, what looks like a piece of
Styrofoam that has been cut out and spray-painted a shimmery
gold, the lines cut at a unique angle, the letter a stylized *E*.

The design is just like my sister's pendant.

And in front of the letter are bouquets that others have left
behind. But the bouquets are dead, just like the one I received
at the hotel. Each bunch of camellias is wilted and rotting and
forgotten on the ground.

TWENTY-SEVEN

The flowers. Alex is sending me a message—he must be. He knows... or someone out there knows.

But Carmen remains fixated on the Styrofoam *E*. It has not escaped her, the familiar pattern.

"Did you do that?" she asks.

And I shoot her a look. "No. I told you I haven't been here yet."

"It could be one of our friends," Carmen says. "I'll ask. Or maybe it's someone from the magazine." She stares at the memorial. "It's nice, though. Taking the time to remember a piece of Ellie's jewelry. It's also pretty spot-on, don't you think? Whoever this was really took their time."

I nod. It's almost too spot-on.

The same jewelry my sister was wearing when she died. The same necklace that dangled at her neck as her body remained hidden for years. The detective said he would return that necklace to me.

The pendant. Someone knew Ellie well enough to make this for her, to leave it at the memorial. *To take their time*, as Carmen said.

They studied her closely enough to know the kind of jewelry she wore, how important the gift from our parents was, how she never took it off.

Someone watched her, memorizing parts of her. They looked closely at her photographs and studied every inch.

"Those flowers," I whisper.

And Carmen gives me a look. "You don't think?" She waves her hand. "No, it can't be. They've been out here for days. Maybe the neighbors brought them. They've been wilting in the sun."

She's trying to convince me.

"And look at the balloon," Carmen adds. "It's been here for days too."

The balloon is made of foil, the words *With Sympathy* stretched across the center, and it's sagging—it's been losing air for days. A white ribbon attaches it to the chain link fence.

I can't help it; I shudder. "I still don't like it."

"We'll clear the flowers," Carmen says, and she drops to her knees, immediately scooping up the bouquets and picking up the scattered petals. "We'll come back and bring new ones."

But I shake my head. I don't think I will ever come here again.

As Carmen stacks the flowers in the crook of her arm, a woman hurries toward us—it's not the police officer, but someone in a navy suit, a glittering brooch attached to her lapel.

"Are you Lauren Capshaw?" she asks, and her tone, along with her carefully styled hair and smart clothes, tells me she's a reporter. I flinch. And I must give myself away because she waves her hand to a videographer who stands nearby. He hustles over holding a news camera.

"No comment," I tell her.

"We're bringing back new ones," Carmen says, as if needing to justify why we're taking away the flowers. We turn and walk, but that doesn't stop the reporter from following us.

"Do you want to make a comment about the discovery of your sister's body?" she asks.

I don't respond.

"Mrs. Capshaw, can you tell us how this is impacting your family? What can you tell us about the investigation?"

Carmen grabs my elbow. She's protective, leading me to the car even though I don't need the assistance. I'm ready to go. I am ready to leave this place forever.

Carmen fumbles with her key fob, the plastic wrapping of the bouquets scratching against her arms. Several more dead flower petals crack and break off, the wilted, half-moon shapes leaving a dismal trail at our feet.

She pops open the trunk and throws everything in, but the reporter is practically at my heels. I have to sidestep her to reach the passenger door. "Leave me alone."

She doesn't stop. "Are there any leads on what happened to your sister? Was it a lovers' fall"—so the word is out about the police finding the second body—"or did he kill her before jumping to his own death?"

The videographer catches up, and he's winded, panting slightly, and I'm almost certain the camera is powered on. He could be recording the whole thing.

I fling open the door. "I told you, no comment."

Carmen says to me, "Get in," and she starts up the engine.

But the woman grips the edge of my door, her fingers holding tight, her knuckles whitening. It's a dangerous move, and I stare at her, at how reckless she's being. How persistent. I could slam the door on her bony fingers this very second.

But she stares at me. She doesn't think I will do it—and I really don't want to. She refuses to move as she peppers me with questions.

When I still don't give her anything, she tries tact next. "Mrs. Capshaw, we're so sorry for your loss. We truly are. But is there anything you can tell us? Anything at all? What are the police saying about the bodies?"

I grit my teeth. "Please remove your hand."

"Your sister and Clive Capshaw. This man's relationship to your husband. What does he know? Why has your husband kept this from you?"

"Please let go of the door."

And Carmen pulls forward, a sudden tap on the accelerator, and the car jerks ahead. The reporter jumps back, a startled cry, her eyebrows lifted in surprise. And I almost laugh at her, her indignation and frustration in the face of my grief. I slam the door and we take off.

Carmen turns at the next corner, and that's when I spot him: Alex is standing there. He's on the curb, watching us leave.

"Stop!" I shout. "Pull over."

Carmen jumps. She doesn't understand what I'm asking since we're supposed to be racing away from the house, from that reporter, but then she looks up and spots Alex too.

"You don't need to talk to him," she says, but she pulls over to stop the car, tucking us between a minivan and a small moving truck, hiding us from the reporter's view.

"You don't need to be around him," Carmen repeats.

But my fingers are already on the door handle. "I've had enough. Every time I'm ready to confront him, he runs away. Not anymore."

Alex sees me, and he approaches the car, his looming shape growing nearer in the side view mirror.

I step out to face him. "How did you know I'd be here?"

"My brother," he says, and he turns slightly. "This house."

And of course he's here. This was his brother's resting place for so many years too.

"I had to see where..." He looks down, his face pinched with so much hurt. Grief too.

Despite everything, I find myself wanting to reach out and comfort him. We have both lost loved ones, and the shock is too much.

"Did you know?" I ask. "Did you know about Clive?"

"No. I just found out."

"Are you sure?"

"Yes, I'm sure." He glares at me, dumbfounded. "The police told me earlier, and I can't believe it... it's horrible..." His face reddens with tears.

Alex hasn't shaved since I last saw him. His clean-cut look is gone, the edges of his jaw now filling in with scruff, and I wonder if that was all a ruse anyway, if he will let his hair grow out now that he doesn't have to pretend anymore. The game is up.

"All these years, and I kept thinking that he might be okay. I kept hoping Clive was okay. But he's gone, Lauren. Same as Ellie."

"He was never heading to Texas."

"I thought he was."

"How could you think that?"

"That's where he said he was going. But then he stopped calling, and I should have acted sooner. I should have searched better. I will always regret that."

That's all *you will regret?* I want to scream.

"It got so complicated. Meeting you, then finding out that was your younger sister we spent time with. I couldn't tell you we were around Ellie when she went missing, and I definitely didn't want you to know we were in New Orleans back then. I couldn't have anyone thinking Clive could be connected— because he's not. He wouldn't hurt anyone." He stares at his shoes. "I had no idea my brother's been gone this whole time. He was just a kid, just a kid," he weeps.

I wrap my arms around my chest. Ellie was just a kid too.

"I really wish you could have met him," he says, looking at me. "Clive was such a good guy, so sweet. Maybe a little bit lost, but he was trying to figure out his life, you know? I really thought he was traveling, that maybe he'd gone back to Mexico, and he would have loved that. I didn't think this was what had happened to him."

Well, neither did I.

I glance quickly over my shoulder. Behind us, Carmen sits patiently, the engine kept running. She's waiting, and I wonder how much she can hear.

"The flowers," I say, lowering my voice. "Why are you leaving me dead flowers?"

His hand jitters at his side.

"Why would you put them outside my hotel room? Dead flowers at the memorial too. How could you?"

"It's not me. Someone else had feelings for Ellie. Clearly. Think about it. Someone made that memorial for her. And the photographs—someone was following your sister. The detective told me about them, how someone was sneaking photos of Ellie. That's who the police need to be looking for, someone who might have been angry that she was hanging out with Clive. They did something to her that night, to Clive also. They killed them."

I shake my head. I don't know if I can believe him. Because Alex is the only one who would choose the pink camellias. He's the only one left in our group to know about them.

"How long were you in New Orleans?" I ask. "How long were you and Clive really around my sister?"

"I already told you—"

"Tell me the truth."

The bar we stood outside that cool November evening. Ellie and I waiting together as the bass pulsed from the front entrance.

"Did you spend time with her the night before she disappeared, or did you really only meet her at brunch?" I ask. "Did you see who else she was hanging out with?"

Lauren, why are you being so secretive? Ellie said to me. *Who is this crush you're meeting up with?*

I stare at Alex, convinced that he's taunting me, still keeping secrets from me. He's not telling me everything.

Was Alex around that night? Does he know what everyone was getting up to? *Did he see?*

And Alex smirks. But it's with such disdain, the look he's giving me full of such contempt—those gray, soulful eyes that I once loved and stared into, but that love and kindness is suddenly gone. Vanished. His gaze hardens, and I wonder if his feelings were ever true in the first place.

Standing here, he flashes me a peculiar, flat smile.

I startle. I stand back, a new wave of panic settling in, the implications that are starting to dawn on me too, the goosebumps surfacing along my flesh.

My husband stares with an expression I've never seen before, and a shiver runs across my scalp. I really don't know this man anymore. I don't know what else he's hiding.

And he smiles. "It looks like you're finally putting it together, Lauren. Good for you. You're wondering what else I know. What you've kept hidden, not just me."

TWENTY-EIGHT

I tell Carmen that I've changed my mind. I don't want to go to her place—I don't want Carmen and her fiancé to feel like they need to hover over me and worry—and I ask her to take me to a new hotel.

"Do you want me to come in with you?" Carmen asks. "I can stay and make sure you're all right."

I grab my suitcase from the backseat, the New Orleans heat coursing again upon my head, my body still tremoring from the conversation I just had with Alex. We drove away, leaving him on the sidewalk. I tell her, "I'll be okay."

You're wondering what else I know.

I thought I was careful. I thought I covered my tracks.

Didn't I? Wasn't I careful? What did I miss?

"Call me," Carmen says. "I'll drop everything, Lauren, if you need anything. I mean it. I will sit with you."

I force a weak smile. "Thank you, Carmen. For everything. But I think I need to be on my own for a little while. But I'll call you, okay? I'll get in touch later tonight."

She looks at me. She's not convinced. "Stay away from Alex, okay? Until you hear more from the police?"

I nod.

"Promise?" she says before she checks her side mirror for traffic.

"I promise."

She pulls away, and I watch her go, telling myself what is another white lie on top of everything else?

The view from my room isn't as nice as the hotel from this morning; it doesn't have a courtyard that extends to a back gate, and there's no fountain. But there is a small, private patio and a couple of tables and chairs for guests to enjoy sitting in the sun. The patio is empty.

I take comfort in knowing that I found a first-floor room, that I'm not facing a side street where a reporter could peer in at me from the sidewalk. There is no steady eye of a camera.

I'm not staying at the same hotel as my husband either.

The hall leading to my room is empty and quiet for now, and I lock the door behind me, pulling the latch across tightly, shoving my suitcase to one side.

It's been a few hours, and surely the police have had a chance to check the security footage by now. The detective may have been able to determine who stood in the hall to make those deliveries, who crept down the corridor before disappearing around the corner. The mysterious photographs slid beneath my door. The bearer of wilted flowers.

"Mrs. Capshaw," the detective says, answering the phone.

"The security video," I ask. "Does it show who's harassing me? Is it Alex?"

"He's not the one who delivered the flowers, no. It was a delivery worker from a floral shop in Mid-City. Someone left an envelope with cash and instructions for the bouquet to be left at your room, and not the front desk. But the shop doesn't have a security camera, and there isn't a street camera either. The delivery worker was told to bang on your door to get your attention."

"But Alex could have placed the order, right?"

"Yes," he says. "Even though he denies it." And then: "He's been advised to stay away from you and anyone else related to the case for the time being."

"And what about the photographs? Who dropped off the folder? Do you know who was following my sister?"

"Someone was in the hall wearing a hooded jacket and earbuds. He pulled the folder out from under his jacket and slid it beneath your door. He's tall, about six two, six three, slender build, white male. But he kept his phone lifted to his face as if he was reading something, but it was to cover himself. He left the hotel through a door at the end of the hall."

"Was it Connor from the magazine?"

"No, we confirmed he's been at the office all day. Connor isn't as tall as the individual seen on the camera either. But we're looking for Riley Simmons. You met with him, right? He works at the magazine. He would have had access to material left at the office. He may know something."

Are you sure we don't have anything left? Riley asked. *I could have sworn there was some stuff the editors decided to keep.* He's tall too. I had to look up at him when we spoke for those few minutes in the break room.

"What did he tell you?"

"We've been trying to get ahold of him," the detective says, "but he hasn't shown up to work. His phone is switched off. We think he may be the one who left you those pictures. He may know who followed your sister. It's important we talk to him."

My phone lights up—it could be Alex, my dad, the Broussards, the next round of reporters still circling around the city, looking for a comment.

The Caller ID displays a New Orleans number across my screen.

"Lauren, this is Riley Simmons," he says. "We need to talk."

I don't know this man. I only met him yesterday. But he might hold one of the biggest pieces to this puzzle, and so I ask, "Riley, what is going on? Was that you who brought me the pictures?"

"Yes."

"Why—"

"I should have told you it was me, but I didn't want to get into trouble. Not at work. Not caught up with the cops." His breath is labored when it releases. "I didn't mean to scare you. But I'm ready to show you everything now. The police have been calling me. I need to come forward with the rest."

"The rest of what? More photos?"

"Yes."

My shoulders tighten.

"I can come pick you up. Tell me where you are. I'll show you where everything is. Where it's been kept hidden."

"No," I tell him. "I'll meet you."

"Okay," he says. "Meet me at the magazine office. Most of the staff will be leaving for the day so it's a good time. Connor will be gone by now too."

"So it *is* Connor?" I ask. "Is he the one who took the photos? Was he stalking her—"

"You'll see."

Riley hangs up, and I'm left sitting in silence, staring at my phone. I'm not sure if I should go there by myself. I'm not sure if I want to see these photos.

Because if Connor was following my sister, if he went to the concert that night, what else did he capture? What else does he know?

. . .

It's late afternoon and the humidity has lightened somewhat, a mild breeze sweeping through the air as dusk approaches, the city of New Orleans settling in for the evening. Over the rooftops, the sun hangs low behind gauzy bits of cloud, a reddish-gold hue bordering the skyline.

Only a few cars remain in the magazine parking lot, and the front offices are dark, a single lamp glowing inside the lobby. The Uber driver pulls away, and I'm left standing and staring at the building.

The double doors push open as Riley greets me. He's still wearing the hooded jacket the detective described in the video, but the hood is pushed down, and the earbuds are gone. His face is drawn tight as he ushers me inside. "Thank you for meeting me," he says.

"What is it?" I ask. "What else have you found?"

"This way," is all he tells me.

The hall is quiet: a meeting room is closed off and so is a large corner office, a studio left dark with lettering on the glass indicating that's where they record the *Nola* podcast.

But somewhere in the back of the building comes the sound of a vacuum, a high-pitched whine from someone in the janitorial crew. In the staff room with the larger cubicles and desks, every one of the fluorescent lights is on, and I crane my neck until I spot the top of someone's head. They're working late. Whoever it is, they're hustling to make deadline.

I'm relieved to not be alone with Riley.

He leads me to the other side of the building, past several more closed offices, until we're in a second break room. A coffee pot is left in the sink and filled with sudsy water. The linoleum floor has been mopped with a strong waft of bleach and lemon striking my nose.

"It's back here," Riley says.

Beyond the kitchen is a small staff room, and it's filled with gray, metal lockers that are lined against the back wall and similar to the ones I had in high school, the ones you see at the gym. The locks are looped through each catch with a spin combination to keep them secure.

The top row is closed, with several of the lockers decorated with a staff person's name or band stickers and radio station decals. A few on the bottom row are left open and empty, waiting for the next new hire.

I've been in this room before.

"Ellie had one," I remind Riley. "Someone cleared out her locker and sent us her things."

"I know. But I kept thinking there might be some other stuff that was stored away. And after you left, I found Connor standing here. He stood really still right in front of this locker, and I had to look."

He reaches for the lock and holds it tight. Exerting a bit of pressure on the latch, he turns the dial and leans forward. It's not how I remember opening my locks before.

"We used to do this at school sometimes," he explains. "I'm not proud of it, but we'd break into people's lockers and take their lunches." He gives me a sheepish look. "Steal their homework."

"And this one belongs to Connor?"

He glances to the side. "The main one he uses is over there. But this locker was always reserved, which never made any sense. I never saw anyone use it, not until Connor."

He fiddles with the lock. "If you add the right amount of pressure, you turn it slowly until it clicks. You keep the tension. It should click one time and then you have the first number in the combination."

I scoff. "You're kidding."

"Then you spin the lock the other way, keeping the pressure, until it clicks, and that's the next number. You do this until you find the third, and then"—he pulls, and the latch pops open —"you're in."

He tugs at the door, the locker yawning open.

Riley steps out of my way so I can approach. I slowly peer in.

The locker is filled with papers, it's crammed with them, the pages loose and piled together in a thick stack. I leaf through the pages and find that they're mostly printouts, articles from the magazine's website. I look for Ellie's byline, or even Connor's, but don't find any. The articles seem to have been written more recently.

I dig through the stack again. Photocopies and other bits of scrap paper are piled in here too, as if everything has been scooped out of the recycling bin and tossed into the space. I realize the paper may have been used to cover up something.

I find a folder at the bottom: it's not red like the one that was left behind at my room, but a traditional bank folder, brown in color, a string wrapped around it multiple times to keep the contents secure.

I glance at Riley, and he slowly nods. "Open it."

The first item is a single sheet of loose-leaf, and on it is a pencil sketch of a letter that someone has drafted—a stylized letter E.

My sister's pendant.

Connor would have seen Ellie wearing it. And now I know, he was the one who followed her. He was clearly obsessed. Connor made the letter E and brought it to her memorial.

I flip the loose-leaf over, but nothing is written on the back. When I look inside the rest of the folder, there are plenty more items tucked away, plenty of snapshots.

It's additional pictures of Ellie. Ellie returning to her apartment. Sitting at a red-and-white checkered table with Carmen as they share a pizza. They're having a beer. They have no idea that someone is on the other side of the street taking their pictures. Carmen will hate knowing she was being watched too.

The next shot is of Ellie standing outside a bar, a local beer sign glowing purple in the window behind her, the rest of the window layered with black tint. She's wearing the jean jacket she loves, and I look closely.

Is this from the night she was reported missing? Did Connor follow her to the run-down house next?

But Ellie isn't standing in front of the music hall. And beneath the jean jacket, she's wearing a different outfit: a pair of black leggings with a T-shirt, the outfit she wore the night before. The night I was with her.

I flip to the next photograph and the next, my hands trembling, aware that Riley can hear my haggard breath. Because I'm not just scared of what I'm about to learn about my sister. I'm terrified of what we might see in the next shot. That it could be a picture of me in New Orleans the weekend Ellie died. That it could be proof I was there and never said a thing.

TWENTY-NINE

Is that why Riley brought me here? He's wondering when these photos were taken? He's figured it out somehow, my secret, but he's giving me a chance to explain, to tell him my reasons why I never told anyone about my location? The reasons I've wanted it kept hidden.

I haven't told anyone because I'm afraid. I've been afraid for years.

Riley is silent, and he hangs back as if to give me space. I watch him out of the corner of my eye anyway. Nothing about him seems accusatory. It's like he wants to give me the benefit of the doubt, and I'm starting to think he left the photographs at my room as a way of giving me a heads-up. He's letting me know that Connor might have taken my picture too.

I flip through the next series of snapshots: a man walks toward my sister. He's holding out wristbands, to show he's paid for their cover fees, and Ellie takes hers, smiling. She puts her wristband on.

It's Clive Capshaw—it's undeniably Clive—with his loose-fitting jeans and confident, eager smile. He looks so happy to be there. He looks so happy to be with Ellie.

And someone else stands behind him. He rests his hand on Clive's shoulder, then steps forward to greet Ellie. He gives her a hug, but her eyes widen, a look of surprise to see him pulling away. In the next shot, he steps back, and her hand lifts to him as if in a shy wave. She's telling him goodbye.

On my sister's face, is that a look of disappointment? Is Ellie actually sad to see him go? She is left standing with Clive.

I scan the photographs. And where was I for all of this? How did I miss this encounter?

It's because I was down the block. I was grabbing more cash from the ATM, knowing our cover fees were being paid for but wanting to have enough cash to cover our drinks.

I hadn't returned yet, but I remember hurrying down the sidewalk. I remember picking up the pace, wanting to see the band, wanting to return and be with my sister and Clive.

While I hurried, I had no idea that Alex had just been there, that he'd already left. That my future husband, the man who would eventually find me and grow close to me, had been right there standing on that curb.

Where did Alex go next? Did he stick around a little bit longer?

And a couple of things hit me at once:

Alex lied about exactly when he met Ellie. It wasn't the following day at brunch.

He also lied about where he was that night, the night before she disappeared.

I flip to the end—there are no more photographs. I've reached the bottom of the stack, and I manage to let my shoulders relax somewhat. This means that Connor, Riley—the police—have no idea I was there that night too.

I stack the photos and return them to the folder. Placing the loose-leaf with the pencil sketch on top, I wrap the string around the folder once, twice, doing my best to keep my body from trembling, to keep my composure intact.

"That's Alex Capshaw, right?" Riley says. "Your husband?"

I don't respond. It takes everything in my being to not flip through the photos again, to make sure there's not something there—my profile, my face coming into view, evidence of me hovering in the background.

Riley says, "It shows that Alex was with them. Did you know about this? That he could have been around them before they died?"

I head back through the break room, the folder clutched to my chest.

Riley slams the locker door behind me, the click of the lock slotting into place. He hurries into the hall. "I think Alex might know more than he's letting on. I wanted you to see this, Lauren. It's important that you know everything."

"Thank you for showing me," I tell him, but I keep moving. In the hallway—with its well-worn carpet, the great length of it —the fluorescent lights beam a washed-out glow against the walls, making me dizzy. It's a lifetime before I find my way to the lobby.

Riley keeps up. "It's not good what Connor did. Taking photos of your sister like that. Following her and frightening her. But your husband has a lot more to answer for, don't you think? You're bringing those pictures to the police, right?"

You're finally putting it together... That's what Alex said. That strange smirk, that interesting expression on his face.

Does he know my true intentions for that weekend?

Alex stepped away from my sister and crossed the street. Perhaps he looked back one more time. He saw me hurrying along the sidewalk. He watched me join my sister. He saw as I tried to get Clive's attention and smile, the shadowed, traitorous look that soon dropped over my face when I realized Clive was only smiling for my sister.

. . .

I push out of the office double doors until we're in the parking lot. Fumbling for my phone, I'm thinking about calling an Uber. I'll ask Alex about these additional photographs. I'll show them to him while wondering if I should contact the detective.

I might be in trouble; Alex is certainly in trouble, and with Connor pulling into the parking lot at this very moment, he is a problem too. My anger rushes over me as I watch him step out of the car, and he's shocked, his eyebrows lifted, to see us standing there.

I shake the folder at him. "Coming back for this?"

He glances at what's in my hand before the flicker of recognition slowly takes over. "Whatever you think about me, I can explain. I didn't hurt Ellie. I would never do anything to hurt Ellie."

"But you followed her. You stalked her. You took photos of my sister at her house, where she went out to eat. It's creepy. It's wrong."

"I know it is," he says, and he slides a look at Riley. "You're the one who found the pictures, aren't you? It's okay, Riley, I get it. I understand. I shouldn't have taken them without her consent. I know what I did is bad."

Connor stares at his feet. "I just really liked her. I really liked looking at her." He shrugs, but it's so casual, so half-hearted, that I want to scream. "I just wanted to be around her, you know? Taking the pictures was the closest I could get to Ellie, and I'm sorry I did that. I've known that for a long time."

"Stalking is a crime, Connor," I say. "She was frightened; she knew she was being watched. And then that sketch of my sister's necklace? You made that E look just like her pendant. You brought it to Ellie's memorial."

"I made it because I cared about her. I cared about her a lot. I'm devastated this has happened." For once, he actually does look sorry. Remorseful.

"Is there anything else?" I ask. "Other photographs?" I lift the folder, needing to know, needing to be certain. "Anything that you might have left in a different locker or at your house?"

"No, you've found the last of them. And now that you've seen them, you know who else was there." He meets my gaze. "I didn't put any of it together until the cops came out with those details, the information about your husband and his brother. I didn't realize it was them."

"Did you see Alex any other time?" I ask. And this time, I say the words slowly, treading carefully. "Do you have any other proof?"

My heart slows as I wait for his response. This could be the moment I've feared for years.

THIRTY
TWELVE YEARS AGO

"Is that him?" Ellie grabs my arm. "Over there. Standing by the hostess stand."

My eyes race to the restaurant entrance, and even though I've been checking every fifteen seconds, my pulse hammering along with my nerves, of course my sister would be the one to spot him.

There he is: Clive. After so many months of emails, we finally get to meet.

"I still can't believe you're doing this," Ellie says. "My God, you don't know anything about this guy. But he's cute. That's a good start," she adds with a giggle.

And I shush her, already feeling the heat in my cheeks.

Dark hair, just like he said, and he's wearing an Arcade Fire T-shirt, the recognizable feather swirl logo from their *Funeral* album across the front.

I wave, but it's awkward, and my sister's smile is so big that she's beaming at him, she's beaming for us, and I wonder if her smile will crack her cheeks at the edges. I tell myself to stop. She's eager, she is super thrilled for me, and she lifts her hand high to call him over.

I try not to die of embarrassment.

"You must be the mystery man," she gushes when he approaches our table.

"Lauren?" he says.

And I hold up a finger. "No, that's me. I'm Lauren."

His eyes glide to mine. "Hi." He looks again at her. "The two of you look so much alike." And he tilts his head. "But different, you know?"

"We're sisters," I tell him. "I meant to say that my sister lives here. That she'd be joining us." I motion clumsily at the empty chair beside me. "Please sit."

Is it just my imagination or does his gaze slide back to Ellie? Does he catch another look at her before sitting down?

It's true: Ellie's light has always shone brighter than mine, and I bunch the material of my jeans at the sides of my thighs. It's the feeling of being overlooked.

My sister keeps smiling. She's pretending to be absorbed by her menu, not wanting to steal the show and bombard this mystery man with too many questions, even though I can tell she's dying to know his story from start to finish. She will want to interrogate him, vet him for me, make sure that I know everything about his life before it goes any further, before I hint at the end of the night that perhaps he can stay with me at the hotel.

"So, how was your drive?" I ask.

He shrugs. "Not bad, only a few hours. You're the one with the long drive."

"It was long," I admit. "But not so bad. A lot of cool places to stop along the way, a quick stop in Memphis too. There's a lot of good music there. A lot of bars."

He nods. "Memphis is on my bucket list to see one day. But I've got to save up. Everything costs money, you know?"

Ellie nods, I do too, and I'm sure of it this time—he steals another glance at my sister, then at the water glass that I made sure was ready on the table for him. "But staying here and finding something to do instead could be fun."

Ellie flips over her menu, acting like she didn't hear his comment.

"Like getting a job here?" I ask.

Another casual shrug. "Maybe. I don't know. I just got here." He gives me a broad smile before he takes a sip of his water. "I'm not tied to anything, so anything could happen."

My paranoia kicks up another notch. "It's a great place," I say.

"You could check out Chicago too," Ellie says, and she looks up, bursting at the seams to finally join the conversation, to help me out. "Lauren lives north of there. She's in Evanston. It's got a great vibe too."

"But nothing like New Orleans, right?" he says.

"True," she answers. "I do love it here. I've loved it since the day we visited with our parents—remember that, Lauren? And after that, I was hooked. I knew I had to be here for school."

"Well, college didn't work out for me," Clive says. "But that's okay. I bet I could find something to do here, some work."

"There's always the service industry," Ellie says. "There are a lot of bars."

"And speaking of which, what are your plans for tonight?" he asks, and I'm happy to see his attention returning to me.

"There's a band, a really great one," I tell him. "I lined up another show for us tomorrow night too."

"Will you be able to join us?" he asks Ellie.

"Tonight I can"—she gives me a cautious look—"I mean, if that's okay."

"Absolutely," I tell her.

"But I can't tomorrow. I'm heading to Crossroads. It's a music hall," she explains to Clive. "I'm reviewing a band for a write-up that I'm doing."

"Very cool," he says. "Do you get to go backstage?"

She smiles. "Of course. But I've covered these guys before. I have enough quotes. I just need to drop by and see if they've got any new songs tomorrow."

THIRTY-ONE

Clive is ghosting me. He's not answering my texts, and I send another email from my hotel room. He doesn't respond to that either.

After leaving the restaurant and checking out the bar, we had a good time, even though I had way too much to drink and might have embarrassed myself a little bit, but so did my sister as she knocked back a few beers and a whiskey and Coke, and so did Clive. Now, with my head pounding, it doesn't feel like I handled it as well as them. I might have tried a little too hard to convince Clive that I was fun, that my sister didn't need to be the center of our attention the whole time.

We watched the band, and by the end of the night, I was left alone, disappointed when Clive turned me down about joining me in my hotel room. He said he had another place to stay and walked off in the other direction. He mentioned catching up with me later.

Well, now it's later. And there's still no word.

Could Clive be meeting up with my sister instead of me tonight? I know it's a ridiculous thought, and I hate the worry that has bubbled into my brain, that the two of them would go behind my back like that, especially my sister, but I saw the way they acted together, or at least the spark that kept coming from Clive. The undeniable interest.

And despite what Ellie told me—that he's more my type, that he came into town to see me and not her, that he was just trying to get on the sister's good side to impress me, to win some extra points—I don't like it. It doesn't feel right.

Ellie's effect has always been so magical and effortless.

I should have told Clive to meet me at a specific place tonight. I should have locked in the details before we parted so he'd know where I'd be. I shouldn't have included my sister at dinner.

I stare at the screen, my phone that remains blank and empty, my paranoia mounting. The painful rejection. Clive still hasn't answered.

I might have driven all this way to only see Clive for one night, and it's enough to drive nails into my skin, to make me feel like a fool, a sad and very desperate fool. I'm letting someone I barely know embarrass me.

In order to avoid the chance of Ellie being around us again, I remind her that Clive and I have the other band to check out, a bar on the outskirts of the French Quarter in the Marigny, and I'll catch up with her tomorrow. She reminds me about her going to Crossroads to cover that band for work, that she'll be busy, but she wants to see me before I go. I only have a limited time in New Orleans.

A few hours later, I receive a text from Ellie.

Where were you?

I write back:

What do you mean?

Why weren't you at brunch?

What brunch?

I stare dumbfounded at my phone, the seconds ticking by. I have no idea what she's talking about. I get a response:

You didn't show up. But it's no problem. You needed to sleep in. Let's talk later.

I consider responding and asking for more details. Did we talk about getting together for brunch? Did I forget about our plans? But she said that she had to run into the office for a few hours today, that it was a good time to catch up on work since it was the weekend and the office wouldn't be as busy.

I slide my phone inside my pocket, hoping the next time it buzzes it will be a phone call from Clive. But it's past 7 p.m. when he finally decides to respond, and my heart leaps then crashes when I see his message.

Do you mind if we get together tomorrow? Something's come up.

My stomach drops. What came up? What could have possibly arisen that he would need to break our plans? After all, this was supposed to be our weekend. Didn't I make that clear enough? Why did it take him all day before he had the courtesy of telling me?

A hotel door slams in the hall, loud conversations of guests erupting in front of the elevator. It sounds like a group of friends getting themselves ready for the evening, their laughter spilling down the corridor as one of them calls out for the others to wait up.

I settle against the bed, and my heart hurts; my disappointment is soul-crushing. I have nothing to do tonight. I have driven all this way, and now I'm alone, in this hotel room, in this exciting city with nowhere to go and no one to spend it with.

I could head out and see the band in the Marigny, the one I wanted to take Clive to, but the idea of going by myself is a depressing one. It reminds me of the weekend that is falling apart before my eyes.

I could grab dinner somewhere. Ask for a table for one.

I could stay under the covers and cry.

A few hours later, Ellie sends me a text.

I stopped by the apartment after work to change clothes. Carmen's heading back to her boyfriend's, so if you guys change your minds or you want to see a better show (lol!), come hang out with me. I'm telling you, this band is incredible. You guys will love it.

So maybe she's not meeting with Clive after all. Maybe I can still find a way to salvage this weekend. After all, family comes first.

It takes me a long time to decide what to do, and when I arrive, the parking lot is full, and I have to circle the block several times before I find a spot on a nearby street. A couple, holding hands, they look like college students, walk quickly in the direction of the music hall. I can already hear the steady drumbeat of the band, the speakers blaring, and people clapping, a few whistling. The show is well underway.

I'm about to open my door, car keys in hand, when on the other side of the street, a flash of denim appears in the night. Long red hair spills past the woman's shoulders, and she walks quickly, her chin lowered. But she's heading in the opposite direction, away from the music, away from the noise.

It's my sister, Ellie. She wears the jean jacket she loves so much.

But where is she going? Why is she leaving the concert so early?

I'm about to call out her name when someone steps into the shadows behind her—they're following her. They're about twenty feet behind, then ten, then five. They're gaining on her and my hackles rise. I should protect her. I should tell this guy to take off.

But Ellie stops and turns, and this man must have said something, maybe even her name, because it's grabbed her attention. I'm about to run toward her anyway when I see the man's face. I see exactly who it is.

It's not always good to be right about certain things.

I'm not sure who is more startled, Ellie or me, to see that it's Clive Capshaw standing there. He's on the sidewalk. He lied to me so he could see Ellie. He wants to be with her. It's the only explanation.

I've been passed over for my younger sister.

But I'm not sure that Ellie expected to see him show up, and in her defense, she certainly looks surprised, almost jolted by his appearance. She looks past him to the street as if to see who else he's with. She's looking for me.

She must ask, but it's difficult to hear what she's saying, what he's saying too. Maybe she thinks we decided to show up after all, to join her.

Not even close.

I get out of the car and shut the car door with a hard click. They don't see me watching from down the block, and for now, I hope it stays that way. Ellie gestures ahead as if she's heading somewhere, she's going for a walk, and he falls into step alongside her. My jealousy, the regrettable curiosity that exists within my lungs, and it beats harder.

I follow. I have no choice.

Crossing the street, I make sure to keep to the shadows, stepping around the occasional cones of light that shine from the streetlamps above. I watch as Ellie and Clive round the corner. It's several more paces before they stop.

They're in front of a dark and looming house, and it's much quieter here, a much quieter stretch along this darker street, far more desolate. The neighbors' houses are either unoccupied or the residents have gone to bed already as it's getting late. The nearest porch light beams half a block away.

I peer into the dark, straining to see Ellie and Clive, to hear them, but I can only make out murmurs, the light tinkle of Ellie's laugh. I can't imagine what he's telling her, his reasons for showing up like this.

My sister gestures toward the house, to something at the top. A chain link fence wraps around the base of the property, and I squint, the signs reading dire warnings: *No Trespassing* and *Stay Out.*

Ellie points higher, to a section that is above the rest of the house, a lookout area with its own wraparound balcony. The property is abandoned, I can tell that much; the house is in poor shape. But beneath the blanket of navy ink sky, the light shimmer of moonlight drifts down through the treetops, and I can see where the house might have once been in better condition. The neighborhood may have been more prominent years ago with its location at the curve of the Mississippi River.

But things have changed over time, and the area has flooded, once, twice, the neighborhoods shifting north, then west. It looks like several of the residents have moved elsewhere too.

I should go to them. I should say something, ask Ellie and Clive what they're doing. Demand to know why Clive didn't include me.

But how embarrassing for them to know that I'm watching them, that I followed them here. That I've been left alone. They will wonder why I'm standing back here and hiding in the shadows. It would seem so creepy.

It will also be unbearable to admit in front of my sister that Clive skipped out on our plans, that he wanted to find her instead. Ellie will look down; she'll feel awkward as the reality hits, as she sees my disappointment, listens to Clive's excuses. She'll feel sorry for me. Once again, she'll wait for me to speak up, to stand up for myself.

I can't see a good way of how this will go, so I remain in the shadows instead. And I'm not sure why I do this, why I stay here and watch them. Maybe it's to add extra salt to my already existing wound, watching them amid my own misery, needing to see what the two of them will get up to next.

I also need to know why Ellie has walked here, what lured her to this abandoned house in the first place.

I duck behind the streetlamp, letting only my eyes peek around the corner. In this quiet, still night, I manage to keep my breath soft and shallow.

They continue to talk, but about what, I still don't know. The orange sulfur glow from the streetlamp brightens a small patch of sidewalk in front of me, but it's not enough, and the light eventually runs out where it meets the grass. It gives way to darkness, the darkness stretching toward the house, to the sight of the broken windows and a battered roof.

Ellie must beckon for Clive to follow because he moves behind her. She bursts across the yard, Clive running to keep up as they scamper toward the chain link fence. The two of them laugh, even as Ellie tries to shush him, while she tries to shush them both. But she can't help it, and another giggle escapes from her mouth.

I clench my jaw, fighting each wave of betrayal. They would make terrible robbers, I think. They would make horrible intruders with their clumsy footsteps and clang and screech of the chain link fence that they pull back and push through to the other side. Whatever they are thinking, their covert operation is anything but.

Clive gives another laugh as he helps Ellie to her feet.

My throat burns. *Of all the men in the world, why did it have to be this one, Ellie?*

But it's not entirely my sister's fault, I know it isn't. She didn't know he'd turn up tonight without me. She can't help that Clive followed her, that she is so magnetic. That I can be so easily overlooked.

They walk quickly up the steps, ascending what appears to be an exterior staircase, the stairs leading them to the top, to that balcony. They reach the cupola, and they're so high, at least three stories, and I wonder if Ellie will be reminded of our treehouse.

I stay right where I am, my feet frozen to the grass, my body unmoving. I don't understand how she can like heights so much, why she would ever want to go up there. I shudder just to see them there.

Ellie and Clive move toward the front of the balcony, the boards squeaking and sagging beneath their steps, beneath their weight, the rickety structure protesting at this unwanted arrival. But to me, the groans sound more like a warning. The wood is weak in so many places and it must be filled with dry rot.

But Clive and Ellie don't seem to care, or notice, and they step around the brittle areas, the wood jostling with every move-ment. They find the balcony railing and lean against it, Ellie pointing out the view, the neighborhood beyond, quite likely the river also.

With the next breeze, the humidity is replaced with some-thing cooler, and the wind rustles my hair. But along with that comes the muddy silt stench of the Mississippi River, the damp odor of soil decay, the wet earthiness of the riverbank. The grass that surrounds us is damp too. Somewhere in the distance, a dog barks.

I listen for the band, for the music to drift toward us with the breeze, but it's silent here. Only the frogs croak in their haphazard chorus, the dog finally quieting in the distance.

Ellie and Clive talk, and it infuriates me that I still can't hear them. It's infuriating they would stand so close together too.

They keep their elbows propped against the railing while the plywood beneath them moans. I can see where the balcony is bowed so drastically in the middle, the posts beneath the railing tilted to one side, and nothing about this structure looks safe. It's a huge hazard that Ellie has gone to this place, that she's brought him here.

Ellie, my younger sister, who has always been more reckless.

But, I realize, she must have been here before. The way she stepped around that balcony, the way she guided Clive: she's tested it before. She knows the right boards and where to stand. She instructed Clive to follow in her footsteps. With the chain link fence below, she knew exactly where to push through.

My sister's love of heights—her need for constant adventure, her zest for high, then higher, places—has led her here once again to explore.

I'm trying too! I want to shout from below. *I'm stepping outside my box*, I want her to know.

I watch them.

How long will they stay on that balcony? How long should I punish myself by watching?

Again, I consider stepping forward and making myself known. I can ask them what they're doing. I can put Clive in his place. But I'm not ready to reveal myself just yet, and I stand back in the shadow to lift my phone.

I will call Ellie, suddenly curious to see if she will answer while also hoping this could break up her time with Clive.

I can tell her I'm on my way to the show, that plans have changed. Can she meet me at the front entrance? The two of them will run down the stairs and Ellie will head back to the concert.

What will Clive say or do then? Will he stick around? Will he hide from me?

But my sister doesn't acknowledge her phone ringing. If she can hear it, she doesn't move to answer it, and I'm thinking that she might not have it on her. She might have left it at the apartment. She might have left her phone at the show.

I call Clive next, my heart racing to see if he will pick up, if he will break away his attention to see who's calling. Seconds pass before he pulls his phone from his pocket.

But he only stares at the screen, the glow lighting up his face for one brief but significant second. And there it is: there is just enough light that I think I see Clive frown.

He pockets his phone, dismissing me. He ignores the call.

He looks at Ellie and turns to kiss her.

THIRTY-TWO

I should leave. I should go back to my car and return to the hotel. I will ignore Clive's messages tomorrow—*if* he even bothers to send me a message. I will drive back to Northwestern and find a way to get over this.

But Ellie doesn't want Clive to kiss her, and though she steps back, her hands lifted, Clive tries again. My sister says something, she points, as if to distract him, perhaps making another comment about the view, but Clive takes hold of her arm. He pulls her toward him, and Ellie pushes back, her voice rising sharply to say the word *no*.

And that's enough for me—I run from my hiding spot, bolting forward, calling my sister's name. I dash across the yard, finding the spot in the fence where they crawled through, the chain link that is bent in from the other trespassers.

"Lauren?" Ellie says, leaning over the balcony. "Is that you?"

"How do I get to the stairs?" I shout, and scramble to the rear of the house.

"What are you doing here?" she says.

"Is that your sister?" Clive calls, and I nearly stop in my tracks.

Your sister. Not Lauren. Not the person he's been emailing for months, the woman he's supposed to be out with tonight. I breathe hard, my anger boiling, my adrenaline pumping with each strike of my heart.

I find the staircase and start to climb, and I'm dizzy, faltering once, then twice, but pushing through. I finally make it to the top. Ellie and Clive are standing at the rear of the balcony to face me.

"Are you okay?" I ask, and I shift my eyes from Ellie to Clive, then back to Ellie again.

The plywood sags beneath my feet, the boards pliable in so many places that it's precarious at best, and far more dangerous than I even realized, with every movement. I try not to imagine the scarce number of nails that are fighting to keep this structure together.

"Careful," Ellie warns. "You need to watch where you're going."

I test another board, and just as I assumed, large sections of it are filled with dry rot. "Jesus, Ellie, how did you find this place?"

"I read about it. They're letting the whole place fall apart, and it's a shame. But this view..." She glances over her shoulder. "Isn't it something?"

I don't look, I can't come close to enjoying that view, and glare at Clive instead. To my satisfaction, he looks a bit shell-shocked, sheepish to know he's been discovered.

The boards creak again, and I gulp, daring myself to peer over the railing and the drastic drop below. I wonder how much damage it would cause if someone were to fall all the way down, if they were to plummet toward that hard, solid ground, the dirt and grass that are almost bathed in darkness.

The balcony shifts, it leans with an even louder protest, and

I fight to steady myself. It's as if we're on a boat that's swaying dangerously with the tide, the boat keeling over.

"How did you know I was here?" Ellie asks.

"I thought I could find you," I tell her. "That I could see you tonight, hang out with you. Because Clive"—and I shoot him a look—"said he wanted to meet up with me tomorrow. He blew me off. He..." I bite down at my anger, at my embarrassment, fighting the tears as I stare at him. "I didn't think you'd be here... that you'd be with my sister."

"He's *not* with me," Ellie says at the same time that Clive proclaims, "It's not like that."

What else could it be? I want to shout.

"I'm here for work," Ellie says. "Remember? I've seen this band before, and I remembered about this place being nearby, and it's so creepy. I love it. You know how much I love weird places. Places with a view." Ellie smiles, and I wince that she's trying so hard to lighten the mood.

"We should go," I tell her, and then I say to Clive, "By the way, if my sister doesn't want to be kissed, she doesn't want to be kissed. You got it? You should back off."

He runs his hand along the back of his neck. "Wait a minute... were you standing out there watching us?"

"I wasn't watching." But my voice cracks, betraying me, and the flush rises to my cheeks. I'm thankful for the cover of darkness, concealing the anguish that stretches across my face. "I wondered what the hell you guys were doing out here, that's all. I wanted to make sure my sister was safe, that she'd be okay. I'm glad I came."

"I'm fine," Ellie insists.

"But you blew me off." I keep my gaze focused on Clive. "You pushed yourself onto Ellie."

"I didn't push—"

"That's not how this looks."

Ellie sighs. She says to Clive, "Just leave. Go away. I want you to go." She reaches for my hand. "Lauren, I'll show you where to step so you don't break through."

But Clive says, "Wait for me," and he calls Ellie's name. He reaches for her even as she draws back.

I whip out my arm to stop him, and he loses his balance, the boards releasing a high-pitched screeching sound, the railing cracking and splitting behind him.

He wobbles, fighting to keep his balance. *"What the hell?"*

My eyes widen. My heartbeat is in my throat. I didn't mean to push him like that. I didn't mean to push him so hard, to push anyone so hard. Not again. I just want him to leave Ellie alone.

Clive catches his breath. He glances over the railing as if to contemplate how far he could have fallen, that steady, long drop, then stares at me, a look which says how reckless I was. He shakes his head. As if he has any right to be disappointed with me.

But he's fine. He's safe. Clive didn't go over the edge, not like that other boy on that warm summer's day. No broken arms and legs. Clive will be okay.

Ellie says to me, "Let's go."

But Clive tries again. "Wait. You can't leave me out here."

"You'll be fine," I tell him. "You can find your own way back."

"But, Ellie..."

To hear him call her name again—not mine—and the rip of anger races through me.

"Get out of New Orleans," Ellie says to him. "We don't want you around anymore."

"But..." And he reaches for her again.

"What part of *no* do you not understand?" I yell, and my arm flies up, my elbow locked tighter than before as I shove him harder.

I strike him something fierce; there's something deep inside my belly that needs to lash out at Clive, against another stupid boy, my need to defend myself and my sister. *Don't touch her*, I want to scream. *You can't have her, especially when you didn't want me.*

Clive staggers. He stumbles on a rotten piece of plywood, his shoe pressing through, nearly falling to the other side. The weight of his hips lands squarely against the damaged railing, and he rocks back, the wood splitting with a deafening crack, like the ripping of Velcro but a hundred times louder.

Clive shouts—he reaches for us. He reaches for anything to hold onto, his long, pointed fingers finding nothing but air, and the section of the railing behind him breaks free. There is no stopping gravity, and Clive plunges over the side.

I don't look. I can't bear to watch this time, to see someone else fall.

It's over in an instant, a sharp yelp from Clive, a terrified, cut-off cry, before the sickening thud of his body against the ground. Like a sack of potatoes, Clive hits the earth.

I freeze where I stand. "Oh my God." But I don't want to move. I don't dare to move an inch and see what I've done. Instead, I stare at the great yawning hole where Clive and that part of the balcony once stood.

Ellie covers her mouth with her hands. She makes a choking sound. But she is able to move, and she ventures forward, one timid toe in front of the other until she reaches the next piece of plywood and cranes her neck to look over.

The slightest moan from Clive drifts into the night air toward us.

Ellie meets my eyes—he's alive. He's badly hurt, but the fall didn't kill him. We can get him some help. We can get help just like what happened last time. Those paramedics fixed that Jacob kid right up.

"I didn't mean to," I tell Ellie. "I don't know what happened."

"It's okay," she says, but even as she speaks, she glances

around for any lights that have turned on, for anyone who has heard the noise and is rushing out here to investigate. Maybe they will call for help instead.

But everything remains still and quiet.

Ellie says, "Lauren, you need to get out of here. You need to go now."

"I can't leave—"

"I'll take care of this, don't worry. I'll take care of Clive. I know some people who can come over here and help."

"Help with *what*?" I ask. "What are you talking about? We should call for an ambulance. They can be here in minutes."

"No," she says, and she presses her hands against her stomach. From below, Clive's moans grow faint. "What if he doesn't make it? What if he..." She whispers, "What if he dies?"

My blood runs cold. No, that cannot happen. Jacob didn't die, which means Clive can't die. Jacob healed, and he got better. We still have enough time for paramedics and a team of doctors and nurses to put him back together again. This time, I will admit what I've done. I'll tell the police. I can apologize over and over.

But Ellie pleads with me with her eyes. She must have seen how bad Clive looks. When she peered over, she must have spotted his injuries, how he is in much worse shape than I realized.

I should go down there and check on Clive myself. I should run down those steps and help him, surmise the extent of his injuries, but I'm frightened. I can't look. The sweat gathers at my neck.

I can't bear witness to another tragedy.

The balcony shifts beneath us, the already fragile balance of the wood moaning and creaking, greatly disturbed by all this movement.

"Go," Ellie says, and she meets my eyes again. "Drive back to the hotel. Try not to worry. I'll take care of everything. I'll tell the cops that he fell, that it was an accident. You were never here."

"You're calling nine-one-one?"

She doesn't answer my question but looks off into the distance. The dog barks once again.

"We'll get him the help he needs," she says. "But you, I need you to get out of here."

The balcony shudders beneath our feet.

"Go now," she says. "Quickly. This place isn't going to last much longer. But I know where to step, how to move around this thing."

I don't want to leave. I can't leave her. I also can't have my sister cleaning up my mess.

Ellie squeezes my hand. "*Now*, Lauren."

"Okay." A sob clutches my throat. I hesitate. "I'm so sorry, Ellie." And I run. I stumble-trip down the steps, my vision tilting sideways until I reach the bottom.

Running to the side of the house, I scramble through the piece of broken chain link fence.

I don't look up. I don't look to see if my sister has moved. If she's coming down the stairs next, if she's searching the ground to assess Clive.

I also don't look for his mangled body. I can't bear to see him up close, to hear his agonizing moans.

"Go," I hear Ellie calling to me from the top.

And I stagger across the grass. I'm terrified, but I'm also filled with a relief that I can get away, I can gain some distance from this place. Ellie will help him, just like she said. An ambulance will show up and Clive's body will be repaired. If he says anything about me pushing him, we'll do what Ellie told me: we'll tell them it was an accident. *You were never here.*

For the second time, maybe I won't have to confess.

I run from that house, my heart in my mouth. I run and run until after a few more streets, I reach the safety of my car.

I should have stopped. I should have looked back. I should have waited for my sister to appear around the corner, but I didn't.

It's only after I'm behind the steering wheel and driving to the hotel that I remember Ellie doesn't have her phone on her. She doesn't have a way of calling for help. Maybe she'll realize this and she'll run to find a neighbor.

Her last words echo through my mind:

Go.

I'll take care of everything.

It's a hope I cling to.

THIRTY-THREE

Alex hides behind a tree. He is crouched within the shadows, making sure to stay low.

He has held himself back, not wanting to be seen, not wanting anyone to know he has followed them too. It is only when he hears the commotion, the rumble and crack of wood, the frightened shouts and cries from the young women, that he rises from his hiding spot.

He sees her rushing across the yard, but it isn't Ellie—it's the older sister, with the same long red hair. She runs from the house, her hand covering her mouth as she... sobs?

Alex looks up. Why is she crying? What's happening up there?

Where are Ellie and Clive? Why aren't they rushing down the balcony next?

Alex hadn't planned on following his brother tonight. When Clive left the hotel, he mentioned something about seeing a girl, and Alex assumed it was the girl he'd been email-ing, the one who suggested they meet up in New Orleans to check out some bands. He found himself wanting to see her again.

Last night, Alex only met up with his brother for a few minutes. He hadn't wanted to get in the way of Clive's date, especially when the brothers had plenty of time to explore the French Quarter later in the weekend.

He greeted Clive at that bar off Magazine Street, the one Clive had told him about, then left to grab some dinner at a bistro around the corner. He dined alone since he didn't want to hang around the concert. He didn't want to be his brother's awkward third wheel.

Standing in front of the bar, Clive was with a woman, but it wasn't the one he was meeting, and Clive explained that she was the younger sister, Ellie. Lauren had gone down the block to the ATM, and the younger sister had unexpectedly joined them for dinner. She was gorgeous: Alex could see that immediately. Stunning, with the shine of her red hair falling past her shoulders, the wink of her bright green eyes that flashed up at him.

And Alex remembered thinking that if she and her older sister looked anything alike, Clive was in good hands. His brother was a lucky man.

Alex considered joining them, and getting to know the younger sister for himself, but Ellie said she might be meeting up with work friends, and she didn't extend an invitation for him to join. And neither did Clive, and that was that. Alex wasn't going to insist on staying.

But when Alex hugged her, he felt it—he was almost positive she felt it too—the spark in her embrace as she held onto him a little bit tighter than he'd expected, the sigh from her lips when he pulled away.

Was it just his imagination or did Ellie look saddened to see him go? He found himself not wanting to leave.

The moment was brief, possibly a flash in the dark, and certainly disappeared when Clive said to him, a little more obviously than he needed to, "Enjoy your dinner, Alex. I'll catch up with you later."

So he left. Alex enjoyed every bite of his New Orleans BBQ shrimp, the decadent bread pudding. But for every bite of his food, for every sip of his wine, he thought about that girl. He thought about Ellie.

Alex returned to the hotel and was surprised to see Clive returning later that night too. He didn't stay at the hotel with the older sister, with either of the young women, which Alex had assumed his brother would have done. They must not have invited him.

The next morning, the brothers woke early, both of them in search of coffee as they meandered Chartres Street, then on to Bourbon. They browsed shop windows before Clive said he'd invited someone to brunch. But it wasn't the girl he'd been emailing, the one he'd driven into town to spend time with.

"Lauren and I had a great time," Clive said. "And she's great." He grinned. "But her younger sister is a lot of fun too."

And that's when Alex realized that it was Ellie who would be joining them, the young woman he'd met last night, and he couldn't help the bubble of excitement that fizzed right through him, the anticipation to be able to see her again.

On their way, with to-go coffees in their hands, Clive stopped at a corner market, where he picked up a bouquet of flowers. "These are nice," he said, holding up the pink camellias. "We can give them to her."

Ellie met them at the restaurant, and she was surprised, maybe a little caught off-guard, to find her sister wasn't there. She glanced at the flowers.

"I thought Lauren was joining us," Ellie said. But Clive told her that no, Lauren was probably still hungover and she wanted to sleep. Alex wondered how Clive would know that when he hadn't stayed in her room, but maybe he'd talked to her. Maybe they'd touched base and she'd declined meeting them at the restaurant.

Or maybe his younger brother was only saying this in order to see the younger sister.

Ellie reached for her phone like she was going to check on Lauren and make sure she was all right, but Clive insisted that her sister shouldn't be disturbed.

"We'll call her later," Clive said.

Over plates of eggs Benedict and Bloody Marys, Clive asked Ellie about all sorts of things: about her classes at Loyola, about any job opportunities if he were to stay in New Orleans instead of moving on to Houston. She said there wasn't anything available at the magazine that she knew of, not at the moment, but there should be plenty of other job listings, lots of restaurants and bars, that he should look them up himself.

While she ate, she periodically checked her phone to see if a message had come through from her sister, but there was nothing.

Alex imagined Lauren fast asleep at her hotel, cocooned within the soft blankets, tucked away from the harsh light blocked behind the blackout curtains. If she really was hungover, she would need an aspirin or two for when she woke up later.

Ellie lightened up over time with conversation, especially with the Bloody Mary seeping into her bloodstream. And at one point, Clive asked if she wanted another, but Ellie said that she shouldn't drink any more, that she was going to work afterwards for an article she was prepping, a band she was covering that night at a place called Crossroads. She lifted a Nikon camera out of her bag.

"I'm dropping this thing off at work," Ellie said. "I don't need it tonight. But while I've got it here, let's take a photo."

Ellie asked the server to take it, and the young man stepped back, expertly eyeing St. Louis Cathedral in the background, the angle of Jackson Square beyond the railing. Alex could tell he'd accepted many photo requests before as the server knew exactly where to stand.

Clive pulled his chair closer to Ellie's while Alex looked down at his plate, then turned his head, his hand lifted as if he wasn't quite ready for the camera. The shutter snapped.

"Oh," the server said, looking at Alex. "Let's try that again."

Alex lifted his eyes, and the shutter clicked again.

Ellie thanked him and she returned the camera to her bag. "I'll print these for my sister," she said to them with a wink. "We can remind her of how she was silly not to join us."

In the dark and surrounded by damp grass and crickets, the house groans, a slow and foreboding rumble that seems to be coming from the top of the house, the tremble spiraling downward, then out, the railing tilting even more around the cupola.

Alex's heart beats faster. Whatever is happening up there, Ellie and Clive need to climb down fast. They need to leave immediately.

The older sister had the right idea when she barreled down those steps. Lauren took off, and the slap of her feet against the concrete has long since disappeared. She fled around the corner.

Alex stares at the house. Where is his brother? Why isn't Ellie following Lauren to safer ground?

Another rumble, and it's louder, the distinct sound of wood cracking and splitting, beams breaking apart, rusted nails yanking from their holds.

He hears a cry—*is* that someone crying? Did he hear someone fall, the desperate pitch of a yelp?

The rocking and splitting fills his ears, but he thinks he hears a thud. But is that the thud of the railing—a broken piece of the house? Or is it someone?

Alex runs. His brother might need him. Ellie might need him too.

His breath is lodged in his throat as he dashes to the fence, finding the same area of chain link from where Lauren fled. He scrambles through and runs to one side of the house, finding nothing. He runs to the other side, and that's when he cries out.

A few feet away, Clive is curled on the ground, his body broken, his legs bent sideways, his shoulders hunched. A great patch of blood spills from his head, the blood seeping into the grass. Pieces of plywood are scattered around him. A heavy board has fallen across his back.

Debris fills the air with dust, chunks of wood giving off an earthy rotting scent, and it's the same debris that covers Clive's hands and legs, the pieces pinning large portions of his body.

Whatever happened, it happened to Clive before that section of balcony gave way. His brother plummeted to the ground before those pieces collapsed on top of him.

Was that the thud he heard moments ago—his brother falling? Or was that Ellie?

Because when he looks nearby, he sees her body lying only a few feet away.

Alex rushes to his brother first. He wants to scream for Clive to wake up, to move, but nothing comes out of his mouth. The screams are trapped inside his throat. He stares at Clive's skin. It's paling so quickly; so much blood has already poured from his head.

Alex can only hear his own breathing. The other houses remain silent, and no one has come out to inspect. Besides Alex, there is no one here to bear witness.

He crawls over to Ellie, her body that is twisted on the ground also, her blood spilling from her mouth. A streak of crimson trickles from her lips.

He checks for her breath, for a pulse... and it's there, but faint. Ellie is still alive.

He doesn't dare move her. He doesn't know what to do, but he must find a way to stop the bleeding. He must do something to help. It's too late for Clive, but maybe he can save Ellie.

His hands shake as he scans her body. He has no idea how bad her internal injuries are, the broken bones, but the paramedics can fix her, right? The surgeons can sort her out at the hospital. God willing, Ellie will make it.

But the blood seeps from Ellie's ears now, and she moans something, something unintelligible with the blood gurgling thick in her throat. She coughs up a little bit of the blood that pools at the corners of her mouth.

Alex searches for his phone, pats at his jeans pockets desperately until he finds it. He lifts it to his face, jabs at the screen... and no... it can't be. His phone is dead.

Alex shakes it as if he's about to go mad. Why isn't it turning on? How did he not have it charged? Because he and Clive spent the rest of the day drinking, that's why. After brunch, and a couple more of those Bloody Marys, they were already in the French Quarter so why not follow it up with a few beers, then a hurricane or two, a good time had by two brothers.

Ellie opens her eyes, and Alex gasps. He's shocked to see her staring at him, and she fixes him with her gaze. She blinks painfully, then moans, and he wants to sob, her moan cutting right through him.

He touches her hair, hoping he can find a way to comfort her, to ease her anguish. He pats at her hair that fans across the grass, but it's awful. The blood is darkening her scalp.

Alex's eyes fill with tears. He can't bear to see her suffering like this, to see anyone suffering like this.

He searches around him again, looking for help.

He can run and find someone, that's what he'll do. Someone must be home in one of these houses. Someone will be inside. He can bang on doors and wake them up. They will call 9-1-1.

Alex is about to leave, he will do this, he will search for help, when Ellie's eyes widen, and she's either flinching from the pain or from the fact that she thinks he's leaving. She begs him with her look—she doesn't want him to go. He feels it, he knows it, that she doesn't want to be left alone. And Alex can't blame her.

He watches as her eyes drift closed, and he fears that Ellie might be losing consciousness. He's terrified that she's not going to make it, that she will spend her last few minutes in more pain than anyone deserves. She will die before he has the chance to call for an ambulance. She could die before he's able to return to the house and sit with her.

He can't leave Ellie by herself, he just can't. He can't leave her to suffer alone, not when she's still aware of what's happening.

He sobs—damn his phone and this god-awful situation. Damn whatever it was they were doing up there in the first place, their reason for climbing to the top of this house. He has lost his one and only brother.

Ellie's breaths grow shorter. She's bleeding from her nose now as she tries to whisper. But Alex can't hear what she's saying, and her voice is too soft, it's too raspy, and he presses his face closer to hear. He smells the sweetness of her shampoo, the sweat that clings to her skin.

She whispers, "I'm not..."

His breath catches in his throat. "What is it, Ellie? What are you trying to say?"

With every inhale, her breath rattles and wheezes. "I can't do this." Her eyes flutter closed.

Alex rears back. *No, don't give up*, he wants to say. He wants to shake her shoulders and keep her there.

But she knows that she's not going to make it, and the pain must be excruciating. He stares. Ellie knows she won't last while he runs off and calls for help. She wants him to hold her hand with the few minutes she has left.

And he does. He holds her hand and he cries for this girl he barely knows. With no other options left, he will do this and sit with her.

She's gone. Ellie has stopped breathing, and Alex sobs in the dark. He is frightened and alone.

Ellie was alive just moments ago, his brother too. They were right there, their hearts beating, their thoughts whipping together with terror as the boards beneath their feet split, and now they're gone.

He sits back on his heels. What should he do? Should he call the police?

But then he scampers back, dropping her hand.

What if the police don't believe him? What if they don't believe that Ellie's and Clive's deaths were caused by an accident? What if they think Alex pushed them, and it's his fault?

He looks over at his brother's body and gasps. The police will want to pin their deaths on someone.

Right now, no one knows that he's here. No one knows his plans. Lauren didn't see him hiding in the bushes, and not a single neighbor has come out to inspect. He doesn't need to reach out to Lauren and tell her what he saw, that he saw her tonight too. She will think she was the last one here.

He must leave. He must get out of this place, and his fear drops over his body like a dead weight. Like a bucket of ice water. He scurries back a few feet more, then rises to his feet, his hand clutched over his mouth.

He must run, the same way Lauren did. She left. She has no idea what's happened to her sister, to Clive. Alex must leave this area immediately too. He must not get caught.

Clive and Ellie were the only ones here, the only ones to know what happened. Only them.

. . .

The house makes the final decision for him. The rest of the cupola and balcony rattles and shakes above, and Alex anxiously looks up. The violent splitting of wood erupts as another chunk of the balcony gives way, the intense buckling of boards soon followed by the railing tearing away from the house. The wood slides toward the earth.

Alex scrambles back even further—and he scrambles back just in time, as a chunk of plywood narrowly misses landing on his head and crushing him. Beams clatter, boards tumble. They collapse with a crash. The balcony comes apart and lands on his brother, covering him.

Alex shouts the word, "Noooo!" and this time, the cry does escape from his lungs, the pure horror at watching all of that wood crash upon their bodies.

He scrambles to one side of the debris and checks for any signs of his brother, for a hand sticking out, or Ellie's hair escaping between pieces of wood, but there is nothing. He can no longer see his brother's face. He can no longer tell where Ellie is, and he thinks he's going to be sick.

He looks up at the great hole where the cupola and balcony once stood. The top of the house no longer exists, and Alex cries out again. He pulls at the plywood, his actions desperate, not caring if the nails tear at his skin. He will haul the pieces aside.

But his shoulders lift, his head rears back—footsteps on the street, and his gaze jerks in that direction. Is someone walking across the yard? Have they arrived to see what's happening? Someone is, in fact, at home and heard the commotion?

This person could soon find him, and he will have to explain. He will have to explain why he followed his brother and this young woman out here in the dark, why he stood by and watched them. That he didn't realize the thudding sounds were their bodies. He didn't run and get help in time.

He tells himself that no one will believe him.

And Alex bolts. Just like Lauren did, he runs as fast as he

can from this house. But unlike Lauren, he knows their fate, what's happened on this dark, horrible night.

Alex takes off and he whispers, "Please forgive me," and he doesn't look back.

He says a silent prayer that this night will never catch up to him.

* * *

Across town, Lauren sits on the edge of the bed with the hotel curtains pulled shut. She is crying and alone and tormenting herself with what Clive must be going through at this very moment, the pain and haziness of slipping in and out of consciousness. She agonizes over what her sister might be doing to take care of things.

Lauren waits for Ellie to call, for her sister to say that Clive is recovering at the hospital and the police believe it was an accident, that Lauren is in the clear. Clive will be on the mend soon enough, and he will make it. Lauren waits for this huge amount of mercy.

But her sister doesn't call, and Lauren remembers that Ellie doesn't have her phone on her, that she might have to wait until morning when she can use Carmen's phone when she returns from staying at her boyfriend's.

But the call doesn't come. Ellie doesn't tell her what's happening, and Lauren is too terrified to contact the hospitals and check for herself. She considers going to Ellie's apartment where she could stand outside and wait, but what if it takes Ellie hours to return?

What if Carmen gets back before her sister does? Will Carmen look at Lauren oddly? Will she know that something is wrong, that Lauren knows more than she's saying? That she couldn't have possibly come into town without seeing Ellie, without knowing where she is?

Lauren can't take it any longer, and the loud chatter and buzz is too much in her ears. She packs her things. She must leave. She must get out of here.

She makes the long, insufferable drive back to Chicago, not stopping, the blackness of the night surrounding her, still hoping, still believing that at any second, after mile after mile of mile markers, she will finally hear from Ellie. Her sister will say that everything is okay. They can move on. Lauren repeats this to herself for every town and mile that comes between her and the Crescent City. She believes that Ellie has worked her magic once again, that she will persevere through this. Both of them again.

That, as always, time can repair things.

THIRTY-FOUR

I keep the additional photographs that Connor took, the additional evidence that proves Alex was with my sister the night before she died. Riley thinks I will show these photographs to the police, and Connor does too.

But when I return to the hotel, I don't pick up the phone to call Detective Rayburn; instead, I slide the folder inside my suitcase.

I'm not certain if it matters anymore, if the detective needs to see these additional pictures. He already has proof that Alex was with her the same day she died from what was found inside Ellie's pocket. Does it matter that Alex hasn't fessed up to me completely, or to the police, that meeting Ellie at brunch wasn't his one and only encounter? My husband has lied to us about so many things.

But so have I.

I've lied for such a long time, withholding information, clutching desperately to my own monumental secret. Terrified of the truth coming out about what I did to Clive.

I was frightened to say anything at first because what if Ellie had done something to him? What if she got rid of Clive to cover up for my actions, and she did this to protect me? Or what if she *did* help Clive and I needed to be patient? I needed to wait hour by hour until she called to give me the all-clear.

Ellie was alive and well when I ran from that house, I know that for a fact. I heard her tell me to go before I sprinted from the property. What happened to my sister afterwards? Did a board crack and split moments later, a gaping hole opening up beneath her just like it did for Clive, and she fell to the ground too?

The rest of the balcony collapsed after I left, I know that now. I must have already been in my car, returning to the hotel, my emotions coming out in short, stuttered breaths. I remember my hands shaking as I inserted the car keys.

When Carmen called me hours later, I was silent. She was worried, but I remained calm. And it's funny how our minds will do this, how they will have a way of continuing with our lies, the ongoing delusion.

Maybe it's a defense mechanism. It's self-preservation. But it's cowardice, plain and simple. It's not facing the facts.

I listened to Carmen, still waiting, still hoping that Ellie would show up, that she would return home. When days passed and there was still no word, I was frozen, paralyzed by my own fear and guilt. When we searched for Ellie, I made sure to avoid those neighborhoods. I refused to see that place again. She got out of there; Clive did too.

I told myself Ellie and Clive were no longer at that house, that they had left. My sister was fine, and she sought help. Clive wasn't as injured as I thought.

Denial can make you believe almost anything. Hope can also.

And so can those whispers in your ear.

You're finally putting it together, Alex said. *You're wondering what else I know*.

There is no proof to indicate that Alex came along afterwards, that after I fled, Alex was near the house that night. But he must have been. He must have seen. He wouldn't have told me something like that otherwise. The chill of his words, that look, wouldn't have reached my spine.

He knows that I abandoned my sister and his brother.

He knows that I didn't help.

And during the smack of my feet against pavement, I should have considered that someone else was out there, that someone else could have been watching, staying hidden. I just never dreamed this person would be someone who would work themselves into my life many months later. They would work themselves into my heart. My bed.

Everyone thinks Alex has been hiding the truth from me. But the fact is, it's the other way around.

I think he's been waiting for me to confess for years.

Detective Rayburn calls to say I can take Ellie's body home, that I can bring her back to Chicago and plan the funeral. He says that Alex will be doing the same for his brother, and I assume he will plan a small service for Clive in Florida. Needless to say, I won't be attending.

Detective Rayburn tells me that he'll be in touch, that the investigation is not yet finished.

And every time my phone rings, my lungs tighten, and I wonder if it's him, if it will be my husband. Or it's Connor and Riley asking if I've shown the detective the additional photographs yet. But besides the ongoing calls from the reporters, it's mostly been messages from Carmen and the Broussards checking up on me, the group of us getting together for a quiet dinner before I head back to Chicago. They will travel north in a few days' time and join us for Ellie's funeral.

.   .   .

Within hours of my arrival, I return to the senior living center to see my dad. I brace myself: this next conversation will be brutal, discussing Ellie's funeral, contacting her friends, and I'm thankful that Sheryl sits with us and brings us comfort.

It's difficult talking to my father about flowers and caskets, which songs Ellie would prefer, while the guilt weighs heavy inside the pit of my stomach. I fear the truth is written all over my face, that he can see.

The detective has filled my dad in on most everything about the case by now, but Dad still has a lot of questions. It doesn't take long before he brings up Alex.

"You don't think...?" he says, and he gazes at me with such watery eyes, such grief. "You don't think that he would...?"

"What? Hurt Ellie?" I flinch. "No. God, I hope not. There's no proof that Alex would do that." But my voice chokes on those last few words.

My dad's eyes stray toward the window, at the birds that are fluttering about and pecking at the bird feeder. "What's going to happen now?" he asks. "What are we going to do?"

And I blow out a long, painful breath. "We'll have Ellie's funeral and we'll bury her next to Mom. And then I don't know, Dad. I honestly don't know."

After my sister's funeral, after the heartbreak of burying Ellie and saying goodbye, Alex returns home. And although I've been expecting it, to hear the turn of his key in the lock, for the front door to swing wide open—after all, it's his house too—it's difficult to hide my shock when I see him standing there.

The vase that once held flowers, his gifts to me, the hand-blown glass that rests near the front door, is empty. We were away for so long, the petals wilted, the water left gray and cloudy and drifting with debris, and I threw them out. I don't know if there will be flowers in that vase again.

Alex finds me in the kitchen, and I turn slowly to face him, the two of us assessing one another for a long and weighted time, neither one of us wanting to speak first, to admit anything first.

I reach for the pendant at my neck, as if I can draw on my own resolve, I can draw on my sister for strength, gripping the letter *E* between my fingertips. Detective Rayburn came through with his promise and returned Ellie's necklace to me.

Alex looks at me for such a long time. "So, what now?" he says, and he stands very still.

I shake my head. I still don't have an answer to that question, not for my dad, and certainly not for Alex. I'm not ready to confirm anything with him either.

Because I didn't kill his brother. Yes, I pushed him, I hurt Clive gravely, but I didn't kill him. I'm guilty for leaving and not making sure that my sister and Clive were all right.

And Alex didn't hurt my sister. He's not the reason the rest of that balcony collapsed and she tumbled down next to Clive. But he must have seen me there. He must have seen me run. Alex followed his brother out that night. He thinks that I left my sister and Clive on the ground, that I left them buried beneath all that rubble.

So why didn't Alex run to the police? Why didn't he tell them? Why not let the police know about their bodies and their whereabouts?

But I didn't breathe a word either, and we're both guilty of that. We're guilty of leaving them in a shrouded tomb, not wanting anyone to pin their deaths on us.

I stare at Alex, at my husband, thinking that maybe we truly are suited for each other.

He says, "I really do love you, you know. I really did fall in love with you."

I nod.

"And I don't regret finding you and then marrying you. Creating this life we have together."

I bite my lip to swallow the pain.

"I'm sorry that I ran from you near the cathedral too, that I scared you, that I had someone deliver those flowers."

And I almost laugh—a shrill, terrified sound that begs to be released, it needs to be released, my bottled-up nerves asking for an escape—because that day in the French Quarter, and that moment when I opened the door and saw the dead bouquet, those are the least of our concerns.

But I don't make a sound. There is no laugh, no shrill comeback to my husband, only a shiver. Because at that moment, I realize we are never going to talk about it. We're never going to confess to one another.

We will keep carrying on as usual, our marriage together, *our life together*, as he put it, as if each of us doesn't have a clue as to what the other is hiding.

Neither of us dares to say anything first, and in that way, we will remain silent. We will hold onto each other's fears as collateral.

Alex lifts his suitcase, his hand wrapping around the handle, and in that silence, we are confirming everything. "I'll go upstairs and unpack, shall I?"

THIRTY-FIVE

My alarm clock is seconds away from sounding. Another Monday morning, the start of another week of sitting in our home office and answering emails.

Alex is already at the foot of our bed holding my cup of coffee, the way he always does. It's the mug I like, my favorite one, the one with the large red heart and thick white handle, the mug my husband reserves just for me.

He sets the coffee on the bedside table and says good morning as I sit up and slowly prop the pillows behind my back. I try not to look at him, not acknowledging how strange this is, how peculiar and otherworldly this feels, our daily routines continuing, despite everything. It's eerie.

We have slowly but surely slipped back into our old lives, pretending that everything is normal, that everything is the way it's always been. Except that we know my sister and his brother are gone, that everyone knows this now. We are grieving.

Though I didn't know I'd married Clive's older brother, Alex knew exactly who I was, my relation to Ellie. We are trapped in this strange and convoluted life together.

And perhaps it's the only way we know how to be around

each other, that pretending, that carrying on in this way, is better than confessing. There is no jail time and accusations from other people at least. Alex and I don't have to reveal every ugly truth about ourselves to each other.

My husband sits on the edge of the bed, and he smiles. And this close, I can smell the Irish Spring soap from his shower, the fabric softener he loves to use, the sweatshirt he's pulled over his head.

Through the window: a bright, vibrant blue across our beautiful neighborhood. The neighbors' kids will be out there playing later this afternoon.

I look down at my hand with the tattoo of my sister's name and run my finger back and forth, the delicate script of the *E* and the two looping *l*s.

Sitting here, having coffee, is this what it's going to be like from now on? Is this how my life is going to look with my husband? We will work at our opposing desks. We will make small talk and acknowledge the condolences of our loss from others.

We will explain that Alex being in those photographs with my sister was a misunderstanding. That he didn't know who she was. He didn't realize that same young woman went missing, and it was the craziest fluke of all to meet and then marry her sister.

Alex looks to the window, then back to me. "Let's go see your dad today," he says. "He'll like that. We can head there after work."

And I nod. I agree, because I don't know what else to do. "Yes," I tell him. "We can bring him some dinner."

And this plan—my acquiescence to Alex's suggestion—pleases him. He smiles bigger, and I know how much he also loves going to see my dad. He loves talking to him, this additional family that he's built.

Nurse Sheryl will stand there and greet us like she always

does. She'll watch from the doorway and smile because Alex has returned, we're working our way through this.

But my husband frowns, and he must notice that I'm not drinking my coffee, that I'm not taking part in the usual morning order of things. He nudges the mug, but I'm not sure if I want it. I have another awful feeling, another premonition of sorts that something is about to happen, that our world, once again, is about to change. That no matter what, we can't pretend our way out of everything.

Life should have already taught us that.

A call comes through on my phone.

I no longer keep the ringer on high. There's no need to jump at every alert, no need to learn what's happened to my sister, to hear any other news that I don't want to know.

But New Orleans Police flashes across my screen, and my phone emits another buzz.

I lock eyes with Alex, knowing I should answer.

His face pales, the noose closing in on us tighter.

It was only a matter of time before we heard back from Detective Rayburn. Only a matter of time before the police learned something else. Who were we kidding?

I take a deep breath, my stomach twisting, knowing that Alex and I convincing ourselves that we could move forward, that we could keep lying to ourselves—to everyone—is one tremble away from our world falling down. It will collapse on us like a house of cards. Like that house, that balcony.

I answer.

"Mrs. Capshaw?" the detective says. "Are you and Mr. Capshaw together right now?"

I hear the tone of the detective's voice, the sense of urgency that is always there.

"Yes, we're together." I put the detective on speaker.

"Is there something else you were supposed to tell me? Additional photographs you were supposed to show me?"

I shut my eyes.

"Extra prints that you were given and I should have already seen them by now?" the detective adds.

I swallow. Riley or Connor checked in with him just like I knew they would. They want answers, and it was ridiculous of me to think otherwise, that Alex and I could continue this ruse.

"In light of what Connor has done, the harassment and the stalking, the following of your sister, he's being very helpful. You have Connor's original prints," the detective says, "but he's kept all the negatives. He went back through them after you left, and he showed us the rest. There are more photographs, Mr. and Mrs. Capshaw. Photographs that show both of you. You were both there."

My shoulders hunch forward, because when I look at Alex, he makes a face. *What is he talking about?* he mouths as he has no idea what the detective is saying. He knows nothing about these other prints as I have not yet shown these photographs to him.

"Alex Capshaw," the detective says, "we can see you on the sidewalk with your brother and Ellie the night before they disappeared, the night before we think they died. But Lauren Capshaw, you're in these photographs too. Why didn't you disclose this to us before? Why didn't you tell us that you were in New Orleans?"

I don't answer.

The detective clears his throat. "I'm sending you the images right now."

And my phone dings, one after the other, the images proving the additional verification we wanted so much to hide. That hazy night, and the music that poured from the building, out of the bar windows.

The detective says, "Please let me know when you see them, when the images come through."

And I watch as my husband peers at the screen.

And there it is, that sliver of time, those few seconds, the missed opportunity when we could have met. It was so many years earlier, the moment Alex stepped away from the bar in search of dinner while I hurried along on the sidewalk seconds later, cash in hand from the ATM, my sister standing with Clive. The look on my face that didn't hide my disappointment that the man I drove all that way to visit was keeping his eyes on Ellie instead.

By the next night, they would both be dead.

Alex sucks in his breath. He looks at me, and his expression sharpens. The police know now.

"Mr. and Mrs. Capshaw," the detective says. "Would either of you care to explain this to me? Can you tell us what's going on?"

Alex rises to his feet, and I look at him, alarmed. Where is he going? He's not leaving me, is he? He's not going to bolt and run?

"Because the Evanston police are on their way," the detective says. "They will be there in minutes, so I suggest you not do anything but sit tight and wait."

Alex takes another step toward the hall. And I stand, knocking my coffee mug to the ground, the hot liquid spilling across the floor and shattering the rest of our morning, this horrific Groundhog Day where we thought we could carry on.

I glare at Alex. If he's thinking about leaving, if he thinks he can take off to protect himself, then he's misjudged me. Because I can leave too. I've spent years hiding my secrets. The police will have way too many questions, but I might have some answers.

In the distance, the first wail of a siren, the pitch lifting into the air and getting close.

My husband and I lock eyes again. Then we turn toward the staircase, the front of the house where there is a loud bang from below.

"Police! Open up."

"I'm downstairs," the detective says to us, and he's still on speakerphone. "The two of you have a lot to explain. Obstruction of justice, not coming clean about your siblings, their deaths."

Another bang at the door.

The detective says, "It's time that the two of you told us everything."

I stare at my husband and wonder which one of us will confess first.

A LETTER FROM GEORGINA

Dearest reader,

Thank you for reading my books, as being an author has always been my dream and I'm able to experience this dream because of readers like you. I thank you with heartfelt appreciation.

And thank you for reading *My Perfect Husband*—the idea came to me in the form of a photograph, as pictures can reveal a shocking secret. Just when you think you know someone, images taken many years ago might tell you a completely different story. This domestic psychological thriller unfolds from a tranquil neighborhood north of Chicago to my old stomping grounds of growing up in New Orleans. Plenty of ghost stories and haunting chills in this city too. I hope you enjoy!

If you'd like to keep up to date with all my latest releases, please sign up at the following link. Your email address will never be shared and you can unsubscribe at any time.

www.bookouture.com/georgina-cross

And if you enjoy my books, I'd absolutely love if you could leave a review. Getting feedback from readers is amazing and it also helps to persuade other readers to pick up one of my books for the first time.

Thank you so much. And happy suspenseful reading!

Georgina

KEEP IN TOUCH WITH GEORGINA

www.georgina-cross-author.com

facebook.com/GeorginaCrossAuthor

x.com/GCrossAuthor

instagram.com/GeorginaCrossAuthor

goodreads.com/georginacross

bookbub.com/profile/georgina-cross

ACKNOWLEDGMENTS

This is my sixth published novel and just saying that feels like a dream come true. Thank you to Bookouture for helping me get started and for helping me to become a published author. Huge thanks to my editor, Maisie Lawrence, for reading my pitch and guiding my first book, *The Stepdaughter*, into the special, thrilling book that it is. I hope my latest novel is just as compelling for you, dear readers, as it's always so much fun to come up with more twists.

Growing up near New Orleans, I have a great affinity for this city, with there being so much to write about and describe. By placing a large portion of this book in and around the streets of the French Quarter, the Garden District, and along St. Charles, I was able to pull in my memories of dancing in music halls just like the ones featured in this book; sunny brunches on the balcony at Muriel's Restaurant, a special place for our beloved Susie; my dad's office along Conti Street and our walks through the French Quarter to Mr. B.'s; the French shops with their gorgeous hats and dresses; and the breakdance performers whose routines in Jackson Square never got old. Writing this book was a fun-filled blast through my past, and being able to use New Orleans as a setting was my dream come true.

This book is dedicated to my friends, neighbors, classmates, and teachers who I remember fondly from the Dell, along with our escapades to New Orleans and Baton Rouge and back again. We had such great times dancing to the Dirty Dozen Brass Band, catching Mardi Gras beads, attending Jazz Fest, and S.I.N. nights at Tipitina's. Let's be grateful we didn't have social media back then.

Enormous gratitude to my agent, Rachel Beck, with Liza Dawson Associates, for her invaluable support to me over these last few years as we continue to brainstorm more books together. Rachel, thank you for giving me the space to breathe and pursue my love of writing while also juggling family life. Each day is getting stronger for us, and I appreciate you.

And thank you to my family, who continues to champion my writing career by asking, *Which book is it now? And how many?* Who would have thought we'd be counting on our fingers to tally the latest—with many more books to come! Just allow me to continue taking over the kitchen table with all my stuff, and don't get too creeped out when it seems all I watch and read are true crime documentaries and suspense thrillers. It's called research, everyone, and I'm sticking to that belief. I love you.

PUBLISHING TEAM

Turning a manuscript into a book requires the efforts of many people. The publishing team at Bookouture would like to acknowledge everyone who contributed to this publication.

Audio
Alba Proko
Sinead O'Connor
Melissa Tran

Commercial
Lauren Morrissette
Hannah Richmond
Imogen Allport

Cover design
The Brewster Project

Data and analysis
Mark Alder
Mohamed Bussuri

Editorial
Maisie Lawrence
Ria Clare

Copyeditor
DeAndra Lupu

Proofreader
Becca Allen

Marketing
Alex Crow
Melanie Price
Occy Carr
Cíara Rosney
Martyna Młynarska

Operations and distribution
Marina Valles
Stephanie Straub

Production
Hannah Snetsinger
Mandy Kullar
Jen Shannon

Publicity
Kim Nash
Noelle Holten
Jess Readett
Sarah Hardy

Rights and contracts
Peta Nightingale
Richard King
Saidah Graham

Made in the USA
Middletown, DE
25 May 2024

54865041R00172